THE HORSE IN THE GRAY FLANNEL SUIT is a wacky, warm story of a father's attempt to win the love and respect of his teenage daughter, who has eyes only for a horse. Freddie Bolton is a charming, harassed, suburban ad executive playing—and losing —Madison Avenue's favorite sport of living beyond his income. Nothing is too good for his daughter, but when Hellie asks for a horse of her own, he has an adman's brainstorm. The insanity that ensues among the delightful cast of characters—including a beer-guzzling horse—provides an hilarious and unusual story.

ERIC HATCH has written for radio, television and movies, and has published numerous books, articles and plays. He is an expert horseman and a well-known judge and steward of the American Horse Shows Association.

THE LAUREL-LEAF LIBRARY brings together under a single imprint outstanding works of fiction and non-fiction particularly suitable for young adult readers, both in and out of the classroom. This series is under the editorship of M. Jerry Weiss, Chairman, Department of English, Jersey City State College; in association with Ned E. Hoopes, Associate Professor, Pace College; and Charles Reasoner, Associate Professor, Elementary Education, New York University.

The Horse
in the
Gray Flannel Suit

(*formerly:* THE YEAR OF THE HORSE)

by Eric Hatch

To the Memory of Helen C. Castles
this book is fondly dedicated

Published by DELL PUBLISHING CO., INC.
750 Third Avenue
New York, N.Y. 10017

Reprinted by arrangement with
Crown Publishers, Inc., New York

Laurel-Leaf Library ® TM 766734

Printed in the United States of America

The movie, *The Horse in the
Gray Flannel Suit,* © 1968, Walt Disney Productions

First Laurel printing—October 1968

MONTHS AFTERWARD, just for the hell of it, I looked up my horoscope for that particular day. It said:

> Scorpios [that's me] should regard today with caution. Beware of entering into negotiations or making hasty decisions, for they are liable to have wide-ranging and unexpected results.

Had I looked at it that morning . . . but no, it would have made no difference. After all, who would consider conducting a perfectly normal conversation with his own wife "negotiating"; and as for "hasty decisions," such as agreeing to do something she wanted to do, I go along with her darn near all the time anyway. There wasn't one blasted thing to alert me. I was in the car all set to drive to the station when Mary stuck her head out the front door.

"Oh, Freddie, Helen's simply mad to have riding lessons. I said I'd have to ask your permission. Is it okay with you?"

The gods on high were pitching me a celestial curve, but I didn't know it.

I made an expansive gesture through the car window. "Why not? She's had every other kind of lesson you've been able to dream up."

Mary, an attractive woman at almost any other hour of the day, smiled—and in spite of pink plastic hair rollers became immediately attractive.

"They're a little expensive. . . ."

"Forget it. The best's none too good for *my* family. I can afford it."

This of course was a black lie. I couldn't afford anything we had. Mary's car, my car, the semidemi-split-level colonial ranch house—at least that's what the real-estate man called it when we bought it five years ago—the color television set, the expensive commuting community, Helen's school, Helen herself, to say nothing of Mary. In fact, after my substantial salary had been divvied up among the revenue agents, the moon-shot boys, the highway department, the board of education, and all the rest of the gang who bit off a chunk as it sped past, I couldn't even afford myself. Naturally, I live way beyond my income. Why not? To live any other way here in the Westport area would be thought ostentatious—and probably vulgar.

"You're a lamb," said Mary. "A sweet darling lamb, and I love you very much."

"I love you very much. Even if you have got a guilty conscience."

"Guilty conscience, Freddie? About what?"

She looked so worried for a second that I wondered if I had accidentally hit home. Mary's a wonderful woman—even if overly given to civic virtue and being chairman of things, if they seemed social enough. If she really had something to feel guilty about, I didn't want to know it.

"I just meant you *ought* to have a guilty conscience, springing something like that on me just when I'm leaving for the train."

She grinned now and blew me a kiss, and I drove off reassured and happy for the moment, with my wife, my daughter—well, with all the things I couldn't afford. With my life. I should worry about riding lessons. They wouldn't last any longer than the ballet lessons, the violin lessons, the watercolor lessons, or any of the other lessons. And Helen hasn't had the slightest talent for most of the things Mary had her taught. Which is just as well. Talent just makes people unhappy. I ought to know. I'm lousy with talent, and it makes me miserable a good deal of the time.

You see, my particular talent is writing, directing, and producing television commercials. The awful kind that sell millions of dollars' worth of a product and make everyone watching want to throw up. Take my latest about the fizzy drink that comes in handy tablet form and settles your stomach. Aspercel. I ought to get an award for that one. It's what you might call the "reciprocating double-action" type of commercial. Not only does it sell to people who feel punk; it makes healthy people feel so sick it creates a new market.

But I was talking about Helen. The riding-lesson bit began almost at once, in September. I didn't pay much attention to it at first. For one thing, Hellie'd already *had* riding lessons of a sort. In Montclair, where we lived before I went with the Tomes Agency in New York, there was a crummy livery stable or riding academy where kids flopped about on what looked like samples of living dog food nobody'd got around to canning yet. And of course since she was five she'd cut out every picture of a horse she could find and pasted them on the walls of her room. Also, she'd read most of the print off *Black Beauty* and *My Friend Flicka* and *My Friend Flicka's Daughter* and every other series about red stallions and black stallions and their children and their children's children she could lay her hands on. But by November the horse thing had gone way beyond a normal obsession.

What first tipped me off was my sensitive nose. As a kid I used to ride around my old man's tumbledown farm outside Buffalo, but ever since growing up, for some reason horses invariably make me sneeze. Now the minute I got home I started sneezing. And began finding horsehairs on the livingroom sofa, and then bits of what could only be described as horse—well, manure—scattered all over. I began listening to Helen's conversation at dinner—something I rarely do, being still wrapped up in the day's business—and found I could understand only about every third word. Oh, I knew the meaning of most of the words, but not in the context she and Mary used them. Words like *quarters* and *thrush* and *splints* and *curbs* and *gags* and *coolers*. Why do you suppose it is that horse words all seem to have simple everyday meanings that have nothing to do with horses?

Not only did she talk a language I couldn't understand but she prattled on about people I'd never heard of. Especially a girl named Judy and someone named Wolfgang. Judy, I gathered, was a schoolmate; I learned she had a horse of her own and lived only a couple of miles away with the horse and, purely for reasons of expedience, with her father and mother as well. It was at Judy's that Helen collected most of the horsehair and manure.

About this horse thing, I played my cards wrong from the beginning. Since I was ashamed to admit I didn't know what Hellie and Mary were talking about most of the time, I pretended to be bored, which took hardly any pretending, and kept me from giving away my appalling ignorance. The sneezing helped here. It was a legitimate excuse for not talking, but after a while it got so bad I couldn't stand it. I went to see our company doctor. It was a brief conference.

"Hi, Doc," I said. "Every time my daughter comes anywhere near me, I sneeze."

He nodded, putting on those wise looks they get, and said, "Reverse Oedipus complex, eh? You're in love with your wife."

"Why not? She's an attractive woman."

"And so you resent your daughter because she comes between you. So you sneeze, unconsciously claiming your wife's attention."

"No, Doc," I said, "I sneeze because my daughter smells like a horse."

He cocked his head to one side. "Sure you're not imagining this? Any reason you know of why she should smell like a horse?"

"Sure, because she's covered with horsehair." I saw his eyebrows cock up. "Don't get me wrong, Doc. She gets it from horses and all the—stuff—she trails through the house. But what can I do about it?"

He grinned, wrote out a prescription for a hundred antihistamine pills, and that was that.

The pills took care of my physical problem. They did nothing for a few other problems I had, like the debts that were beginning to make me feel like Atlas with the world on his shoulders. I was getting deeper in hock every day, and my job was beginning to get my goat. I'd been with Tomes for ten years—producing those commercials, and acting as account executive, without commission, for the past five. All around me I saw men zooming past me on the way up. Somehow I had to get off the treadmill and start getting up in the world myself.

But these were ancillary problems. What worried me most was that ever since the horse lessons Helen was acting less and less like a girl, and because of this, I guess, every day we seemed to drift further apart. Unlike a lot of guys, while Hellie was cooking in the oven I hadn't been wanting a son. I'd wanted a daughter. What had I got? A jockey! I blamed Mary for encouraging her to be interested in all the wrong things instead of the right things—like boys. Helen was fifteen, close to sixteen. Instead of riding, what she needed was the kind of lessons they teach at places like the fashionable girls' prep schools or Katharine Gibbs: lessons about how to wear your hair and how to dress and how to talk and how to move your legs and what to do with the other parts of yourself. Helen has everything else she

8

needs. She's perfectly well built, and she isn't homely. I mean, she doesn't have pimples or a big blobby nose or anything like that. She just manages to *look* homely.

This problem came to a head at Christmastime. There was a junior dance at the country club, and I wanted Hellie to go. She didn't want to go. I insisted. *This* was something girls did. To me it was as simple as that.

I will never forget that evening. I'd bought her a blue dress that the girl in the shop in Westport called a "Junior semicasual formal," which made me think of what the real-estate agent called our house. I came home from the office early that evening to find Mary waiting for me, looking worried. After the briefest sort of kiss, she said: "Freddie, Helen honestly doesn't want to go to this dance. She's scared to death."

"In another six months she'll be sixteen. She *must* want to go to the dance. She's a girl."

"She's scared to death," said Mary again.

"Of what?"

"Just—everything. Appearing in public. Boys. Strangers. Herself."

I couldn't see it. I just wasn't willing to believe *my* daughter could be a misfit.

"Were you scared of things like that when you were almost sixteen?"

Mary produced the funny crinkly smile that I'd always thought cute as hell.

"Well, no—no. But then boys always seemed to—like me. *You* should know. Wait a minute. I was, too, scared about going to my first dance."

"Well, then . . ."

"But *I* was only twelve."

We walked into the little room we called the den for no reason except it wasn't the living room and I sat on the two-place sofa that the decorator, to my disgust, had called a sofette. What Mary had just said disturbed me deeply. Enough so I poured myself a double ration of vodka. I knew from empirical knowledge that Mary had not been precocious. And she was twelve when she had gone through what Helen was going through at fifteen. I swallowed a big hunk of my drink.

"If you're trying to break it to me gently that my daughter's retarded, okay," I said. "What do we do to help her?"

9

Mary looked as if she wanted to laugh but realized this wasn't exactly the sort of thing you should laugh at. She made herself a drink.

"Honey," she said softly, "the fact that you're an idiot doesn't make the slightest difference to me. No, I'm not trying to tell you your daughter is retarded. There isn't anything the matter with her at all. She just happens to like horses better than boys."

"I would say that indicated quite a little the matter with her."

"All it means is that she hasn't gotten to know any boys, and so perfectly naturally she's afraid of them. Do you still insist she go to this dance?"

"Mary, she *has* to begin getting to know boys sometime. In fact, I think it's important that she go to this dance. Is she making a fuss about it?"

"Nobody defies Caesar," Mary said, "not even Caesar's daughter. I'll help her finish getting dressed." In the doorway she turned. "Freddie, promise me one thing. Stay and keep an eye on her at the dance—will you do that?"

I looked at her in astonishment. "Aren't you coming?"

"I'm afraid if I did she wouldn't even try. She'd know that being a woman I'd understand too well how she feels. But I agree with you that since she's agreed to go she ought to make the effort to, well, to behave like a lady. I'll do what I can to help her look the part."

A few minutes later Hellie came into the pantry where I was wolfing down Cooper's sharp American cheese mixed with cellophane. I heard the click as she tripped on the sill; I'd forgotten she wasn't used to wearing very high heels. In fact, I don't think I'd seen her in them since she was about eight and used to sneak a pair of her mother's and sort of ski around in them.

I looked at her. I suppose she wasn't really beautiful, but she looked beautiful to me. And strangely touching. The blue dress with the bouffant skirt and a top that came just off the shoulders; her hair that always looked a little too long to me, done smartly, close to her well-shaped head and drawn back from her face; her eyes, carefully made up just enough by her mother, gave me a shock. She looked— if you didn't look too closely—grown up. But if you looked at her really hard, you saw that the formal dress accented all the little-girl things about her; things like not knowing quite what to do with her arms and hands, the nervous shifting of her weight from one foot to another, the way she unconsciously scrunched up her shoulders as though trying to hide their infinitesimal bareness. What really threw me was that for the first time I saw she looked like Mary. Not the Garden Club Mary, the other one whom I'd met at Bennington seventeen years ago and had fallen in love with and was still in love with.

"Hellie," I said, trying to keep my voice devoid of emotion, "you look perfectly lovely."

She gave me a nervous, twitchy smile. "Thank you, Daddy. I—I wanted to wear my ballet slippers because I feel sort of queer, but Mummy said you wouldn't like it."

"You would look sort of queer in them, honey."

The red lips quivered a moment. "I think I look queer anyway, and that's why I feel queer."

"You look beautiful."

She shook her head. "No, because I'm not beautiful. But it—it's a beautiful dress. And thank you for buying it for me. . . ."

I felt like a brute, an old-fashioned Prussian father. She hated the dress and hated wearing it because she hated going to that damned dance. That fact that she *was* going and was going with good grace made me feel worm-high.

She was teetering wildly on the spike heels. I couldn't subject her to the humiliation of falling flat on her face. "All right, honey girl, let's compromise. Why don't you go up and get those white-and-gold shoes with the little heels you wear to church?"

The high-heeled shoes were off like a shot, and when she came down some of the tension was gone. I got my coat, and Helen put on Mary's beaver and we went out to Mary's gunmetal-colored wagon. I held the door open for Hellie, and she got in, but she didn't know what to do with the bouffant skirt to keep from mussing it when she sat down. I didn't know either, so I suggested she pull the whole thing up and drape it over her shoulders. She blushed crimson at the mere idea. I put the brain to work, and she wound up getting in back, pulling the skirt up over her knees, and she rode kneeling on the seat cushion.

The club was about four miles away. For the first mile she chattered on nervously. Then she ran out of glibness, so for the next mile I chattered. After that, the silence got deeper and deeper. A mile from the club I heard a gulping sound. "Daddy! Stop the car!"

I hit the brakes, heard the tonneau door open and then heard her supper come up. I didn't know whether to try to help or whether to stay put. I decided to stay put. I heard her get back in, and immediately launched into diversionary tactics.

"How's the riding coming along, Helen?"

"Mummy says I'm not to talk about it when you're around because you get upset. Why does it upset you?"

At this point I felt she deserved an honest answer. "I guess because I don't know anything about horses or riding and don't like talk I can't join in."

"But why can't you join in?"

"I can't join in because I'd make a fool of myself."

"You could learn about horses. I have a lot of books." She must have seen my shudder, because she went on. "Oh, I don't mean Black Stallion or Flicka. I mean how-to books. You could learn, Daddy; I *know* you could."

When did I have time to read a book? As it was, I got up at six and worked so hard all day to support her and her mother that by the time I got home and had dinner I was ready for the sack so I could drag myself out again at six to do the same thing all over again. But it would have been cheap to say this.

"Maybe I'll try to learn someday. How *is* the riding coming along?"

"Wolfgang says by April, if I keep going the way I have been, I can start riding in shows. Of course, he'll start me off in some real grundgy ones. That's how Judy did. So I'll get experience in competition. Four-H sort of shows."

I assumed Wolfgang, whoever he was, must be her instructor.

"That's great," I said, my mind wandering. "Who's Judy?"

"Oh, *Popsicles!*" That was a pet name left over from a few years ago—when she'd been a little girl and we'd still been close. It had always made me wince; it still did, but tonight I was glad she felt close enough to use it. *"You* know Judy, Judy Gardner. She's been at our house for dinner lots of times."

"Oh," I said, light breaking, "the manure girl. Of course I know her."

"What did you call her?"

Desperate, I reached way out. "The manor girl," I said. "Gardiner's Manor on Gardiner's Island in the sound.

Those Gardiners were the last authentic lords of the manor in this part of the world."

To my relief she bought it.

"That's cool! Can I tell Judy that's what you call her?"

"No," I said in panic. "Maybe she isn't the same family." I turned into the club driveway. "Well, here we are. All ashore that's going ashore."

One look at her face and I said she could come with me while I parked the car. "Then I'll escort you in the way a gent ought to escort a lady to a dance."

I parked, gave her my arm, and she trembled her way into the clubhouse, where we checked our coats and I turned Helen over to a sort of imitation Mary who was acting as hostess. I waited until I saw Hellie greeted by a couple of girls she knew and the hostess introduce her and the others to some boys who were just coming in; then, just to keep out of sight, I slipped away to the bar. About fifteen minutes later I drifted back to the dance room. The combo was tuning up, and the girls were standing in a bunch giggling, Helen giggling with them. The boys were at the other end of the room, putting their hands in their pockets and taking them out and putting them back and shifting their weight from foot to foot and generally looking unhappy. I hid a grin. I'd never had to go through this country-club-dance bit. Maybe there were some advantages to being a poor boy on a rundown farm.

Helen was obviously okay, so I returned to the bar. I came out once more a little later and everybody seemed to be dancing, so it was back to the bar again. This time I bumped into a couple of guys I saw on the train every night, and we got talking about guess what. Horses? Not on your life. Advertising. The time slipped by. It must have been almost ten when I glanced at my watch and hurried back to the dance.

The four-piece combo was beating out the primitive music all the kids use for the frug, the watusi, the swim, and all the other orgiastic dances that have become fashionable with the younger set. I looked for Hellie but didn't see her among the dancers. She must have gone outside with a boy. That was all right. That was fine, in fact—if she watched her step. I was starting back to the bar when a cleared space opened between the stompers and I saw her. And I felt like a heel for making her come to this dance.

13

She was sitting all by herself at one end of the big bare room in a row of empty chairs. She was ashy pale, gritting her teeth, and at the same time trying to look as if she were having a wonderful time. Every now and then a boy would stroll by on his way to or from the can, and as he'd look down her eyes would get a pleading unwanted puppy look and she'd manage a smile—but the boys would walk on by. Then I saw the blue Alençon lace handkerchief I'd bought her to go with the dress. Without knowing it she'd twisted it to shreds.

I started into the room. I met the hostess, looked her right in the eyes, and said, "If I were your husband I'd beat holy hell out of you!" Then I went to Helen. She had guts all right. She managed to bob a curtsy and say good night to the stunned hostess—and managed to hold onto herself while we got our coats and until we were down the front steps. But then she picked up her skirt and ran straight for the car and completely fell apart.

I drove with one hand, holding her in my right arm all the way home, while she sprayed tears all over Mary's beaver coat. When we got to the house, she pulled herself together—and amazed me.

"Don't tell Mummy how awful it was," she whispered; "it'd just make her sore. What was the matter with Mrs. Harper when I said good night? She looked mighty funny."

"The matter with Mrs. Harper was that I told her if I were her husband I'd beat holy hell out of her—for not making sure no girl was neglected by a bunch of mentally retarded juvenile delinquents too dumb to know their—"

Hellie interrupted me. "I know, Daddy. You don't have to say anything."

She turned in the half-light of the parking area to look at me. The blue eyes were, for a second, a woman's eyes, misty with affection and understanding. I quickly muttered something about putting the wagon away.

I ROCKED ALONG through the winter running as fast as I could on that old treadmill that powers the endless conveyor belt that carries money from the public to the advertisers to Harry Tomes to me, and from me to the First National Stores, the bank, Joe's Service Station, the cleaning woman, the country club, General Motors Acceptance Corp., and half a dozen appliance company finance joints.

By now my creditors and I seemed to be in a neck-and-neck race. The more I owed, the more they pressured me into buying and the less I dared refuse. I was afraid if I didn't play their way they'd gang up and descend on me en masse. As they did business on this same basis with most everyone I knew, I didn't see how *any* of us could survive. By March, before the summer people moved in to take up the slack, it was an even-money bet that the creditors might go broke before the guys who owed them dough did.

Funny part of it was that this hand-to-finance-company existence never seemed to bother Mary at all. Mary's folks, out in Redlands, California, where she was born, had owned orange groves in the good old days before the races at Santa Anita and other places shoved aside growing oranges and making "B" movies as the state's principal industries. Mary had not wanted in her childhood and she had not wanted while she was at college where I met her, and even though her folks were presently on the broke side I was damned if she was going to want now she was married to me. I guess, in a way, Mary was my status symbol. Her old man's beginnings weren't much different from my old man's beginnings, but to me Mary had always been way up there.

By April the financial thing was so acute that I seriously began thinking about selling the semidemi and moving into a bungalow. It was then, as though she had sat down and figured the worst possible moment, that my beloved status symbol hit me on top of the head with a flatiron.

It was at dinner in late April; the kind of warm, pleasant

smell-of-gardens-growing sort of evening that makes a man think about painting his boat and getting his deep-sea reels oiled up. I thought after dinner I'd go out to the garage and sit on an old Coke case and just look at my boat resting there on its little old two-wheel trailer and let myself dream about fishing. Which is sometimes a lot more satisfactory than actually fishing. The big ones don't get away as often in the garage as they do out in the ocean.

"Daddy."

I must have looked way off somewhere because Helen said: "Please pay attention. This is important. This is *it!*"

"Shoot."

"Popsicles." She'd been saying that a lot since the ghastly night of the dance. Mary put her hand over Hellie's. "Don't call your father that, dear. It makes him ill, and then he has to start taking Gelusils and—"

"Mary! Not in front of the child," I protested. "I simply cannot afford to take a chance on her going around even mentioning Gelu—the name of a rival product."

Helen looked at me with fond contempt. "Oh, Father, you think I'm so square I don't know Aspercel is the magic word in this family? That thirty-nine percent of the users of Aspercels have fewer gas pains than—"

I laughed. She was teasing me, but I liked her attitude. Like father like daughter, except for the manure bit. "Hellie, you were starting to say something about this being 'it'?"

The first part was lost in a huge mouthful of mashed potatoes . . . "thinks I'm developing wonderfully. He said this afternoon I have the prettiest hands and seat."

I felt the old adrenalin start pumping. I resented the gall of any man telling my daughter how she was developing and that she had a cute bottom. Then I checked my anger. I should be tickled pink. I forced a phony smile.

"What else did *he* say?"

"He said"—Hellie was bubbling with excitement—"he said he thinks there's just a chance I might make it this fall."

"Of course there's an 'if,' " said Mary. "But that's always true in a thing like that."

"He's willing to let me try. Isn't that wonderful of him?"

I had no idea what my wife and daughter were talking about. But with the self-protective instinct all husbands and fathers develop, I knew I was being set up for the kill. So I temporized.

"That's great," I said. "Good kid, that boy."

I'd overreached. I was supposed to know "him," but apparently wasn't supposed to be on such patronizing terms with him. I sensed from the white, tight-lipped look on my daughter's face that I had committed some dreadful form of *lèse-majesté*. She dissolved into tears.

I turned to Mary for clarification, but nobody gets away with anything with my Mary. She looked down her pert, aristocratic nose at me, her blue eyes accusing.

"Just how many double vodkas did you have in the bar car?"

This was unfair. I hadn't had any. I said so. Down came the nose.

"You honestly don't know who we're talking about?"

"No, but maybe if you'd taught your daughter not to try and talk with her mouth full . . ."

"We were talking about Wolfgang von Roetz—your daughter's riding instructor. I know you must know who *he* is because you've seen his name on the bills he's been sending you every month for the past seven months."

I quibbled. A good quibble sometimes comes in handy. "I've never seen any of the bills. Just the envelopes. His name isn't on them."

"You've never even *opened* the bills?"

"What was the use? I couldn't pay them anyway."

"Oh, Frederick!—really!"

Except on special and usually horrible occasions she hasn't called me Frederick since that day in church seventeen years ago when she said, "I Mary take thee Frederick," and even then she flashed me a grin and said "Freddie" with her lips. She got up from the table.

"Where are you going?" I asked her. "We haven't finished dessert."

"The hell with dessert. I'm going to get you a double vodka. Maybe a triple. Maybe one for myself, too. I need one and you're going to."

17

BACK IN THE DEN, I looked at the bill Mary handed me and I could feel my complexion turn to crimson and then to purple like a disturbed chameleon. I was a damn disturbed chameleon. The billhead said:

THE AUSTRIAN SCHOOL OF EQUITATION IN AMERICA
WOLFGANG VON ROETZ, DIRECTOR

To: Frederick R. Bolton, Esquire
Creek Road
Weston, Connecticut

For Expert (Junior) Instruction:
64 Lessons   @ $10.00 .... $640.00
Horse rental   @ $ 5.00 .... 320.00
Balance due April 1st $960.00

In script was written below:

Thank you,
W. von R.

I looked at the bill and looked at it again. For one thing I could not believe a child of mine could be so dumb it could cost nine hundred and sixty dollars just to teach her to ride a horse. I mean, what the hell, riding a horse! You just get up on it, grab the reins, and say "Giddap" and kick it in the slats. When you want it to stop, you yank on the reins, and if that doesn't work you steer it at the wall of a house or something. That's how I rode when I was a kid, and it hadn't cost my old man any nine hundred and sixty dollars. It hadn't cost him nine dollars and sixty cents. Good thing, too, because most of the time he didn't have nine dollars and sixty cents.

Mary held the triple vodka to my lips. "Swallow. Again.— Now again."

I began to think, and at once had an idea that might explain everything.

"*I* get it. Helen once mentioned something about Madison Square Garden? I mean, I guess circus riders get pretty good pay in the Garden. That could explain this bill. Three, four—maybe even five hundred a week, huh?" I shook my head in wonder. "My little Hellie a circus rider. I can't get over it. An artiste!" A vision floated hazily in front of my eyes. "I guess when the boys get a load of how she looks in that spotlight all done up in tights and spangles and glitter stuff in her hair, that'll be the end of the wallflower stuff. Why, Mary, she'll hardly be able to fight them off."

Mary's voice sounded as if it were coming from a long way off. From outside the asylum gates. "Your daughter," she said slowly and so distinctly there could be no misunderstanding, "has not been studying to become a circus rider."

"She hasn't? Why not?" I hated seeing that bubble burst. Little Hellie had looked so pretty in it. "What in heaven's name for nine hundred and sixty bucks' worth *has* she been studying? How to become a female Eddie Arcaro?"

"She has been studying," said Mary, still with that painfully distinct diction, "what technically is known as 'Equitation, Hunting Seat.'"

"Come again?"

"That's the proper way to ride a hunter. A horse that's known as a hunter."

"A hunter that hunts what? Besides oats?"

"Stop trying to be funny, Frederick. This is very serious."

"Anything that costs nine hundred and sixty dollars is mighty serious. Something you can't see or touch or resell that costs nine hundred and sixty dollars is so serious a thing I don't know that I can bear to talk about it. Can I ask another silly question?"

"I don't see how I can stop you. You're bigger than I am."

"Okay. Where are we going to get the nine hundred and sixty dollars? God knows I haven't got it."

Mary didn't say anything. She picked up her vodka on the rocks and sipped thoughtfully. Mary was a chic thirty-seven, but right now she looked way over forty.

"I'm a flop," I said, and meant it. "Other husbands—guys I see on the train—a little thing like nine hundred and sixty dollars wouldn't mean anything to them. They buy

19

their wives mink coats and diamond bracelets and—"

"That's what *you* think!" Mary interrupted, her eyes flashing. "Don't forget, I *know* their wives—some of them, anyway. Those guys *talk* about buying mink coats and diamond bracelets. If once in a lifetime they actually do produce a mink coat, it's because they've traded expense accounts with some other guy who sells mink coats as a sideline."

This was something to think about—an expense account could be used for barter and trade—but not now. "Where can we raise that dough? I'm in hock to my ears at the bank right now. I even had to hock next year's Christmas bonus to pay Hellie's spring semester bill at Weston Country Day. I feel awful about this, Mary, because I know I said go ahead and give her the lessons." I laughed, but the noise didn't come out sounding like a laugh. "Know what I thought riding lessons cost? About a buck and half, two bucks a shot. That's what they cost when I was a kid. In Buffalo, that is."

"A couple of centuries ago. Poor darling Freddie." She curled her feet under her on the sofa, and sipped her drink. "We could sell the wagon, I suppose, and I could drive you to and from the train in your old car like the young marrieds. That would do it, Freddie. When you get off the train, would you look at me the adoring way those men look at their wives?"

I put my arm around her. "No. And I couldn't let you do that." She dropped her head to my shoulder. "I'll find some way of getting it up."

Suddenly she sat bolt upright. "Oh, God, I forgot. The poor kid! You haven't heard the half of it. *Poor* Hellie! We just can't swing it—and she has her heart set— That's what she was starting to tell you."

The vodka was working, I guess, because the sight of her looking so dejected and hopeless made me say: "It's all right, sweetheart. I'll take care of it somehow. She doesn't have to give up this equi—equi—whatever it is. If that's what she wants more than anything else in this world, okay. After all, she's my daughter, isn't she."

This was, of course, not meant as a question, and, fortunately, was not taken as one.

"But that isn't what she wants more than anything else in the world," said Mary in a funny voice. "She wants a horse of her own. That she can ride in big horse shows. In equitation classes."

"She's dreaming!"

"Of course she is. But didn't you ever want anything so much you just couldn't stand living unless you got it?"

"Yes, I sure did!"

"And did you get it?"

I looked at her with a self-satisfied leer. "Yes, I got it. Seventeen years ago. You and I were married a couple of months later, remember?"

Gently, Mary reminded me we were talking about horses.

"Well, how much *is* a horse? And why can't she rent one?"

"As a matter of fact, she could. But to rent the kind of horse she has to have in the kind of shows she'll be riding in would cost as much as buying one. Honestly, Freddie, I've been over and over this with Wolfgang, and it makes sense. It seems at last we've found the thing that Helen really has an absolute talent for—"

"Yeah, spending money I haven't got. She inherits it from guess who."

Mary glided right over this. "You see, Wolfgang teaches only top riders. He won't let his pupils ride in the big AHSA shows unless he thinks they can at least get in the ribbons. It would louse up his reputation as *the* hotshot instructor. He says Helen's ready. I'll prove it to you."

She ran upstairs and was back inside of two minutes with three crummy little blue ribbons—just single pieces of blue ribbon with a brass safety pin and crummy gold lettering that, wearing off, said "The . . . 4-H Horse Sh . . ." I knew the missing letters had to be "ow" rather than two I would have found more appropriate. They also said, "F . . . st Pr . . . z." Beside them on the coffee table Mary had put two little silver cups, and I mean *little*. They were engraved. One said "Champion." The other said "First Prize." Champion or First Prize where or in what neither of them said.

I opened my mouth to make a crack. I didn't make it. All of a sudden the absurdity of the scene struck me and I was about to laugh, but didn't. This wasn't funny; it was close to being tragic. All the sweating and concentrating and just plain work Hellie had put in—seven long months of it. All that dough I was going to have to get up for good old Wolfie. All the dough I knew right now I was somehow going to have to get up to buy my kid a horse. And to prove the whole bloody performance perfectly justifiable, Mary turns up with what looked like two tin eyewash cups! I sneaked a glance at Mary and saw she was waiting for me to radiate enthusiasm. All at once she looked very much as Hellie had at the dance, looking up hopefully at the boys as they passed by.

"Well?" Mary's voice trembled.

I had to say *some* thing that wouldn't hurt her. Just for the hell of it I told the truth. "I'm overwhelmed."

"Don't try to be funny, Freddie."

"I'm not." I picked up one of the ribbons. "Even cheap gold lettering doesn't wear off unless it's rubbed off. From being slept on under a pillow, maybe? From whatever a little girl does with something that stands for all her cockeyed dreams. You've proved something all right, Mary. Not that Hellie's very much of a rider—yet. What you've proved to me is that it isn't the size of these crummy cups that counts; it's how much Hellie put into winning them."

"They're all Wolfgang's been willing to let her try and win yet. I think her winning them's quite something."

"So do I. I guess they're probably the most expensive eyewash cups in the world. And I guess the horse jazz means a lot more to her than I've suspected. If I can figure out how to swing it, I think we ought to back her up in it. What the heck—a couple of hundred bucks for a horse of her own . . ."

"Well, a little more than that." And Mary bounded off to another angle of persuasion so fast I suddenly felt apprehensive. "There's another reason why having a horse would be a good idea for Helen."

"Keep going."

"Well, you know how worried you've been about how immature she is socially? I mean with practically no poise at all?"

"I would say," I said, after weighing the metaphor, "she has about as much social poise as a giraffe at a cocktail party in a low-ceilinged apartment."

"Yes. Well, Eleanor Gardner tells me that Judy was the same way. Then they bought her a horse, and somehow it made all the difference."

Even though Judy Gardner was Helen's buddy, she hadn't really registered on me because she dressed just the way Helen did and she was at that stage of development where, unless you happen to be their father or their uncle or something, girls seem interchangeable—like army rifle parts—except some are dark and some are light. Now that I really thought about it, she did have more poise than Helen. She'd get up when I came into a room and would hardly giggle at all and would always find something intelligent to say, like, "Isn't it a lovely evening, Mr. Bolton?"

"All right, how much is a horse?"

Mary got up and edged to the doorway. "Less than that little sports car you've been muttering about buying yourself."

This was dirty billiards.

"How much, Mary?"

She seemed unable to get out the words.

"How much is a horse, sweetheart?"

She took a deep breath. "Two thousand dollars, and as Wolfgang says, if we don't spend it and get her a horse, we might as well have put all the money we've spent so far down the W.C."

"Down the what?"

"Wolfgang is very Continental. He means down the john."

I thought I was beginning to see through Wolfie. "And I suppose it just happens that right at the moment, if we act fast, Wolfgang just happens to have exactly the right horse for her?"

"Freddie"—now that I had neither strangled her nor shot myself at the suggestion I go into hock for another two grand, her normal imperiousness returned—"Freddie, this may come as a shock to you, but Wolfgang refuses to sell horses to *any* of his pupils."

This made sense. I thought a little better of Wolfie. Not much, just a little.

"I get it. Obviously all his pupils can't always win ribbons, but since he's sold their dumb parents on the idea that if he teaches them they will, he has to have something to blame. That's where the horses come in. The horse they've bought from somebody other than old reliable Wilhelm Wolfgang von Roetz."

"Freddie"—full confidence in her physical safety restored, she was back beside me on the sofa, one arm around my neck—"you might as well get the whole package. After we've bought the horse we'll have to build a little tiny stable for him and buy a little one-horse trailer—

on time payments, of course—so we can take him to the shows."

"He's a horse; why can't he walk to the shows?"

"Because they have them all over New England and Long Island, and even with the three or four nearby, well, there are hard roads and traffic—and besides, he wouldn't be the kind of horse you ride to places. Only after you get there. We can get a mortgage to build the stable. I've checked. And it only has to be two rooms, one for his stall and . . ."

"And one for you and me. Then we'll have to build one for Hellie because we sure aren't going to be able to afford to live in a house."

Again she rode right over my words. ". . . and one for the saddles, blankets, bridles, dandy brushes, and—"

"Does he have to have dandy brushes? Wouldn't ordinary ones do? Or would that be bad for Wolfgang's reputation?"

"Dandy brush is the name of a certain *kind* of brush. For cleaning his coat."

"Couldn't we use the vacuum cleaner—"

Even as the words were out, it hit me. I held up my hand for silence. "I just got an idea."

"For one of those awful commercials?"

"No. Quiet now. Don't disturb it in gestation."

We sat motionless. My brain whirled; I could all but hear it clicking like a high-speed computer. Say I could acquire . . . not buy, acquire . . . a *five*-thousand-dollar horse. The bank would lend me two thousand on him if he was insured, and then I could pay Wolfie off and make down payments on the trailer and the rest of the stuff we'd need. If I could just acquire—con somebody—sell somebody on the idea of . . . My mouth dropped open in awed admiration of a brain that could produce the plan mine had conceived in that split second.

"I have got it," I said quietly. "I have absolutely got it. I am almost certain that if Helen is as good as you say—good enough to ride against kids who are good enough to ride in Madison Square Garden—I can get her one hell of a horse!"

"Oh, *dar*-ling!"

"On one condition."

"That she take care of it herself? Of course she will."

24

"You're damn right she'll take care of it herself. But that's not the condition."

"Then what *is* the condition?"

I smiled my genius smile. It is a flickering, shy little smile—calculated to make people want to punch me in the nose. I smiled—and said nothing. I really do have a mean streak in me.

4

THE NEXT MORNING I walked out of Grand Central and up Lexington Avenue to the shiny newish building that housed the Tomes Advertising Agency, all three floors of it. I got off at the middle floor (top floors were for top executives, and even after ten years I wasn't a vice-president), crossed a small lobby lighted by a blond receptionist with very short skirts and a handsome front, and turned down a passage that was lined on both sides with what strangers at first took to be cells. Closer examination showed them to be cages, eight-by-six windowless cubicles with arched doorways and grilled gates that theoretically provided privacy for the minor account executives, their secretaries, various research types, copywriters, and other fauna indigenous to the advertising business.

Halfway down the lines of cages I came to mine. I knew it was mine because it was empty and because Miss Clemens, my secretary, was in the adjoining one. She nodded to me as I passed and I nodded to her, then went into my cage and closed the openwork "door" behind me. I wanted the illusion of privacy. I picked up the phone and dialed the boss's secretary. When she came on the line I told her I wanted to make an appointment to see Harry Tomes. She suggested three o'clock a week from this coming Friday, subject to later confirmation of course. Taking my life in my hands, I said that unfortunately I was booked solid all next week and the rest of this one but to buzz him on the intercom and tell him I had an idea for a new kind of image creation and subliminal advertising that had been illegal until I worked out how to legalize it and that it might serve as a pattern for the whole industry and would he have lunch with me today at Toots Shor's.

There was a brief wait; then she was back on the line.

"Did you say you had a new idea for handling image creation for one of our accounts that used to be illegal until you thought of how to legalize it? Mr. Tomes wanted to be sure I had it right."

"Not for one account, for lots of them. As a matter of

fact, I have an appointment set up with the Allied Drug and Food people for this afternoon. I gave them only a clue on the phone, but they jumped at it—tentatively, of course."

A second later Harry Tomes's elegant voice came on the line, and I knew he'd been listening. I'd figured he might be, my inviting him to lunch being a real attention grabber. The hired help normally didn't do that.

"Freddie?"

"Hi, Harry." It was that kind of agency. You had to make appointments a week ahead through a third party to talk with the boss, but the agency image demanded you call him by his first name just as if he were a friend. "What say?"

"Look, Freddie, I'll be glad to lunch with you today, but do we have to go to Toots Shor's?"

"Well, no. We could go to Sardi's. Shor's and Sardi's are the only places where you let me have an expense account."

I heard the secretary who was still on the line gasp and click off. Then I heard Harry chuckle.

"You want to take *me* to lunch on *your* expense account?"

"If I took you any other way you'd have to eat corned beef and cabbage on Third Avenue. You might not like that."

"Look, I have a better idea. You have lunch with me on *my* expense account."

"If you insist."

"All right, meet me at the University Club. Twelve fifteen, right?"

"Yes, sir!"

"And Freddie—you didn't dream up this idea you say you have as an excuse to get me alone to talk to me about something else? Like a raise?"

"I promise you that if *you* want to talk about a raise I'll be willing to listen, but *I* want to talk to *you* about what I said I wanted to talk to you about."

"Sorry. Your crack about corned beef and cabbage, you know?"

"Well, I'm not kidding about that, either."

"No." His voice sounded thoughtful. "No, I suppose not. Well, okay, twelve fifteen."

"Right, sir."

I buzzed for my secretary. I was supposed to buzz for

her even though she was only a pane of glass away. It would have been much easier to yell, "Hi Suzie" or just to tap on the glass, and beckon. But even minor executives didn't do that sort of thing at the Tomes agency. I watched her pull her skirt down over her knees, pat her hair, sneak a look in the thin little mirror she kept glued to the back of her desk calendar, and generally prepare for the long voyage to my cubicle four steps away.

After she'd made her entrance I said, "Would you by any chance know anything about . . ." I stopped, looking at her. Like everything at the Tomes Agency—the rugs, the draperies, the furniture, the iron grillwork on the cubicle doors—the secretaries were chic, glossy, and expensive-looking, and matched the décor. Oddly enough, all of them could type superbly, but their individual personalities, if any, were completely submerged. They didn't even look sexy in spite of their stage makeup, because to look sexy a girl has to look human. I changed my mind. "No, I guess you wouldn't," I said.

"I might."

"The odds are all against it."

"Why don't you ask me, Mr. Bolton? I know about lots of things you probably don't think I know about. Because I don't look as if I knew about anything except being a secretary."

This intrigued me. Suzie had been my secretary for a year. For the first time, I realized she probably ate and went to the bathroom and things like that just as people do. It had never occurred to me before. I somehow must have felt that when she wasn't being my secretary she was probably covered up for the night like the electric typewriters.

"It's a long shot, but you wouldn't by any wild chance happen to know anything about horses?"

The effect of this simple question was astonishing. The Katharine Gibbs mold cracked, revealing a girl called Suzie Clemens who happened to be a secretary in an advertising agency daytimes; but when evening came, turned into a real live, animated girl you didn't just cover up and—well, I suppose you did, if it were cold.

"Horses!" she cried. "What kind?"

I was a little taken aback. "Well, what kinds are there?"

"Oh." She sat down on the little chair beside my desk. "Well, there're Appaloosas, Arabians, Morgans, palominos, thoroughbred and Standard Bred, parade, quarter horses, working stock horses, jumpers, hunters, Hackneys, five-gaited, Tennessee—"

"Whoa! You said the one I want. Hunters, that's the one. You know anything about hunters, Suzie?"

An expression of mild distaste came to the lips that I could see now really were lips. Quite attractive, almost kissable lips. Or would be if you troweled off enough Revlon.

"Hunters," she said. "I'm a quarter-horse girl." Her eyes lighted up. "Barrel bending and cloverleaf are my specialty. I know a little about hunters, of course. But why hunters, Mr. Bolton? Quarter horses are so much more—"

"Because I'm—acquiring one for my daughter."

"Oh, too bad."

"What does that mean?"

"She'd have so much more fun with a horse like mine."

"You own a horse? Of your very own?"

"Of course."

How could she own a horse? My first thought was that she was being kept by some rich nut. But she no longer looked like the sort of girl who'd go in for that sort of thing.

"Please don't be offended if I ask you a personal question. About your horse, that is."

"Of course not."

"How much did you pay for him?"

"He's a her. I paid two hundred and fifty dollars. But she was green, of course, and a three-year-old. Completely unschooled. That makes a difference. I made her myself. Why don't you change your mind and get your daughter a quarter horse?"

Two hundred and fifty dollars! One tenth of what I was supposed to pay. Suzie was still rattling on about her horse.

"My bedroom's just full of ribbons—blues and reds and yellows—and trophies we've won. I'd love you to see them sometime." She must have caught a look in my eye, because far down under the pancake she was blushing. I wouldn't have known except that the lobes of her ears turned as pink as a rabbit's. "It would be perfectly all right, Mr. Bolton. I have a girl friend visiting me."

"I'd love to see them even if you didn't have a girl friend. Now tell me, did you ever hear of a character called Wolfgang von Roetz?"

"Did I! I guess everybody has. Why?"

"He's been teaching my daughter to ride."

Suzie whistled. "She must be tops. Is she?"

"I don't know. I've never seen her ride."

"But that's just awful. That's downright cruel, Mr. Bolton!" This time her lobes turned scarlet.

That was not the sort of thing Katharine Gibbs taught secretaries to say to their bosses. Of course, it had just slipped out, so it didn't bother me. But the fact I suddenly saw it was true did bother me. It bothered me like hell. Hellie and I had been drifting apart for two or three years, I guess, ever since her mother got going on all those weird lessons—ballet lessons and painting lessons and violin lessons. Before that, she and I used to have a swell time together talking, for instance, about fish. But she'd lost interest in fish and all the things that went with them, like the smell of the sea and the heave and roll of a deck, while for my part I hadn't been able to work up much of a sweat about ballet or watercolors or fiddles. Where I'd guessed wrong about the horse lessons was in thinking they were like all the other stuff Mary had dreamed up; now I knew it really was Helen who had been mad for the riding lessons. I felt scared all of a sudden. Was I losing Hellie? Last night, I knew, I'd gone a long way toward losing her.

This situation I would change. In a hurry.

Suzie was still looking scared and miserable.

"Suzie, I'm grateful to you for saying what you did. Fathers, all fathers I guess, forget now and then to at least pretend to share their kids' interests. They get wrapped up in trying to make enough money to feed everybody and dreaming up deals and, well, you know. Besides, nowadays I don't even know what Hellie's talking about half the time, and I have to take pills whenever she comes anywhere near." I saw Suzie's eyes widening. "Most of the time Hellie smells like a horse. I'm allergic to horses; they make me sneeze—and that's all I know about them. Now tell me something. It would appear that my daughter's got to have a horse she can ride in something called Equitation Hunting Seat classes in horse shows. She has to because her heart is going to break if she doesn't. Is there any reason why she couldn't do what you did and get one for two hundred and fifty dollars?"

"One of von Roetz's pupils ride in AHSA shows on a two-hundred-and-fifty-dollar horse?" She sounded aghast at such an outlandish thought. "Why, Mr. Bolton, rather than see that happen he'd give her a horse himself."

"Not a bad idea, if worse comes to worst. How much do *you* think she'd have to pay for a horse she could maybe win on in AHSA shows, whatever they are?"

"American Horse Shows Association. The Big Leagues of the show world. A hunter?" She thought for a second. "Well, it would have to be a three-quarter-bred, probably; thoroughbred might be too hot for her." Her jaws moved thoughtfully, chewing an imaginary straw, country fashion. "Oh, I'd say she'd have to pay somewhere between two thousand and four thousand dollars. More than that and the judges would just write 'push button' or 'passenger' on their card, and she'd be out on her can."

I gritted my teeth. "Suzie, at home I *have* to listen to all this talk I don't understand. Here I don't. Now just what do you mean by 'push button' and 'passenger'?"

"Just what it sounds like. The kids don't have to do anything except sit. The horse does it all."

"I get it. Now tell me something else. What do horses wear—in public, I mean?"

"Tack." I guess she saw my blank look. "That's the saddle and bridle and stuff."

This didn't fit in with my big subliminal advertising plan. Thinking out loud now, I said, "I don't suppose they could have their names painted on their sterns? Like boats? In gold leaf maybe?"

Suzie swallowed hard, started to speak, remembered I was her boss, and said, "Well, Mr. Bolton I've never *heard* of it being done."

"What would a horse-show judge think of that idea? Make it easy for him to tell which was which."

Suzie seemed to be suffering from some strong emotion she was having difficulty keeping under control. "I—I don't think Wolfgang von Roetz would stand for it, Mr. Bolton. Maybe if you'll tell me what you've got in mind I can help you."

"I'm having lunch with the boss. I want to get somebody in the art department to whip up a quick layout that I can take along to show him and the Allied Drug and Food people. Anybody in the art department know how to draw a horse?"

"They must. If they don't I can do it. I draw pretty well

and I want to art school for a while." She smiled. "Of course, if I drew your horse it would turn out to look like a quarter horse."

I looked at her. In the last ten minutes she had become a very pretty girl. I wondered I'd never noticed it before. "Suzie."

"Yes, Mr. Bolton?"

It had been on the tip of my tongue to ask her where she lived. It had occurred to me that dropping in to see all those trophies she'd won bending barrels might be a worthwhile experience. Then it occurred to me I might become one of them.

"Let's go along to the art department."

5

I STUCK IT OUT in my office as long as I could, growing more nervous every second. By eleven o'clock the enormity of asking the boss to lunch—my sheer gall in thinking I could pull off the deal I'd cooked up for Allied—had given me acute palpitations. I was sure I'd overreached in trying to take a flying leap off the treadmill and into the big time. I was frantic with fear I'd get fired—and then financially I'd go under in less than a week.

By eleven fifteen I got up, stuck my head in Suzie's room, said, "Lunching with Tomes. University Club," and took a powder. When I got out in the street I walked fast, heading uptown. Although the University Club was at Fifty-fourth and Fifth, I went past to Fifty-ninth, where Central Park begins. I walked around in the spring sunshine, looking at the homeless bums on the benches, the shiny baby carriages pushed by smartly uniformed nursemaids, at assorted dogs being perambulated by owners, at pigeons and squirrels hanging around looking for handouts. It soothed me, and by the time the University Club came in sight I was all right. Good thing, too, because Harry Tomes was waiting for me just inside the front door.

Harry was miscast as head of an advertising agency. For one thing, he was a gentleman of the old school, and for another he spoke English, which made it a little hard for his fellow executives to know what he was talking about sometimes. He didn't dress the part, either. Instead of the sharp form-fit suits his vice-presidents wore, he had on a sloppy, baggy green tweedy arrangement that must have cost a fortune. No tailor possibly could have been willing to make such an awful-looking suit for less than four hundred dollars. Like Wolfgang, they too have to think about their reputations.

We went up to the dining-room floor and had a cocktail. A cocktail only, which was something else that made him stand out, lunch being a par-three hole in our business. After a while we ordered and went into the big quiet dining room overlooking Fifty-fourth Street. "I haven't seen you in quite a while, Freddie," he said when we were settled down, "but I've been getting good reports on you. That last Aspercel commercial you did, the one where you hired—I can't think of his name—not John Gielgud—but that other really famous actor to play the part of the man with the upset stomach. A stroke of genius. I saw it once at home, by mistake. I hate to admit it, Freddie, but it made me feel so sick I actually had to leave the room and take some bic—" he caught himself. "Some Aspercel. How's the family?"

"Fine," I said. "That is, generally."

His permanently bronzed forehead, beneath wavy white senator-type hair, wrinkled. "Generally? No domestic trouble, I hope."

"No, not domestic. Horse."

He scowled, and the set of his mouth showed he had plenty of the hardness it took to reach the high places.

"I don't like the sound of that. I expect my—associates —to run into debt, to live a little beyond their incomes because that's one of the greatest incentives I know to keep a man on his toes. The boss doesn't have to keep after him; his conscience and his creditors do that. But to run into debt betting on horses—I do not approve of that. In fact, I won't stand for it. I'm not against it morally, but I don't want men associated with me on the executive level who are so dumb they can't recognize the impossibility of beating any system where you've lost fifteen percent of your money to the state and the track before the race even starts. That's why I *own* racehorses instead of betting on them. How deep are you in for?"

"Mr. Tomes." It slipped out. "I mean, Harry. I have never bet on a horse race in my life. I have never seen a horse race except on television, where I watch them to keep up with the commercial content of the programs, and I have no intention of seeing one. In fact, all horses do is make me sneeze."

"I beg your pardon, son. I must have misheard you. I thought you said you had horse trouble."

"I did. Maybe I'd better put it another way and say I have daughter-horse trouble. I'll go even stronger and say I have daughter- and daughter's-mother—that is, daughter- and wife-horse trouble."

He smiled. "You live somewhere around Westport, don't

34

you?" I nodded. "Where the status symbol was born and is saluted like the flag."

"Status symbols I can handle, I think they're funny. This isn't funny. My daughter, it seems, is nuts about horses. She's had about a grand worth of lessons from God, and God says if she has her own horse she'll get good enough to maybe get a shot at Madison Square Garden next fall. My wife's ganged up with her, so now Helen gets a horse."

"So you do want a raise after all. To buy a horse?"

I shook my head. "Everybody always wants a raise. But you couldn't give me a raise that taxes would leave me enough of to buy the sort of horse God says Helen has to have."

"God being?"

"Wolfgang von Roetz."

I was astonished because Harry whistled just the way Suzie had. "You really do have a problem."

I told him I thought I had it solved.

He arched well-trimmed eyebrows. "You have the bank you're going to rob all picked out?"

"Too complicated. And you have to hang on to the money too long before you dare spend it. No, I have—and, well, you may agree with me that the idea transcends"—I added the word like chili sauce—"mere talent and approaches a special category. My daughter Helen is going to buy an extremely well-known—maybe even famous—horse called Aspercel."

"Aspercel—Aspercel? Well known? *I* never heard of any horse called Aspercel."

"No, sir, but I think you're going to. I think quite a few million people are going to. Here's the layout." I reached into my pocket and pulled out a piece of proof paper. On it was a slick line drawing. It showed a girl something like Helen wearing a big grin, carrying a silver tray in one hand, and with the other leading the fanciest-looking horse Suzie and the art department of the Tomes Agency had been able to dream up, which, it being a pretty fancy agency, was a pretty fancy horse. It was wearing a fancy blanket that had imprinted on it, in big block letters, AS-PERCEL. In the background was an equally fancy one-horse trailer. Blazoned on its side was ASPERCEL.

Harry Tomes looked at the layout. Then he looked up at

35

and through me. "So? All this means is that I've got a pretty good art department that can work out a nice layout." He looked harder at the picture, holding his pince-nez over the layout like a magnifying glass, his expression getting sourer by the second. "And," he growled, "one that doesn't seem to know a horse's noseband goes inside the reins, not outside." He looked up at me again. "I wouldn't expect you to know that. Of course, you could have looked it up."

"I'm a producer and account executive, not a research man." I was sore at Suzie, so I was snapping at the boss. It was not a good way to carve out a career for myself. "Sorry, sir, of course I should have checked this thing myself. *I'm* the one who can't afford to let Allied Drug and Food see a presentation with inaccuracies in it. I'm extremely grateful to you, sir, for catching it."

"Now, if I may ask a foolish question, this is supposed to be a presentation of what?"

I touched my napkin to my forehead, delicately shoved some drops of ice-cold perspiration to one side. I'd never made a presentation directly to the head man before. I thought he was just cutting me down to size for the fun of it; I didn't know that what he was really doing was transforming himself for the moment into the client, saying the things the client would say, knocking the presentation before it was fully presented to throw the salesman off balance so he would be buying a sound buy and not some supersalesmanship. I didn't know then that Harry Tomes did this on every major presentation that went out of the agency. I was really shook; this deal I *had* to put over.

I got a grip on myself. "I'm asking you to visualize what the art department can only suggest." I gave him a sheepish smile. "Somewhat inaccurately."

"Damned inaccurately!" He looked at me quizzically. "Do you sell presentations this way when you call on clients?"

I had to grin. "Most of our clients aren't quite as tough to sell as you are, Boss. They seem to go on the assumption that I wouldn't be calling on them and taking up their time unless what I had to offer was pretty darn good."

To my infinite relief he laughed. "Okay, Freddie. You put me properly in my place. I'll quit picking on you. Start fresh."

"Right." I pointed to the drawing. "Your wife and a few

million other upper-class wives subscribe, say, to *Town and Country* or *Harper's Bazaar* or *Sports Illustrated* or, like the really upper crusters, to *The Chronicle of the Horse* and even to the *Illustrated London News* and *Paris Match*. You see a photograph of this horse in the news section of these mags—nowhere near the ads—with a caption under it that reads: 'Aspercel wins again. Miss Helen Bolton leading her famous hunter Aspercel from the ring at Piping Rock after winning the John Q. Public Memorial Trophy.' Next week or next month in one of the other mags you see another picture. The horse has on that plaid horsecoat or whatever you call it in this picture and the caption says, 'Miss Helen Bolton and Aspercel, Show Champion, having lunch after winning the Status Memorial Cup at Fairfield. Miss Bolton is the daughter of Mr. Freddie Bolton, the well-known advertising executive.' Crap like that. My God, Harry, can you see the subliminal image of Aspercel-the-product this sort of thing will create? Without a word of paid advertising this campaign will make the word Aspercel synonymous with health, wealth, swank, sportsmanship, youth—you name it! Do you know any other way you can hit the snob market with what, when you come right down to it, is a gas-pain pill to make you burp? You get the seal of snob approval and automatically you get mass market. You can't do that with paid advertising. You *can* do it by making Aspercel news!" I paused for breath. "Well, sir?"

He gave me a deadpan look that chilled the marrow of my bones. The look lasted for maybe two minutes. Letting me sit there in his nice club dying by inches. I wondered if when in the course of the next minute I finally did die he'd help carry my body out or just let the waiters do it.

"Well, son," he said slowly, as I snapped to attention, "it strikes me that you and I and Allied Drug are going to share a lot of money. On most unequal terms, of course. This one we don't have to light a rocket under to see if it will blast off." He looked sheepish. "Beg your pardon, Freddie, but I've been reading a novel about the advertising business. Your idea, well, I think it's great. Even if I do see one big stumbling block."

"Like what?"

"Simply this. How could you possibly persuade your daughter to ride a horse with, God forgive me, such a silly name? People would kid hell out of her."

"Sir," I said, "my daughter would agree to ride a horse called Lyndon B. Goldwater if that was the only way she could get one. As a matter of fact, if I know Hellie, she'll think Aspercel's a cute name for a horse. Of course, I may have to work on her a little."

"I'll bet. All right, what's the package?"

"Well, with the client's permission we divert enough money from his radio and television advertising to cover the cost of the horse and trailer. Peanuts. I'd guess around ten thousand, plus the cost of the expense account the Tomes Agency would give me to defray some of the costs of hay, oats, horseshoes, and entry fees at the shows. Or I can hock the horse at the Weston Bank."

He smiled. "I should imagine your local banks own an interest in a considerable number of horses." He paused, obviously mulling. "No, son, I think Allied will want to pay the expenses for maintenance and the rest. After all, it will be their horse."

"Harry—" I looked him right in the eye, which, considering he had eyes like pieces of flint chipped off a pawnbroker's heart on a cold day, took quite some doing. "Harry, you could not be more mistaken. This will not be the client's horse nor your horse nor my horse. This deal is on the level. This will be my daughter Helen's horse. That's the only way I'll go into it. Maybe you haven't caught on to the real point here. No magazine or newspaper would give free publicity even under pressure to a horse called Aspercel that was even indirectly owned and operated by the company that makes Aspercel. They couldn't, too obvious. But with the deal on the level and on the strength of the total yearly advertising dough we steer their way anyway, we can tactfully pressure a dozen magazines and all the New York newspapers into running lots of pictures of a kid's horse called Aspercel. But there's a more important reason why it will be Helen's horse."

"Yes?"

"I promised her it would be."

His mouth loosened up, and the ice melted out of his eyes. "I'm glad you said that," he said. "The old verities get kicked around so much nowadays it's refreshing to stumble across genuine corn. By the way, you've got to let *me* go up to Allied Drug and close this thing for you this afternoon. Not you."

"But they expect me. I set up the conference. . . ."

"Son, I assure you I'm quite capable of handling it."

"But you don't think I am?"

"I don't think you're capable of telling them with a straight face that you persuaded yourself to accept a free horse for your daughter to ride in horse shows. Somehow that wouldn't carry much weight with me. But if I tell them one of our vice-presidents has a daughter who's a show rider and I've persuaded him to call her new horse Aspercel as part of a legal subliminal advertising campaign that will cost x dollars . . . By the way, Freddie, you won't mind my referring to you as one of our vice-presidents, will you? It strengthens the—er—pitch."

This stopped me cold for all of ten seconds. But Harry had said he liked stumbling across old corny verities, so I let him have another. "I'll mind if it isn't the truth."

He grinned. "Let's put it this way. If they go for this new brainstorm of yours, it will be the truth. Because you'll have earned it." He chuckled. "And by the way, I wouldn't like one of our new vice-presidents to have to hock his daughter's horse with the Weston Bank. A bit undignified, don't you think?"

We ate lunch then. We'd just been taking bites up to now. When we parted in front of the building, he said if he went straight home from the conference he'd call in and let me know who won.

6

THAT EVENING on the way home I didn't ride in the bar car. I wanted to be alone, which, on a commuting train, means sitting with a few hundred people you don't know instead of congregating with the dozen or so whom you do. I went all the way to the back of the train and out onto the rear platform and stood there, watching the rails flow behind me and wondering why buildings and towers seem to get bigger as you go away from them and then all of a sudden shrink. I knew why the parallel rails gave the impression of getting closer together the farther you got from them. That was because this particular railroad was broke and the rails weren't always quite as parallel as they ought to be and sometimes did just what they looked as if they were doing. I wanted to be alone because this had been an emotional day.

I drove slowly home from the station through the spring twilight. It was nice to see trees shooting out tiny green leaves and to hear the water still in spring spate burbling under bridges and to see men mowing evening grass again. Every now and then—I guess it happens only when you're on the brink of forty—a day turns up that you would like to prolong beyond its normal span. This was that sort of day, and driving very slowly seemed a step in that direction. I turned into the driveway of our place, stopped for a moment to admire the four acres of weeds that surrounded a postage-stamp lawn and the house, the whole ringed by trees, giving a false impression of remoteness. Then I thought about Helen and Mary waiting breathlessly for the return of the lord and master from the wars with news of the battle, and went on up the drive and into the garage. Empty. I walked toward the house. Even before I reached it, it felt empty.

I banged inside, snapped on lights, and went into the pantry. There was a note stuck in the top of the vodka bottle.

Darling, knew you'd find this first thing if I left it here!

Helen and I are out with Jack Gardner and Wolfgang looking at horses. Meet us at their house for cocktails.

We L. U.

H. & M.

Here's a map. P.S. The Gardners are nice people. You know Judy.

Somehow I no longer cared about prolonging this particular day. I was sore and disappointed. I poured myself a slug, splashed some water in it, and tossed it off. Then I studied the map. The Jack Gardners. Jack Gardner, Judy's father. That made him a fellow sufferer. I downed another drink, neat this time, and looked at the note. No, Mary and Helen were off with Jack Gardner looking at horses; it didn't say anything about Mrs. Gardner. That meant he was the nut in that family.

I went out to the garage and sat down on an empty Coke case and stared at my boat. But there seemed to be a barrier between us, and the fish dreams wouldn't come, so I got into the car and drove off under the mistaken impression I had the map of how to get to the Gardners' house photographed in my mind. I managed to get lost in no time at all. It was almost seven before I reached their low white farmhouse with rail-fenced paddocks and a little show-ring with horse jumps in it, and, set back in a grove of trees, a stable.

The front door of the house opened and a woman with pepper-and-salt very short hair and wearing tailored blue slacks and a man's white shirt came onto the flagstone front porch, and smiled.

"I'm Eleanor Gardner. You're Freddie Bolton and you probably need a drink."

She was a tall, slim woman, five, maybe even ten, years older than Mary. Her face, until she smiled a welcome, was quite plain and almost mannish, with features that were too pointed and big black eyes that were too black and strikingly large. But when she smiled, she became surprisingly attractive and thoroughly feminine.

"To be candid," I said, "I do not need a drink, but I would very much like to have one."

"Come on in." She led the way into a wide hall whose walls were hung with old and I guess very valuable steeple-chasing and fox-hunting prints. "Mary telephoned a few minutes ago. She and Jack and Wolfgang are on their way back from the Sheridans', but they stopped to throw hot dogs and milk into the kids."

We went down two steps into a big, gracefully proportioned living room. In a bay window was a table with a splendid assortment of bottles and glasses and ice cubes in a silver bowl.

"You're the man of the moment, so you fix drinks, won't you? I'd like Scotch and soda on the rocks. Tolerably strong."

I fixed the drinks, handed hers to her, and realized she was staring at me. There was an expression of friendly concern in the big black eyes, that amused, tolerant look women reserve for inspecting other women's babies.

She walked across the room to a yellow sofa with a leather-topped mahogany coffee table in front of it and sat down. "You're upset about something aren't you?" It wasn't really a question. "Did something horrible happen in town today?"

I suppose I should have been sore at her, asking me something like that when she hadn't known me over three minutes, but I wasn't. For one thing, she was the sort of woman who made you feel the moment you met her that you'd known her all your life. For another, I was really desperate to tell *somebody* about getting promoted. So I told her the whole story, and when it was over she sounded more disappointed than I that Mary hadn't been home.

I even told her about going out to the garage to visit my boat, but instead of laughing at me she said she understood.

"I used to fish a lot, but then I caught"—she suppressed a giggle—"I caught Jack. Maybe we could go fishing sometime in the fall if this horse bit ever quiets down for five minutes. Honestly, I will be mighty thankful when Judy gets to be eighteen and, according to the rules, will become ineligible for this Hunter Seat Equitation racket. If she'd only get interested in boys. I used to think she was queer for horses. But I've grown hopeful again. I've realized a surprising number of them do seem to end up finally married and pregnant and things, so I suppose it does pass eventually—like measles."

This was like having been shipwrecked in the Sahara Desert and bumping into somebody who's also been

42

shipwrecked in the Sahara Desert. "I thought maybe I was queer for thinking Hellie queer."

Eleanor Gardner shook her head. "Oh, no, our number is legion."

All of a sudden we were friends, laughing together.

"I take it, Mrs. Gardner, that you yourself are not exactly what you might call an equiphile?"

"You take it right! I was once but no more. And the perfectly awful part of it is I have to go along to every single horse show there is anywhere."

"But if you don't like it, why go?"

"Well, theoretically I go to take care of Judy. But the truth is I go because I can drive the horse trailer and Jack can't. He's got a complex about it. So because I love him I suppose, I go. I go to every single show every single weekend from now until the end of October. Just the way you're going to do."

"*Me?* I won't be having anything to do with this horse-show stuff—except to get up the scratch."

She put her left hand on my shoulder. She had a surprisingly strong grip. "My boy, my heart bleeds for your innocence. From what I hear, you, fellow equiphobe, are also going to every horse show from hell to Newfoundland this summer. Starting practically immediately. You play gin or canasta or casino or backgammon?"

"Sometimes."

"Well then, you and I may get very expert at gin, canasta, backgammon, and casino and maybe even chess before this summer is over. I think you're going to be a great comfort to me."

"You're kidding, aren't you? About me really having to go to all these horse shows?"

"No, dear, I am not. Now, brace yourself while I explain how I know. This morning, just for practice and at Jack's suggestion, your wife tried driving our horse trailer. Without the horse in it, thank God."

"And?" I didn't need to ask. So I just inquired how much I owed her.

"Nothing. It was insured at fifty dollars deductible and your wife insisted on paying the fifty." I winced. "But believe me, Freddie Bolton, when you get the nice two-thousand-dollar trailer your wife's picked out for you, you'd *better* do the driving."

"Two thousand!"

"You're a big wheel at Tomes now, remember?"

I'd forgotten all about that. She handed me her glass, and I returned to the reassuring array of bottles. A minute later the front door opened and Mary, looking shot as mothers are apt to look after a long afternoon with kids and before their evening Martinis, drooped into the room.

"Hi, Eleanor. Well, we found a horse. Jack was sweet to come along."

I started to say hello, but before I could Eleanor Gardner said, "Mary, like you to meet a friend of mine. A Mr. Bolton."

Mary, smiling a funny smile, bobbed a curtsy. "How do you do, Mr. Bolton?"

I waved. Eleanor went on. "Mr. Bolton's with the Tomes Agency. You know, advertising?"

"Oh?"

"Yes. And he's very highly thought of there."

"How nice."

"As a matter of fact, he's one of their vice-presidents."

The game ended in a shout: *"What?* Freddie, is this true?" I nodded. "But darling, why didn't you tell me?"

"I wanted to, Mary."

One thing about Mary—she was not dumb. I mean about little things the way "brains" sometimes can be.

"How perfectly awful, our not being home," she cried. "But I never dreamed . . . How did it happen?"

I grinned. "For once the boss led with his chin, and I trapped him."

Before I could go into it, the front door opened again, running feet came through, and a second later something that was all length and legs and arms and flying hair and glowing eyes was hanging around my neck.

"Oh, Daddy! I've found *the* horse!"

"Only if your father approves, Helen," Mary reminded her.

"I schooled him over four feet in the Sheridans' indoor ring, and Wolfgang says he's just perfect for me. *Please,* Daddy, say it's all right for me to have him!"

This was all too sudden. With Helen still holding my hands, I looked over her shoulder at Mary.

"Honey, weren't you—er—anticipating a little?"

"I told Helen we ought to wait before we even started looking, but . . . can I tell him what you said, Helen? . . . Freddie, your daughter said, 'My father said he

44

thought he could arrange for me to have one hell of a horse, and I have more faith in my father than in anybody else in the world and that's why it's all right to start looking.' So—we looked."

I suddenly remembered what Suzie said about my never having taken the time or trouble to watch Hellie ride. And my kid felt like that about me! I hugged her to me tight, so tight it made her gasp. I bent so my lips were right next to her ear, and whispered, "I'll have to decide whether you've picked the right horse, but it *is* all right, Helen."

I thought Helen was going to faint. Instead, as an outlet for God knows how many months of pent-up hopes and fears and wonderings, she burst into a cascade of tears and clung to me even tighter than I'd clung to her.

Again I put my lips right next to her ear. "Hellie. Hellie, listen to me. It's about the horse's name." She stopped crying instantly. "Whatever he's called now, if you want him, *you* have to name him Aspercel. It's—it's a business thing. Can—can you bear to?"

"Aspercel?" she whispered back. "But that's a beautiful name for a horse, Daddy! It's a much nicer name for a horse than it is for a . . . and I can call him Aspie for short. Oh, Daddy, I just love you to death."

She started to dissolve again, but Eleanor Gardner told us to break it up. "Here come Judy and Jack *and* good old Wolfgang."

I looked toward the doorway. God in person, I wanted to meet.

7

JUDY GARDNER came into the room, shook hands, and said: "Oh, Mr. Bolton, we had the most wonderful afternoon! And it's so wonderful about your buying Hellie that wonderful horse! And isn't it a lovely evening?"

Here was a load of the "poise" again. I found myself responding in kind. "Why, thank you, and it was—I mean is —a lovely evening and I'm glad you had a wonderful afternoon."

She giggled, which I had been too polite to do when she'd made the same asinine comments. Then she kissed her mother and, with Hellie, faded out of sight. Naturally, having only been together for eight or nine hours they had a lot of unfinished business to go over.

Jack Gardner came in next. You got the feeling that his warm, friendly smile came into the room first and he just followed it. He was maybe ten years older than I, with sparse, neat gray hair, and a roundish face except for his square chin. He was of middle height, and both his clothes —tweed jacket and gray slacks—and ruddy complexion made him look like the successful country real-estate broker he was. He also looked Yale. He greeted me heartily, apologized for not being home when I arrived, gave his wife a kiss, and said he hoped I'd been properly taken care of in his absence.

"I suppose Helen told you we found a real nice horse for her. Of course, it was late when we got to Sheridan's. Been to a lot of other stables first. And Tim Riley, a pro-dealer who uses the stables there and in exchange manages the place for the Sheridans, had the horse all tacked up and waiting outside the ring, so we didn't take the time to strip him down and vet him. But he went great for little Helen, just great!"

"She said she'd jumped four feet. Is that high? For a horse, I mean? I ask because at college *I* used to jump six feet."

Jack Gardner grinned. "It's low for a good horse but it's high for a kid on a horse."

"What is high for a horse?"

"Anything over five feet is too high for most horses. Our top open jumpers can squeeze over just about seven feet. The record high jump is eight feet and an inch or so."

"You think he's the right horse for Helen?"

Jack Gardner shrugged, then laughed. "I'll take the fifth on that one, Freddie. I said he went great for Helen in the ring—and he did. But there's an awful lot more to a kid owning a horse than just riding him. A heck of a lot depends on the *kind* of a horse he is."

"I thought he was supposed to be a hunter."

"Sure, but technically anyway that's only a type. When I say, 'What kind of a horse,' I mean the same thing you mean when you ask, 'What kind of a guy is he'?"

"And you didn't have a chance to find out what kind of a guy this horse is?"

Gardner gave me the kind of look I've grown used to from Mary and once in a while from Harry Tomes. Speculative. "Wolf ought to be here in a second. He stopped to wash his hands."

"In the W.C.?"

Again the look.

"He's very anxious to meet you."

I was going to suggest that was probably mostly because I owed him nine hundred and sixty dollars when Wilhelm Wolfgang Heinrich von Roetz sauntered across the hall and down the steps into the room.

With a name like that and with the horsy reputation and whatnot I'd expected him to march in looking like one of the old Kaiser's Uhlans, preceded perhaps by a German band—the way Jack Gardner was preceded by his smile—clicking his heels and bowing from the waist and gargling in his throat and all kinds of Teutonic stuff like that. I felt badly let down when he turned out to be smallish and slim, with neatly trimmed fair hair and blue eyes. Wearing brown slacks, a tan tweed sports jacket, white shirt, and maroon tie, he looked just about like anybody else.

"Wolfgang, like you to meet Freddie Bolton. Freddie, this is Oberkommandant von Roetz of the Uhlans."

"Hi, Mr. Bolton." We shook hands. "I wish Jack would stop trying to startle people with that Prussian-cavalry-officer routine. Some people believe him."

"Well," I said, "with a name like yours—and the European accent—can you blame them?"

"Please believe me, Mr. Bolton, the nearest I ever got to be a cavalry officer *anywhere* was when I made sergeant at Fort Riley just before they took all our horses away and gave us tanks and jeeps instead."

To my horror I found myself liking the guy. In a few minutes, if I wasn't careful, I'd find I was actually enjoying writing out a check for nine hundred and sixty dollars to him. He was lousy with charm.

"Don't let him knock himself to you, Freddie," Jack broke in. "He stayed on in Europe after the war and used his G.I. loans to go to equitation schools like Saumur and the Lippizaner one in Vienna, and he studied under a bunch of German cavalry officers who were tops in dressage. That's where he got the accent."

"Which," said Wolfgang, "just happens to be, shall we say, synthetic? Like the piaffe movement in Grand Prix Dressage. The real accent is Wyoming, but that wouldn't do—after I'd decided to become an imported product—and I hired a ghost writer and a literary agent." He chuckled. "Every professional horseman should have at least one of each. Mr. Bolton, your daughter possibly may have a great gift. I have big plans for her. Big plans!" I guess he saw my face tighten up, because he quickly added, "Provided you approve of them, of course."

Jack handed Wolfgang and Mary drinks. Mary said, "After Helen schooled that strange horse over those big jumps this afternoon, Wolfgang told me that if she has a few really good horses to work with she could be ready for the U.S. Equestrian Team by the time she's eighteen."

This was too thick even for me in my abysmal ignorance to swallow. "I'll bet he tells that to all the girls," I said pleasantly.

From the angry flush that rose into Wolfie's smooth sun-bronzed cheeks I knew he really did tell that to all the girls and most of the boys, too. Of course, this wasn't much worse than some of the slight exaggerations I make about products I advertise, and I realized Wolfie was only selling his own product as best he could. It gave me a line on his character. As a fellow salesman, it did not lower him in my estimation—raised him, if anything. But he leaped in with an alibi.

"Of course, she is only just beginning," he said, "and even I could be wrong about her. I wouldn't want, the first time you see her ride in a show, Mr. Bolton, for you to expect her to look like Billy Steinkraus."

Here was a name I knew. It made me feel secure enough to risk what I thought of as a witticism. "I wouldn't like her to look like Billy Steinkraus either," I said. It lay right where I'd placed it, in the middle of a vast wasteland of silence. I shrugged. "Well, I guess I probably wouldn't understand a lot of your jokes either, so that makes us even. But what I'd like to know, before I get too enthusiastic about horses, is how good is she right now?"

He didn't seem to want to answer this, and his reluctance started a shivery sensation in my stomach.

"Well," he said, "with the right horse, by the end of the summer, she should be winning blue ribbons in equitation classes. With enough luck she could even qualify to ride in the Maclay or the Medal finals in the Garden—as I have already told Mrs. Bolton."

I didn't know what this Medal and Maclay business meant. At the moment I couldn't care less. My stomach began to jump. This was not how Mary had presented his prognosis to me. It certainly didn't fit the pitch I'd made to Harry Tomes and that he had made this very afternoon to Allied Drug.

"But she can't win blue ribbons *now?*"

He gave me a superior smile. "In little 4-H shows, yes. She already has."

"But in real AHSA shows? The—big league?"

"She might."

I could feel my eyes starting to get a metally glint like Harry Tomes's. And when I added my sense of outrage at having been conned into letting Harry and the whole agency down, it made me feel ten feet tall.

" 'Might' isn't good enough, Mr. von Roetz. You told her she was ready to ride in the big-league shows. As a competitor, not a spectator sitting on an expensive horse following the other kids around the ring and then when the ribbons are handed out getting kicked in the teeth."

"She's a beginner, Mr. Bolton. To win blue ribbons in the big shows takes polish, polish, polish!"

"Starting right now," I said, "you are to double or triple the lessons, and you give her that polish, polish, polish. How long will it take you to get her up to where I was told she already is? That is, really ready to compete. Two weeks?"

"Say six weeks?"

I couldn't stall Harry Tomes or Allied Drug that long. "A month."

He shrugged. "We can try."

The tenseness, an almost shocked sort of tenseness I could feel in the silence around us, made me feel sorry. I'd made a scene; that was all right. What wasn't all right was that I'd made it in Eleanor Gardner's living room, and it must have made her terribly uncomfortable. I wanted to apologize but that would only have made it worse. There was another way. I put a hand on Wolfgang's shoulder.

"I'll tell you one thing you *have* done for me for which I'll be eternally grateful, Mr. von Roetz. You've given my daughter a whole new interest in life at a time when she needed it most. You've given *me* a new interest in life too."

Relief flooded his face. He looked like a man who's just escaped being run down by a cavalry charge. "Oh? Have you too become interested in horses, Mr. Bolton?"

I laughed. "No, just in paying for them. I'll write you out a check right now. Should have done it long ago. You've been darn decent about my—forgetting."

"No hurry. I'd appreciate it of course, but . . ."

I went over to a corner desk and wrote out a check. Mary and Wolfgang and Jack drifted into a little knot and began talking horse. Eleanor Gardner disappeared, to knock some dinner together, I guess, and, completely forgotten in my corner, I just listened. At first I felt the way I do when once in a while Mary (she *is* a social climber in a nice way) drags me out to dinner with some Garden Club friends of hers who go to the Riviera every winter and they all unconsciously lapse into French (including Mary), pretending that to such ultra-sophisticated people it is more natural than speaking English. As I am usually the only person at these dinner parties they can conceivably impress, it has always struck me as an awful waste of their time, but flattering.

But this horse bunch might as well have been talking Homeric Greek so far as I was concerned. Just to give you an idea, at one point Jack said, "At Simsbury last Saturday, Wolf, did you notice in the Medal hack-off how Dee was on the wrong diagonal through the first half of her eight?"

"I certainly did," said Wolfie. "And did you notice she carefully changed over so she was still on the wrong one through the last half?"

"No, I didn't," said Jack. "I saw her shift but I thought she'd changed to get on the right one. I guess Joe didn't notice, either, because he pinned her on top. What on earth happened to Potter in that class?"

"You mean the way all of a sudden he started scrubbing?"

"Pumping, I'd call it."

"It's the horse," said Wolfgang. "He doesn't like it indoors. The kid's substituting scrubbing, or pumping if you'd rather, for leg. He hasn't any."

"I don't think he has any hands, either," said Jack.

"He hasn't. Half the time he throws the horse away. Then he snatches."

"Yet he got pinned over Judy."

"I know, Jack. I hollered about it. I thought of filing on that class; but what the heck, Judy got left twice, which would have given the medal to Dee, diagonals or not. Besides, Joe's a friend of mine. He does a good job most of the time. We all slip now and then. . . ."

It was almost eleven when we said good-bye. Hellie rode in the old station wagon with me, snuggled tight against my shoulder. Mary, in her car, got home ahead of us and was waiting outside the garage, looking as if she were about to expire with curiosity. She shooed Hellie up to bed in a hurry, then blocked my way. "Well? If I have to wait another minute to hear how you pulled this off I'll— I'll . . ."

"There was really nothing to it, honey. Just simple genius."

"Frederick!"

I chuckled. "It all hung on my ability to give a fancy show horse a suitable name that would get his picture in the papers. I did."

"Did what?"

"Picked a suitable name—a name so suitable that certain people practically begged me to let them *give* me a horse. I thought the very best name I could think of would be Aspercel."

"Allied Drug and Food!"

"Naturally, and I did agree to let them give me a horse— and a stable—and a trailer and . . ."

"And the vice-president business? Is that for real too?"

"Sure. If you had a guy working for you who could dream up a con job like the one I dreamed up, wouldn't you make him a vice-president?"

"Me? No, I'd marry him!"

"Well, Harry couldn't marry me, you see, so he made me a vice-president. Go on tuck Helen in; then come join me in a drink."

I went into the den for a nightcap. I didn't really want a drink: what I wanted was to sit quietly and think about myself as a vice-president of the Tomes Agency sitting quietly in the den of his country house in fashionable Fairfield County sipping a Scotch and soda. Everything has to have some sort of public image nowadays. Naturally, as an advertising man I had to carry it one step further and have a private image. To be honest, I *hate* Scotch; but that was what fitted my mental picture of myself, so I had it.

I sat quietly and pleasurably contemplating myself for all of ten minutes and then was interrupted by Mary calling, "Come on up. Helen wants to talk to you." I suppose it's the fate of vice-presidents to be interrupted. Mary met me on the way up the stairs. "She's so excited it's going to be hours before she'll go to sleep. Do you think I ought to give her a tranquilizer?"

Mary asking *my* advice! Boy, had I shot up in the world overnight

"She's rattling on about Aspercel," Mary said.

"In this house that's no crime."

"The horse. And about winning Maclay Classes and Medal Classes. I think right this minute she's seeing herself riding that horse in Madison Square Garden at the National Horse Show."

This I understood. I'd been seeing that vice-president sitting quietly in his den sipping that Scotch and soda. "Let her. Likely that's as close as she'll ever come to doing it."

"But it's after midnight. She has to get up at seven for an early lesson at Wolfgang's."

"Good. In that way she can develop stamina. Champions have to have stamina. When she wakes up, feed her The Breakfast of Champions—with some Aspercel for a chaser."

Mary inspected me closely. "You a little drunk?"

I nodded. "But not from liquor."

"Oh, Freddie, you've waited such a long time for today, haven't you?" She kissed me.

I went on up the little flight of stairs to Hellie's room. Her bed lamp was on, throwing a soft glow over a face so happy it returned the glow—with interest. As she was in Madison Square Garden, which was about forty miles away, she naturally hadn't heard me coming up, so I was able to stand in the doorway for a couple of minutes just looking at her and loving her and missing the times we used to have together; then, for some reason I found myself remembering the first time I'd taken her out fishing. She was so little I had to hold her fingers around the rod with mine. I remembered hers were all sweaty and sticky with taffy or something. I wished, I wished—no I didn't! I really didn't want Hellie to stay a child—yet . . .

She was wearing a blue nightgown that was innocently revealing. She was *almost* a young lady. For a jealous second—just one second, mind you—I was glad she was what I considered abnormal about horses instead of normal about boys. Then I was myself again. I flipped my lighter to light a cigarette. The noise roused her and she made the quickest trip on record from Madison Square Garden to Weston.

"Hello, Daddy. Is it really, really true I'm going to have that beautiful horse for my very own?"

"Or its equivalent." The glow faded. "Hellie, my darling"—I found I was talking softly the way I used to when I'd put her to sleep with bedtime stories about fish— *a* fish, rather, named Sam. "Hellie, this horse thing isn't something I can rush into blindfolded. He's got to be good or, well, let's be honest, I'm sunk. I'll have made a fool of myself with the one account I simply cannot afford to make a fool of myself with. For all our sakes."

"But Aspercel *is* good, Daddy. Wolfgang says he's just simply the perfect horse for me."

I sat down on the edge of the bed and took her hand. "Baby, I understand. Better than you'll ever know. But this horse is going to cost a lot of money, and one person's opinion—not even if the person is Wolfgang—isn't enough."

"Mr. Gardner and Mummy saw me ride him. *They* think he's just wonderful. *Please,* Daddy, say I can have him!"

I wanted terribly to say just that, but something was holding me back. A gambler's hunch, maybe. God knows,

53

this whole deal was a whopper of a gamble from the time I'd first thought of it.

"I can't, baby. I have to go to Chicago tomorrow, but Friday, when I get back . . ." I saw the tears start welling up.

"Suppose somebody else buys him while you're away?"

I took out my pocket checkbook. As she watched, I wrote out a check for one hundred dollars payable to the Sheridan Stables and gave it to Helen. She took it, looked horrified as she read the amount.

"Turn it over."

On the back I had written: "Acceptance of this check is agreement to an option of one week to purchase for four thousand dollars the horse offered to and tried out by my daughter, Helen Bolton, at your establishment today."

The brightness came back to her eyes. She lifted her face up to be kissed good night. I kissed her. She snuggled down into bed. I turned out the lamp, and as I tiptoed out of the room heard a soft sigh that was my complete undoing. I went back to the den and got happily crocked with Mary.

8

I GOT BACK to La Guardia at ten Friday morning and took a cab to my office. At least I thought I had. I got out of the elevator at the usual floor, walked down the corridor of glass cubicles with grillwork doors, started to turn into mine, and stopped. A man I could plainly see was not me was sitting at my desk, and the wrong girl was in the adjacent cubicle. I looked up and down the corridor, checking. All the other offices were occupied by the same old people, so this had to be it.

I went up to the strange young man behind the desk and cleverly, I thought, asked if he could tell me where I could find Miss Clemens. And Mr. Bolton. "Freddie Bolton, that is?"

"You mean the horsy guy? The one's just been made a veep?" I nodded. "He's up on the next floor with the other veeps. Nice layout, but Jee-sus!" he shook his head, "is that guy ever nuts about horses!"

" 'Nuts' is an understatement," I said, and carted my suitcase and dispatch case up another flight to what was known as "The Peat Bog," because the carpets were so thick. No glass cubicles here, just glass-paneled secretaries' offices leading to the vice-presidents' private offices. And they were private. Real doors that closed.

I was feeling completely out of place when a familiar voice yelled "Hi!" It was Suzie sounding glad. She must have been feeling as lost as I, because she'd popped out of one of the offices behind me—I'd overshot the runway—and came running toward me. She grabbed my dispatch case and tried to grab my suitcase, but I wrestled it away from her.

"Suzie, what is the matter with you, trying to carry my suitcase?"

"It's your new office, Mr. Bolton! You just don't know how important it makes you seem, sir."

"Well, having you carry my suitcase doesn't make me feel important; it makes me feel like your grandfather.

And it just happens I don't like feeling like your grandfather, Miss Clemens."

She turned up her pert little puss with a woeful expression. *"Please* don't start calling me Miss Clemens. I feel lost enough up here. I don't know any of the girls, and they're all a million years older than I am and . . . oh, Mr. Bolton, I'm so glad to have you back home." Impulsively, like a kid, she grabbed my free hand, tugged it. *"Now* let me show you our wonderful new office."

She let go and swished ahead of me down the corridor, her tight black skirt outlining each small alternating buttock. She turned into an office that obviously was hers—it was considerably larger than *my* office had been in my sub-Peat Bog days—walked across it, opened a door, stepped back, and cried, "There!" waiting for me to act surprised.

I didn't have to act surprised. Except that it did have a sort of desk, although it appeared to be made of satinwood, it didn't look like an office at all. It looked the way I imagined Alfred Vanderbilt's library would look—if he'd happened to go in for hunters and show horses instead of the bangtails.

It was, in a word, magnificent. Bright red carpet, lovely leather sofas and chairs, and a big table in the satinwood motif. Beige drapes at the windows, table lamps whose bases looked frighteningly like authentic ancient Chinese porcelain horse heads and obviously worth much too much money for any office I infested.

One of the walls held a few English fox-hunting prints and, in rows of bookcases, made of satinwood of course, hundreds of books dealing with very refined sports like fox hunting and polo and trout—as opposed to deep-sea—fishing. The other wall was literally covered with photographs of horses in various stages of dress and undress, activity and idleness. There was one whole section devoted to pictures of a child. They were arranged in a series, showing her first as a child on a Shetland pony, then a bigger child on a bigger pony, then on a still bigger pony jumping over fences, then on a horse, the equines, the child, and the fences all growing bigger as the series progressed. I walked up close. The child was Helen! Only Helen in shiny black top boots and a hard sort of jockey cap like the ones the huntsmen in the fox-chase pictures on the other walls were wearing. I blinked.

"Mr. Bolton," Suzie's voice sounded apologetic, "Mr.

Tomes wanted it this way. I drove out to your house, and Mrs. Bolton found some pictures of Helen, and the art department did the rest. They—they did a wonderful job of matching the face to the bodies—don't you think?"

"Suzie, it's a fake!"

"Oh, no, because it *could* have been Helen. Mrs. Bolton told me the highest Helen had jumped was four feet, so I checked with the people where we got the pictures and made sure none of the jumps were any higher than that. The photographer just didn't happen to be around when Helen was jumping, that's all."

"It's still a fake."

"What about you using shaving cream in your TV cake commercials because it looks more like cake frosting than cake frosting looks like cake frosting? Isn't that a fake?"

I could have pulled rank. I could have, if I'd been dumb enough. Instead I laughed and said, "You are a ruthless young lady—"

Just then I spotted the biggest photograph of all. It showed a man in black boots and white breeches wearing a long black riding coat and a stunted high hat. He was riding a black horse over a jump so high it would have challenged a pole vaulter. I moved closer, but I knew who it had to be. It was. Wolfie—in the flesh! Hanging in the star spot in *my* office! At the bottom of the picture was some very high-class lettering:

WILHELM WOLFGANG HEINRICH VON ROETZ

then a lot of German that I could just figure out said he was riding something or other at something called the Aachen Horse Show and that the jump was so many meters high, which it sure was. On the lower-left-hand corner of the mat was written:

> *To Frederick Bolton, Esquire,*
> *Father of my favorite pupil,*
> *With most sincere best wishes,*
> *Wolfgang von R.*

"Where did you get this?"

"Oh, Mr. Tomes called him up and said he wanted a picture of him for your new office—to surprise you."

"It surprises me."

57

"Wolfgang is a very charming man. Don't you think so, Mr. Bolton?"

"What do you mean? You never told me you knew him."

An uncomfortable little green-eyed feeling that I didn't like had come over me. It grew greener when she said: "Oh, I never did until last evening when I went over to his place to get the picture. My, he's got some beautiful horses, even if they are hunters. Why, I must have been there over an hour just looking at them and talking with Wolfgang. Don't you think he's charming?"

"No."

I heard Suzie giggle—I'd made a chump of myself, letting her think I was jealous. But she was to make me feel even worse.

"Mr. Bolton. I did something I shouldn't have."

"I don't want to hear about it," I snapped.

"Oh, it isn't about Wolfgang. It's—well, all these hunters and jumpers, I just couldn't stand it. It made me feel so disloyal to Queenie. Look."

At the bottom of the wall was a row of seven-by-ten glossies of another girl on a horse. The girl was Suzie Clemens done up in skintight pants and a cowboy shirt and hat on a palomino that had to be Queenie. In some of the pictures she was sitting holding enormous silver cups or trays; in others she was galloping all out on the straight or galloping around brightly painted oil barrels, the horse leaning so hard into its turn her inside foot almost scraped the ground. They were impressive, and they were just as real as the ones of Helen were phony. I was touched by the girl's obvious skill, by her loyalty to her wild-looking animal, by her daring—in the pictures—to say nothing of her daring to put them up in my office.

"If you mind, I'll take them down without a fuss, but . . ."

Though I don't approve of that sort of thing in the office, I put my arm around her shoulders. "Suzie, I don't mind one little bit. I think they're terrific. Of course I'll let you leave them up, particularly as I'm about to ask you a rather large favor."

"About us or about horses?"

I'd have given a lot to know what she meant by that question, but I didn't ask. For one reason I didn't have the nerve. But the main reason was that I happened to look up just then and saw Harry Tomes standing in the doorway.

I removed my arm from Suzie's shoulders with such dignity as I could manage and prepared to catch her when she saw Harry Tomes and fainted. She must have sensed my panic button was pressed all the way down, for she turned and calm as anything said: "Hi, Mr. Tomes, I was showing Mr. Bolton our handiwork. I apologized about putting up all those pictures of Queenie, and Mr. Bolton was being awfully kind to me about it."

Harry Tomes looked from her to me, then back to her. His face was inscrutable.

"Is he awfully kind to you very often?"

"No," said Suzie. "He's never been kind to me before."

"How *does* he treat you most of the time?"

"As if I were one of the I.B.M. machines."

His face suddenly became scrutable, and I saw he was holding back laughter. "That's a hell of a way to treat a pretty girl," he said. "No wonder it's taken the poor fellow ten years to make vice-president. Now, Suzie, *I* want to ask you a favor. Can you possibly make room on that wall someplace for one more picture?"

He didn't ask *me;* he asked Suzie!

"Of course, Mr. Tomes. How big is it?"

"Oh, not very big. About the size of that one of von Roetz." Then turning to me: "Picture of one of my race-horses, Jonah, winning the Hampton Gold Cup at Saratoga last year. I feel a little guilty asking Suzie to put it up, but it's good window dressing." He chuckled, a low dirty chuckle. "And after all, you've let Suzie put *her* horse's picture up. . . ."

"Oh, I'm only too glad to have it, sir."

"Suzie, run along to the art department and get it, will you? They're putting on a new mat."

"Yes, sir, Mr. Tomes!"

She was gone. Quivering inside now, I watched Harry Tomes deliberately close the door, drift over to one of the armchairs, and sink down into it. It was the expensive kind of chair that you sit in and not on. For maybe two minutes that was all he did, occasionally looking at me, then looking away again, using silence as a weapon the way the other men use words. He knew perfectly well that I was saying to myself far worse things than he would ever say. And by letting me do his bawling out for him, he didn't get ulcers.

"I wasn't eavesdropping," he said. "You were such a dope you left the door open. However, you can consider the incident closed except for one thing."

"Yes, sir!"

"Just what was that rather large favor you were going to ask Suzie to do for you?"

I breathed again. "This, er . . ." I gestured with my thumb toward his picture on the wall. "This Wolfgang character took Mary and my daughter horse shopping the day before I went to Chicago. They found one; belongs to the Sheridan stables. Wolfgang says it's the ideal horse for her—old Aspercel himself. Now, I could be wrong, Harry, but I don't quite trust Wolfie. So I was going to ask Suzie, if she could make it, to go up to Mount Kisco with me this afternoon and give this horse a thorough physical."

"What's the matter with getting a veterinary?"

"I don't know any," I said. "Besides, any veterinary I got around there would be a pal of Wolfie's. I'd be the outsider. You've no idea how far out, either. Suzie obviously knows all about horses. She's got her own she raised from a pup. And with her I wouldn't be the outsider; Wolfie and his crowd would be the outsiders."

"How come? They're horsemen and she's a horseman."

"She's a quarterhorseman," I said. "She looks down her nose at this hunter crowd."

He was thoughtful for a few seconds. "I think you have something there. This Aspercel horse has to be *right*. If he turned out to be blind or to have three legs, or even five legs, we'd lose the account. By all means take her."

"Thanks." I pointed to all the horse stuff in my office. "Who are we trying to kid? It makes me feel as if I were wearing somebody else's suit."

"Nothing could concern me less than how you feel about it, son. You see, it just happens that Tom Dugan's coming in to chat with me at eleven about applying this subliminal notion of yours to some of their other products. He said that while he was here he would like to meet you. Get the idea?"

I got it all right. Tom Dugan was *the* head man of the Allied Drug and Food Corporation. Aspercel, of course, was only one of a few dozen other big moneymaking products. Tom Dugan was one of the "invisible men"—like the President of the United States. Unless you were richer than he was—something almost impossible to imagine—

more powerful, more socially hot stuff, you couldn't get within three secretaries of him. Unless, of course, you had something he wanted. Tom Dugan wanted to meet *me*.

"Jee-sus!"

Harry chuckled again. "Well, almost. St. Peter, anyway." He paused; then: "I—er—did a pretty good job of selling when I went up to his place to pinch-hit for you last week. I let them know that persuading you to get a new horse for your kid and name it Aspercel was quite a feather in my cap—you being so publicity-shy you'd never let anyone outside your family and immediate business associates know what a horseman you were."

This was too ripe. Before I could reply, the intercom box—also satinwood—spoke mutedly: "Mr. Tomes. Mr. Dugan is here waiting for you."

He was across the room in two seconds, pressed a button, and said, "Thanks, Katherine. Be right there." He turned back to me. "You and Suzie get that racehorse picture right up. Put it next to von Roetz. I'll speak to her on my way out about vetting that horse with you. And better have her stand by now to smoke screen for us if Dugan should turn out to be a horse-show horseman. She has all the lingo."

"But it's quarter-horse lingo," I shouted as he went through the door. "Suppose he's a hunter guy?"

"Then she can confuse him—but good!"

9

IT TURNED OUT, to my astonishment, that Suzie lived at Easton, which is only a twenty-minute drive from the semi-demi in Weston. She'd been living there for the whole year she'd been my secretary and never mentioned it. I couldn't get over it. It made me wonder if I was a lousy boss not to have taken enough interest in my secretary to find out where she lived in case she got sick or anything. But then Suzie hadn't turned into a girl until a week ago, and I.B.M. machines aren't supposed to get sick.

We got off the train at Westport and picked up my junky station car. Then we drove to her house because she said she wouldn't feel right fooling around stables in her office clothes. "Horses know when you don't feel right around them," she said, "and they take advantage of you." I could believe it. I had a low opinion of horses anyway.

I'd pictured Suzie as having a room in someone's house, or at best a two-room apartment over a store in the village. I was hardly prepared for a four-room saltbox, a pretty little house way out in the country; white, red shutters, a rose arbor over the front door, a brick walk with flower beds on each side, and a two-foot-high white picket fence around the whole thing.

There was a catch: About a hundred yards up the road was a corral with four horses wandering around, stomping and twitching at flies, and a dozen or more horses eating their way across a couple of huge fields that lay right back of the house. By the corral was a tumbledown, gray, weatherbeaten stable consisting of two or three rows of interlinking sheds. Horses all over the place! As we pulled up in front of her house, I frantically gulped one of my antihistamines.

"That's the Bar J," she said. "The J stands for Joe Mc-Millen. This house I live in is his. Of course, he has his own farmhouse just across the road where he and his family live. It's a real break, because in exchange for giving riding lessons for him weekends, I get the house and Queenie's and Lambie-Pie's keep for free."

"You have *two* horses?"

"Yes, I just bought another. Queenie's for racing and Lambie-Pie's for western-trail-horse classes. Lambie-Pie's a piebald; that's why I call her Lambie-Pie." She hopped out of the car. "You wouldn't like to buy a book of ten lessons for fifty dollars, would you?"

"Can you imagine what my daughter would say if she found out *I* was taking *cowboy* lessons?"

"Not 'cowboy,' please, Mr. Bolton; Stock Saddle Seat Equitation. And she really wouldn't *have* to find out, would she? That is if you'd like me to give you some lessons. If you would, you know I wouldn't really charge you anything for them."

For just a second I was tempted. And not by the idea of taking cowboy lessons.

"I couldn't, honestly, Suzie."

"Okay." She shrugged. "I'd ask you in to look at my trophies, but then we'd get talking and I'd probably be forever getting ready. But you can see them when you bring me home if you like. I'll only be a minute."

I sat in the car, turned the radio volume way up, and listened to commercials. I'd schooled myself so I didn't have to listen to the music or news—just the commercials. It's probably the same with somebody like Yehudi Menuhin. I'll bet when he listens to a symphony orchestra he hears only the violins. In between commercials I wondered what weird kind of outfit Suzie might decide to put on. I didn't think the cowboy hat and fancy frilly shirt and stuff she wore in those pictures in my office would go over too big at this Sheridan Stables place, which I understood was pretty plush.

She came back in less than five minutes. All the pancake makeup was gone, and the Revlon was down to just a touch, and she was dressed the way Helen dresses most of the time. Only Suzie's blue jeans and powder-blue, man-type wool shirt were tailored, which Helen's certainly are not, and her loafers shone like mahogany.

"Would you like us to take my car since it's such a lovely sunny day?"

"Sure. Why not?"

"It's in a shed in back. I'll go get it."

She ran around the house and I climbed out of the sedan and lighted a cigarette. Moments later I heard a roar. A bright-red slightly vintage topless MGA shot past the corner of the house and slithered to a stop. Back of the wheel was Suzie in goggletype sunglasses. Crossing my fingers I climbed in beside her. "Here!" she said, and handed me a pair of the goggles. "We're off! Grrrrrrr-yah-hoooo!"

She startled me, but not nearly so much as what happened next. We skidded sideways out of the dirt driveway so that when we hit the hard surface of the road and, with a jerk stopped skidding sideways, we were already headed up the road the way we wanted to go. At least the way Suzie wanted to go. I wasn't sure I wanted to go anywhere in this car. As she ran up through the four gears, she yelled at me.

"Sorry about making the yell, Mr. Bolton. That's how I do to start Queenie in the barrel-bending races."

"Does it startle her, too?"

She flashed me a happy kid grin. "It's calculated to. And boy, does it! Hey, put your seat belt on, Mr. Bolton."

I groped for the seat belt and looked at the speedometer out of one eye; I didn't dare face it full on. It seemed to say something like seventy. I saw a corner ahead and snapped my seat belt shut in a hurry. Suzie dropped into third, roared the engine to full power, the tires screamed bloody murder, and the once-smelled-never-to-be-forgotten aura of Naugatuck, Connecticut, where they seem to burn rubber day and night—although they claim to be making it —rose around us. But we got clear of the curve, and a long straight stretch of road lay ahead of us.

"Now I'll slack off on the reins a little and let her go."

She did. Since I couldn't bear to look at either the road or the speedometer, I looked at Suzie. In spite of her intentness and concentration, she was smiling, and with the wind howling around her head, torturing her hair, and the way she was controlling all that speed and doing it so skillfully, she seemed very young and very happy. It seemed impossible then that she could ever get old, but would just go on like that forever, wind whipping her hair, sunlight and shadow crisscrossing her cheeks—Peter Pan at the wheel of a sports car.

I had a hunch that these were things I ought to be feeling about Helen—my daughter—not about my secretary. But except for fleeting moments since the dance, Helen and I had not yet found a common ground other than the relationship that placed us at opposite poles of humanity—

the father-teenage-child one. Suzie and I had found a common one, fleeting as the wind itself perhaps, but there. I wasn't scared any more; I was exhilarated. I wished the car would go a little faster, roar a little louder. But fifteen minutes later we slowed, and I saw that we were on the outskirts of Mount Kisco. It would have taken me at least half an hour to get there in my buggy. Suzie shoved the goggles up on her forehead.

"Like it?"

"After the first mile, yes."

"I'm awfully glad. I'm awfully glad you liked it, because I loved it. Fred . . ." Then, as though she'd just come out of a cloud, she added, "Mr. Bolton."

I grinned at her. "Actually, I loved it too, Miss Clemens."

Her mouth started as a smile but ended as a grimace. "No, I can't. It wouldn't be proper. But please don't start the Miss Clemens bit."

The communications I'd been thinking about were better than I'd realized. "Okay, Suzie."

"Maybe—maybe someday I could."

I suppose we were both perfectly well aware that we weren't really talking about her dropping the "Mr." when we were out of the office.

"There's the sign to Sheridan Stables." She shifted up through the gears as far as third. "I want to make a suggestion, Mr. Bolton, if you won't take offense."

"Shoot."

"When we get to the stables, try to play it dumb, will you? Let me do the talking."

"When I get anywhere near any stable I don't have to play it dumb. I just take my antisneeze pills and try to pretend I'm somewhere else."

"Oh, come on!" She flashed me the grin, and we were back on solid ground. I felt splendid. It was just a warm feeling, like the warmth of the spring sunshine and the feeling that things were bright and shiny, like the spring afternoon—and the little red car.

10

THE SHERIDAN STABLES was the kind of place Diamond Jim Brady would have liked. To live in, that is; it was much too good for horses. You went through an archway into a gravel courtyard that looked as if every pebble were taken up each day and individually scrubbed. Flower beds, filled with tulips at the moment, bordered it, and on all four sides was a wide colonnade of horse veranda. Opening onto this were the deluxe bedroom suites. There was brass everywhere anybody could find an excuse for brass: stall-door hinges, hasps, lamps, hitching rings, water-bucket bindings. And all of it shined every day. When the ground crew were through scrubbing the pebbles, or maybe they did the brass first.

We wandered through the arch. There seemed to be no one around.

"There ought to be sort of an office," Suzie said.

"With bellboys, in case the horses ring for icewater."

She spotted a sign that said OFFICE, and started toward it. When I followed, she shook her head. Smiling, she pointed her forefinger at me. "Stay." I barked. She giggled and said, "You stay! Sit stay!"

I gave quite a nice dog whine. It was easy because our late dog, a Yorkshire terrier, always whined when you commanded him to do anything. Suzie grinned.

"Do you really think that's a proper way for you to speak to your boss?" I said. "Sit stay?"

She turned bright scarlet. "Are you mad with me? You really bark very nicely, Mr. Bolton."

"You know I'm not mad," I said, and barked again, joyously.

A man wearing jodhpurs and turtleneck sweater came out of the office. He looked up and down the colonnade. "Seen a little West Highland White around here anywhere? I thought I heard him just now."

Suzie turned away so the man would not see her giggle. "No, I haven't seen any dog," I said. "Unless you count me. I'm quite a gay dog sometimes."

The man in the jodhpurs—he had the same lean, physically hard look as Wolfgang—stared at me, steadily. "Very funny. You looking for somebody?"

Suzie walked toward him. I stayed where I was, as told. "Yes, we are. Are you Tim Riley, the manager?"

"I'm Riley."

"Hi, I'm Sue Clemens."

The sun-scored face broke into a smile. "Well, the quarter-horse girl! Glad to meet you, Sue." They shook hands. "Saw you ride at Eastern States last September. You know"—he jerked a thumb toward the fancy stalls—"I don't suppose I should admit it, but I get a real kick out of that stock-horse stuff."

"*Quarter*-horse!"

"Pardon. Anyway, I get a real boot out of it. What are *you* doing here? You and your barking boyfriend get lost or something? This is a hunter and jumper stable."

"It's this way, Tim. That horse Wolfgang has for sale here?"

"Which one? He's got three of 'em here right now."

So Wolfgang never sold any of his pupils a horse! No wonder Suzie wanted me to lurk in the background. The horse boys would accept her, the quarter-horse girl, and wouldn't try to kid her too far. I heard her say, "I'd like to see the one the Bolton kid has put down a deposit on."

"What's your interest in the deal, Sue?"

"Her father's my boss. He asked me to see if I thought it would be a good horse for his kid."

Riley scratched his head and looked up at the sky. He spoke quietly, as if talking to himself. "There's a three-hundred-dollar commission that says you think he's the right horse, Sue."

"I couldn't take it, Tim, honest. Not in this case. If I did I'd only turn it over to my boss."

"Oh, he's a good guy, eh?"

"Why, yes," said Sue after a little pause. "He's a wonderful guy—I think."

Riley, who was about my age, smiled down at her in an amused way. I guessed he had kids of his own. "But you're not sure?"

"I—I haven't known him very long."

"Well, you know the old saying—walk softly and carry a long hatpin."

"But I never wear a hat."

"Then just watch your step. Your boyfriend there, what's his interest?"

"Oh, *he's* just interested in my car. You must have heard it come in."

"My ears are still ringing. Well, let's go look at the horse. Want to ride him?"

"After I look." She beckoned me forward. "Tim, this is Freddie. Freddie, Tim."

"Hi, Freddie. You like cars, eh?"

"And boats and fish."

"I get seasick."

"Well, when I get around horses I sneeze." I sneezed, and took another antihistamine.

"Fair enough," said Tim. Then: "Say, Freddie, er, this isn't supposed to be Wolf's horse. It's better for his business if folks think it's my horse. You know how things are. Okay?"

"Sure, I sure do know how things are. I'm a salesman. You have to use angles selling anything."

"What do you sell?"

"Advertising."

"Whereabouts? New York?"

"Yes, I work for the same folks Suzie does."

"Oh." He was thoughtful for a few steps. "You know her boss?"

I looked at Suzie, at the beautiful stables with the sleek heads thrust out at us as we went by the stalls, looking for handouts. I was enjoying myself, but I knew I shouldn't be. Not in these surroundings.

"I've met him," I said. "See quite a lot of him, but I was just thinking, and I decided, no, I don't really know him at all."

"Mystery man?"

"You've got it."

"Here we are. Next stall," said Tim Riley.

Another head, chestnut, with a white diamond mark running down his face, peered at us. Even I could recognize that as horses' heads go this was a handsome one. Suzie started toward the stall door. The ears went back and the big lips, black and padded like catcher's mitts, started to part.

"He's a little nippy with strangers," said Riley. "Don't get too near him, Freddie." The advice was superfluous. I didn't intend to get within twenty feet of him, but as Sue came near, the ears flattened and the upper lip rose, baring the biggest set of oat-choppers I ever saw.

"Watch it!" snapped Riley.

"The hell with him!" said Suzie. "Knock it off, horse!"

The horse lunged at her. So fast you could hardly see it move, her small fist shot out and caught him right on the soft part of his nose. His ears came forward; he made an almost sad whickering noise as if the world had betrayed him, and hung his head. Without a by-your-leave, Suzie unsnapped the catch on the stall door, opened it, and said, "Get back there, you big handsome hunk of Kennel Ration! Baa-ack!"

The horse obediently backed away from the door.

"Okay, Tim, strip him."

Riley stepped into the stall, unsnapped the buckles on the light canvas blanket the horse wore. "I can see now why that stock—pardon, quarter horse you ride is so well trained. You don't let a horse get away with much, do you, Sue?"

"I don't dare. I'm too little to fight them much. When I'm on the ground, that is. I have to stop anything before it starts, or I'm licked."

For some reason Riley grinned at me, and for some reason Sue blushed.

The blanket was off the horse now, and the rest of him looked just as handsome—and just as dangerous—as his head. I couldn't believe that Helen could possibly take care of such a creature herself. I had a quick vision of those huge savage teeth tearing her little arms, and felt sick to my stomach. "Of course, I don't know about these things," I said. "But honestly now, that couldn't be a kid's horse, could it?"

Riley looked up at me. "Matter of fact, it could. He likes kids and he's all right with them. He was fine with the Bolton kid the other day, and although she rides real good —tops for the short time she's been at it—she sure hasn't been around horses in the stable much. That's something Wolf doesn't teach, and he ought to, for my dough. His kids look great in the show-ring, but as horsemen? Pfui!"

"Take him out and hook tie ropes on him, will you, Tim? I want to vet him right." Suzie had walked toward the rear of the stall, her eyes going over the horse like an insect spray.

"Anything special you wanted to look at, Sue?"

"Yes, there is. Just from where I stand, I think four thousand dollars is a silly price to ask for a horse that's supposed to do a lot of jumping if he isn't sound in back."

"You thinking about on the near hind leg, maybe?" She nodded. "What the hell," he said. "Of course, he goes sound enough up till now, and the curb is only just starting, but Wolf ought to know that even if a guy's a real jerk if he's smart enough to be able to pay that kind of money for a horse he's smart enough to have some expert give it a going over."

He stared at the clean straw on the floor of the stall that, like the gravel of the courtyard, looked as if it had been polished blade by blade. From the expression on his face, I guessed he was having a struggle within himself. Presently he looked up.

"I hate to do this to Wolf. It's his pigeon, but then he's loused his own deal. How about going to the other barn and give a look-see at a horse of mine? He has papers, he comes from Canada, and he won the Junior Hunter Championship at the Royal in Toronto last year. He belonged to a kid who won the Equitation Championship on him, too. She traded this one with me for a three-day horse. The one I'm going to show you isn't trained for dressage."

Naturally, I didn't know what a "three-day-horse" or "dressage" was, but it struck me as a good lever to start beating down the price.

"Not trained in dressage, eh?" I shook my head and made belittling noises.

"So what's it to *you*, Freddie?" Tim Riley acted disturbed. "This Bolton guy's daughter isn't schooled in dressage either, is she? From seeing her ride, I would say positively no."

I turned to Suzie. "Is she?"

"No. Of course she isn't, Freddie."

The Freddie slipped out. I liked the sound of it.

"Well," I said, "though it's none of my business, I'd say that since Bolton's daughter isn't schooled in dressage, either, it seems to me it oughtn't to cut down the price of the horse more than by, say, a thousand bucks."

Suzie flashed me a look of glee—and admiration. Tim gave me a dirty look. I was having fun.

"By the way, Tim, before we go look at him, does that horse of yours eat people like this one?"

"Sonny, the horse I'm going to show you is so gentle Bolton could use him for a baby sitter."

"How much?" asked Sue.

"Six thousand dollars—with a new-car warranty."

"Three thousand five hundred is top. I happen to know that," said Suzie. Which she also happened to know was a black lie.

"Fifty-five hundred."

"Four, even," said Sue. She looked at me. I held up one hand where only she could see it, the five fingers spread.

"Not a nickel under five," said Riley.

"Too much," said Sue.

I'd gotten all excited, which was ridiculous, since I didn't have the faintest idea what we were trying to buy or even if I wanted to buy it.

"Four thousand five hundred!" It was torn out of me. Auction fever.

"Sold!" shouted Riley, waving a hand, "to the man in the pinstripe blue suit!"

Sue looked startled.

"A clown!" Riley cried happily. "Damned if you didn't take me in just like you did before with your barking." Laughing, he threw the blanket back on the chestnut, buckled it in place, straightened up. His face had fallen into the creases of serious thought. "You didn't by any chance mean that bid, did you?"

I got cagey. "Why, that wasn't a bid; that was an—an exploratory negotiation. I simply meant that if you wouldn't sell him for four thousand five hundred, I wouldn't waste my time looking at him. And, just for the record, I may bark but I am not a clown. This may seem a fine point. . . ."

Tim reddened. "I beg your pardon, sir. I meant it only in fun."

"Tim," said Suzie. "I think it's time I told you—er—Freddie's last name. This is Mr. Bolton. My boss."

"May God have mercy on my soul!" said Tim.

"I like the sound of this horse of yours," I said. "At forty-five hundred, let's go look at him."

"Right, Mr. Bolton! This way."

He led the way out of the courtyard, down a gravel path to a second stable, not quite so fancy as the first. It was like moving from, oh, the Plaza down to the Astor on

Broadway. No courtyard, no white gravel, no brass. Just a long row of box stalls with an overhang roof that served as a porch. Here again the heads were sticking out of the open top halves of the stall doors, the horses watching us with ears laid back or pricked forward, depending on the nature of the beasts. Tim and Suzie were talking the foreign language my ears were beginning to get used to, though I still was far from tuned into it. I walked along the row of stalls, keeping a safe distance, fingering the antihistamine bottle in my coat pocket. I was about halfway down the line when I heard what I've since learned is called a whickering. I turned around. From the stall I had just passed was thrust a coal-black head with a tiny white star in the middle of the forehead. It was whickering at me, and the great liquid horse eyes were gazing at me with unmistakable reproach. I read him at once. He felt bad because I hadn't stopped to give him a handout or to say howdy. I chuckled and walked back. The ears stayed pricked forward, the whickers came faster. It was very appealing.

"Well, you great big slob!"

Forgetting I might lose an arm, I began stroking the silky muzzle. He leaned his neck way out, reached down to sniff at my coat pockets, obviously hunting for sugar. When he didn't find any, he nudged me gently with his head, which, considering its size, was like being nudged gently by a steam shovel. I reached up and pulled his ears. He lifted his head, rested his chin on the edge of the stall, and blew hot air at me through his nostrils. I went back to stroking his muzzle.

"Well, well, well," I said. "So I've finally found somebody who appreciates me."

The horse heaved an enormous sigh of contentment. It began as a blast of hay-scented air, changed to a whistle, and ended in a grunt as he ran out of breath. I turned, took a step away to call Suzie, and the great silly beast grabbed my sleeve in his teeth and pulled me back. Though his choppers were as big as Wolf's cannibal horse's choppers, for some reason they didn't frighten me. I think it was because of those big, reproachful eyes. Having got me back into position, he rested all eight inches of his chin on the edge of the door again, closed his eyes, and waited for me to start stroking his muzzle.

This, I thought, happily, is for me! A little ashamed, I

said under my breath, "I mean, of course, if I *have* to have a horse at all."

Tim and Suzie came up, and I had the feeling Suzie was laughing at me inside and trying not to show it.

"What's this one?" I asked Tim. "I like him. That is, it seems to me he might make a proper sort of horse for a child."

"Why, this is none other than the one I was bringing you to see. Killarney."

I grinned at Tim. "No," I said, "I think his name is Aspercel."

"There are times, Mr. Bolton, sir, when I almost wish you'd bark rather than talk. You say things that upset me. I should know the name of my own horse, shouldn't I?"

"In this world, Tim, we none of us can ever be certain of anything. Suzie, start giving him his physical."

11

IT WAS SIX O'CLOCK when I dropped Suzie off. I drove to Westport and stopped at the little pint-sized shopping center at the northern edge of the town and telephoned home. Mary answered, thank God.

"Honey, is Helen home?"

"Why yes," she said, sounding puzzled. "Do you want to speak to her?"

"No, I don't! That's why I called. I want very much not to speak to her until I've spoken to you."

"Oh?"

"We have a problem that's going to call for a little togetherness. Can you either get rid of Helen or think up some reason why you should slip out and have a drink with me?"

She dropped her voice to a whisper. "It's something about her horse, isn't it?"

"It certainly is."

"Did the Aspercel people call the deal off or something?"

"No, Mary; I can't talk to you about this on the phone in whispers."

"Where are you?"

"In the booth at our gas station."

"Did you go up to look at the horse or couldn't you find the time?"

"I went up. That's why I've got to talk to you."

Mary was sounding more and more exasperated. I suppose it was understandable, me sounding so mysterious, and women, most of them anyway, being emotionally unlike men and a little unstable.

"Just a minute." I heard her speak to Helen. She sounded as if she were talking through a fur muff. I knew she'd put the telephone against her chest, thinking I wouldn't be able to hear. "Listen, Sweetie, Daddy's being all mysterious and playing games and wants me to slip out and have a drink with him. He's just back from a long trip, and I think we'd better humor him, don't you? What? Yes,

74

he did look at the horse. Did he buy it? Sweetie, I'm afraid not, but . . ."

Having the phone against her chest didn't muffle the wail of pure anguish. When Mary came back on the phone, I burst right in.

"Damn it, Mary, I heard that! That's just exactly what I didn't want to have happen. You've put your foot in it this time, but good. I'm on my way home. You take Helen up to her room and give her a tranquilizer and sit her down at her homework—then you come down to the den. I'll give you ten minutes to get things calmed down. Good-bye."

I hung up. Just like that. I'd never thought I'd want to do that to Mary—or dare. I got in the car, and tuned the radio to the local station, listened to three nice commercials, and started home. It seemed impossible that less than a week ago I'd driven this road slowly because I wanted to postpone the evening. I turned into the driveway and blinked in surprise. The field on the left of the driveway was enclosed with new post-and-rail fencing. On the same side of the house, balancing the garage, was a low white stable. Grass hadn't grown on anyone's feet around here while I'd been in Chicago, that's for sure! To my surprise the post-and-rail fencing and stable did a lot for the place. Gave it a certain éclat missing when it was just another semidemi-split-level colonial ranch house. Mollified, but only slightly, I drove up to the house, parked, and went inside.

More out of bravado than expecting to find Mary, I walked straight to the den. She was there, sitting on the close-coupled sofa with drink fixings on the coffee table. Mary was a lady in the true and old-fashioned sense of the word. But ladies—real ones, like Mary—have never been noted for their lack of spirit.

"I hope you're quite ready to apologize? Here's your drink."

"Thanks, and I am ready to apologize if you think I really should after you've heard what I've got to say. In the first place I was not being mysterious because I wanted to play games. All I wanted was to keep my daughter from getting a crack over the head."

"If that's true, you don't have to apologize."

"All right, we'll skip it, but I need your help, Mary. And you're not going to like what I'm going to say, so let me say first that I know what this riding thing means to Helen and I'm back of her all the way. Unfortunately, I also know that Wolfgang Wilhelm Heinrich von Roetz, who is her god and her idol, is a liar, and by my standards and yours a crook. If Helen finds that out, it'll leave a mark on her she may never quite get over."

I took a deep swallow of the drink Mary had fixed for me. She did the same of hers. There was a long, long silence, and when Mary spoke her voice was not quite steady.

"I don't think that's a very nice thing to say about somebody unless you can prove it. You couldn't just be a little jealous of him because of Helen, could you?"

"Mary, he told you he never sold horses to his pupils?"

"Yes."

"And he told you that horse of Tim Riley's up at Sheridan Stables was absolutely ideal for Helen?"

"Yes."

"Brace yourself, honey. That horse doesn't belong to Tim Riley or Sheridan Stables or anybody except Wolfgang Wilhelm Heinrich von Roetz. Furthermore, though the horse is apparently all right around kids, if strange grown-ups go near him he's liable to tear their arms off."

"Oh, come off it!"

"No, that's a fact, but it's beside the point. What isn't beside the point is that he has what's called a curb—that's a sort of bone thing near his left rear knee or whatever you call it—that will beyond any doubt make him go lame unless he's given cocaine or whatever stuff they use and would make any horseshow judge throw him out of any class where what they call conformation counts—you know what that means. How he's put together, and all that."

"Oh, dear," Mary sighed. "And you wanted me to help you break it to Helen without letting her see the idol's clay feet way down inside his Hessian cavalry boots?"

I nodded.

"Now would you mind telling me how you've become so smart about horses all of a sudden?"

"In a minute. There's just one more thing you ought to know. I did buy a horse, a beautiful horse. If I'd known that pretty stable was already up, I'd have brought him home with me this evening."

Mary actually dropped her drink. Fortunately, the glass was almost empty. "Freddie! Are you telling me you actually went out on your own and bought a horse because you thought it was beautiful? Oh, dear God give me strength! How much did you pay for it?"

"Well," I said calmly, "Tim Riley wanted six thousand dollars for him. I bought him for four thousand five hundred. And he's not only beautiful; he's nice. For a horse, that is. I happen to like him. That weighed heavily with me."

"What do you mean he's 'nice'?"

"Well, he didn't seem to want to bite anybody. Not even me. All he wanted to do was poke his nose in my pockets and hunt for sugar. I borrowed some from Tim and gave it to him, too. Here. Take a look at him."

I took out of my briefcase a Manila envelope with Aspercel's papers in it and half a dozen photos of him leaping fences and winning things. "Tim threw in the pictures free. Decent of him, don't you think?"

She gave me a look—anyone who's ever been married for more than six weeks doesn't need to have me describe the look. Then she slid the stuff out of the envelope and for a long while just looked at the pictures, one by one, then at all of them again. Then, holding the pictures in one hand, like a baton, she said: "But Freddie, this horse is terrific! It's absolutely terrific! I can't believe you did this all by yourself."

"I didn't. I've been holding out on you." I grinned. "I had a very pretty girl with me whose métier is bending barrels. Harry Tomes wanted her to come along."

"What do you mean 'a very pretty girl whose métier is bending barrels'? How many drinks did you have on your way home?"

"Just two," I said, "with Tim Riley and Suzie."

"Suzie? You mean that painted hussy you call your secretary? What was she doing with you?"

"You know she's a horsewoman. She must have told you about it when she stopped here to pick up those snapshots of Helen while I was away."

"But that isn't the same Suzie. That one had on blue jeans and loafers, and I don't think she even had on any lipstick. I'm talking about the Suzie who sits at the typewriter in the cubicle next to yours who's made up an inch thick and who isn't pretty by my standards and whose *métier*, if any, certainly is not bending barrels."

"Mary," I said with delicious slowness, "I don't sit in a

cubicle at the office. I have a huge office of my own that looks like Alfred Vanderbilt's library. You're really mixed up, honey, because the Suzie that stopped here *is* the same Suzie who sits in my secretary's private office."

Then I slipped. "And if you think she isn't pretty, it's because you haven't watched her driving that red MGA of hers around corners at ninety miles an hour."

"I think I'd like another drink, a stiff one," said Mary. "Then I think you'd better give me a blow-by-blow on this thing. Just so I won't get any wrong ideas."

You know, it felt sort of good to be back half in and half out of the doghouse again. Real homey. But as soon as I'd finished the blow-by-blow, play-by-play on my day—tactfully leaving out just a little here and there in the interest of world peace—Mary gave me a demonstration of woman's mind at its sneakiest. Without even pausing to think, she picked up the telephone, dialed a number, and when it answered said, "Wolfgang? . . . Good. If you have any lights turned on in your house, turn them out. . . . Why? Because my husband was captain of the rifle team at Dartmouth. [Completely false!] What's that got to do with you? Well, nothing, except that when I last saw him he was just starting to get his gun—then he was going to look for you. I think he plans to shoot you."

I gasped. She smiled at me, wrinkling her nose. After listening on the phone for maybe a minute, still smiling, she said: "You really must have a guilty conscience, Wolfgang, because all you're talking about is how can I stop him and not sounding one bit surprised that he might feel like shooting you. Not even curious about why he might want to. So I have to assume you know why. You do, don't you? . . . Oh, you think maybe you do. Oh! wait a minute. Here's Freddie now. He's just coming up from the cellar. Freddie, *please* put down your gun and speak to Wolfgang. *Please,* Freddie!"

I gave her a wild look. She ignored it, stamped her foot hard on the floor. Over the phone the noise could easily have sounded like a very angry man slamming down the stock of a gun. She handed me the phone. I took it and held it away for a second, looking at it as if it were an unpleasant object, which, at the moment, it was. I hate fights; they embarrass me. Then all of a sudden I thought about that wail of unhappiness Helen had let out, and I felt that this might be one fight I wouldn't hate. I lifted the phone.

"Von Roetz? Bolton here." He started to talk, but I interrupted him. "No, don't try to explain. The problem is this simple. You've made yourself into the idol of a lot of kids around here. So they don't get hurt you're going to stay an idol if I have to prop you up and wire you onto your pedestal." He gobbled. I went on. "When I hang up you're going to telephone my daughter Helen and you're going to tell her that that horse of yours she tried out a few days ago. . . . No, don't try it on, fellow; I *know* whose horse it is. . . . No, I don't want her to know you lied to her. Idols don't lie, get the pitch?" He got the pitch. "Okay. You're to call her up and tell her that since she rode that horse it's developed a swelling that looks like a what-do-you-call-it and you don't want her to have it."

Wolfgang said: "He has got a curb coming on, but the horse would have carried her, Mr. Bolton. But you're quite right. Do you mind if I say that I think you are being a very good sport? I'll call her up right away. Meanwhile, I'll see if I can find another horse that would be suitable."

"Don't bother," I said. "Tell her you phoned me at my office and told me that you wanted me to look at another horse that would be even better for her and you called up to see how I liked it."

"If you say so, Mr. Bolton. Should I say any particular horse?"

I'd been holding the phone so Mary could hear both ends of the conversation. We grinned at each other.

"Yes, Mr. von Roetz, you should. A Canadian horse named Killarney. Ever hear of him?"

There was a silence, then a faint spluttering of muted German that sounded so instinctive it made me wonder if his accent really were synthetic. Then he laughed a very phony laugh. "That is a nice horse, Mr. Bolton. But I am afraid Helen cannot have him."

"Why not?"

"Because I am buying him for myself to make into a Grand Prix Dressage horse. He has talent, that horse. Too much to waste on a child. I am really sorry."

"Wolfie," I said sweetly, "I don't think you can afford to buy him because the price on him right now is twenty thousand dollars. Do you want to pay that?"

"Someone has been kidding you, Mr. Bolton. I'm buying him for four thousand dollars."

"No, my fine friend, you are not."

"Who says I'm not?"

"I do. Because *I* bought him this afternoon for four thousand five hundred."

There was a tremendous silence. I broke it.

"You've lost a horse, but you still have a chance to save a reputation. I'm going to hang up now so you can call Helen. So long." I hung up.

"We make a pretty good team, don't we?" Mary said. "I scare them to death; then you tromp on them."

I nodded. "Do you think, after Wolfie's talked to her, if he does call her, Helen'd like to take me out and show me her new stable?"

The look in Mary's eyes answered me. Just then the telephone rang.

12

THE HORSE was due to arrive Sunday morning. Tim Riley would have sent him over any time and Helen was in a sweat to have him brought on Saturday, but for once I put my foot down. There were certain logistics to be considered here. I mean it wasn't as if Aspercel could just arrive, unpack his bags, and come on into the house for potluck lunch with the family. For one thing, he wouldn't have any luggage. Except for his halter—that thing that would be a bridle if it had reins and a bit—he would arrive stark naked. Worse than that, unless sudden steps were taken, he would be moving into an empty house, and if that happened we would have a very cross horse on our hands.

This situation led to what was probably the only moment of glory I, the nonhorse member of my suddenly horsey family, had all that summer. I'd been brought up on my old man's farm, remember? Until I was twelve and the old man invented what turned out to be the forerunner of the electric shaver, which moved us across the tracks and got me through Dartmouth, I had done my share of farm chores. I'd pitched too many bales of hay and bags of grain and mucked out too many stalls and cowpens not to have a pretty good idea of what went into and then came out of a cow or horse in an almost continuous flow. As we finished breakfast Saturday morning, I cleared my throat ostentatiously.

"Now, Helen," I said, sounding as pompous as I could in case I never got another chance like this, "go get a pencil and a pad of paper and we'll make out a list of the things we must have stowed away in the barn before sundown."

Helen scampered off to her room. Mary's mouth fell open in surprise. "Why before sundown?"

"Just an old farmer's expression."

"Didn't you have electric lights on your father's farm?"

I had a sudden flash of memory of my father sweating over his account books; of mother mending and remending our clothes; of the unpainted, poverty-ridden barns that housed the cattle and two workhorses somehow kept sleek and fit; of lying in bed and hearing Father dreaming out loud to Mother about his great invention, and Mother, who had no faith in it at all, speaking the encouraging words he so very badly needed to hear.

"Kerosene was cheaper than electricity, Mary."

Helen came back with paper and pencils.

"We'll start with the hardware. Now write: Two galvanized trash barrels to store the oats and bran or whatever fancy horses eat nowadays. One pitchfork. One two-handled basket for carrying manure. Two galvanized buckets. One hay net. One saddle rack to mount on wall. One bridle hook to hang from ceiling for cleaning. One sawhorse for saddle cleaning. One shovel. Hoof pick, curry comb, sweat scraper, rectal thermometer, I mean horse size. Hard bristle brush, soft bristle brush, half a dozen dishcloths, one ton of upper New York State or Vermont hay, two hundred-pound bags of best oats, hoof oil . . ."

The list went on and on as memory after memory came to me. By the time it was completed, I could see that I was going to be the nicest thing that had happened to the purveyors of horse household goods in years. I could also see that the Tomes Agency was going to have to divert a little more of Allied Drug's radio and television money into their subliminal advertising account. A quick calculation told me that Aspercel, counting the cost of himself, the trailer, the stable, and the stuff on our list had already set somebody back almost twenty-five thousand dollars. And we were still in the pits working on the car and hadn't even started the race yet. I fervently hoped that the somebody didn't turn out to be me.

When the list was done I tried to call Jack Gardner to find out where to buy the hay and oats and stuff. They were away at a show, of course, and didn't answer. So I called Suzie. Turning herself into a nice combination of friend, private secretary, and hostler, she said she'd attend to all the stable stuff and see that it was installed, and told me I'd better take the station wagon into New York and go to Miller's on Twenty-fourth Street for Aspercel's personal equipment. She even told me who to ask for and to say I was a friend of hers.

I'd thought Helen would come with me. I should have known I couldn't compete with Aspercel. Here was this gorgeous creature only fifteen miles away, and she'd owned him for more than twelve hours and she hadn't set eyes on him yet. I really couldn't blame her for not wanting to drive into New York with me and pick out the beast's toilet articles. But before I took off she did give me the biggest, slobberiest kiss I'd ever had from anyone except a Great Dane.

From the time I got back late that afternoon, life at the semidemi was like Christmas Eve waiting for Santa Claus to come down the chimney. About 2:00 A.M. Mary finally got Hellie to sleep. By 6:30 A.M. Hellie had us all up again, and at 7:30 she went down to the foot of the drive and sat down to wait for her horse to arrive. I didn't know whether to laugh or cry; she knew Tim Riley had told me he'd van him over around eleven.

At nine thirty I got worried about Hellie, so I walked down to the foot of the drive to see if she'd fainted from excitement. She was sitting on the grass at the side of the road, arms around hunched-up knees, a faraway expression on her face and her eyes staring up the road toward Westport in spite of the fact that she must have known Tim would arrive from the other direction. I didn't say a word. I had the feeling it would be intruding into a child's private world in which older people have no rights, for Hellie had become a child again. I stretched out on the grass, and lying there beside her I found I was pitying her for the agony of her seemingly endless vigil and at the same time envying her with all my heart. Without meaning to, I spoke my thought half aloud.

"It must be wonderful to want something so very much and to *know* that it's going to arrive."

She never took her eyes from the road, but one arm dropped from her knees and a hand groped around in the grass until it found mine. I squeezed the disembodied hand and it squeezed back. For the better part of an hour we stayed like that, scarcely moving, not speaking a word until the sound of a motor coming up the road shot her to her feet. It was the Gardners. A few minutes later, Suzie roared up, and a little after that two men in riding clothes who were friends of the Gardners and a few minutes after that a windblown boy and a girl in shorts none of us knew buzzed up on a Vespa. Until that moment I had no idea I'd bought such an important horse. These people who talked in monosyllables, if at all, had come merely to watch Aspercel arrive at his new home. When the wait began to feel anticlimactic, I invited the whole gang up to the house for drinks, leaving Hellie and Judy, too, of course, to their happy vigil. The experience was heartening. No doubt about it, Aspercel the horse was a promotable product. I felt a trifle easier about the twenty-five grand.

I mixed the drinks, enjoying Mary's discomfiture at being made an involuntary hostess while she still had those curlers in her hair. I got on quite well with Jack's two strange horsemen friends, who turned out to be professionals. Why not? they hadn't been tipped off yet that I was to be treated like a moron. Because I'd been smart enough to buy Killarney-Aspercel, they were downright respectful. They actually asked my opinion about quite a few horse matters, such as what did I think of the AHSA rule that apparently actually says a horse is an animal that stands over 14.2 hands or fifty-eight inches high and that anything under that is a pony unless he happens to be something called an Appaloosa, an Arabian, Morgan, palomino, pinto, or western, in which event he can be a horse and a pony at one and the same time although not in the same show. That was one of the foreign-language bits I'd overheard at the Gardners that night we had the casserole.

"You want to know what I think of that?" I asked. "I think it should either be changed to include Wapiti and Ibex or should be abolished. I mean, why not?"

I saw Jack Graham's eyes go up. The two horsemen looked at each other knowledgeably, nodded, and one of them said: "You've got a point there, Mr. Bolton, even if they are foreign breeds. I'll bring it up at the next PHA meeting. Maybe we can get some action."

Mary, passing me with a bowl of cashew nuts, gave me a smart kick in the calf that made me wince. Then Eleanor cried out, "The van! It's coming up the drive!"

I grabbed an opened bottle of beer—I like it in cans better, but this bottled beer was one of the accounts I handle —and followed the others, who had all gone out to the parking lot where a huge, low-slung nine-horse trailer was just coming to rest with a sighing of air brakes. From inside came a most alarming sound of metal clanging on metal. The driver, a barrel-type red-faced man wearing a faded blue turtleneck jersey, put his hands to his ears.

"All the way from Mount Kisco!" he said. "All the way from Mount Kisco! I ask you, folks, how could we know the Canadian idiot wouldn't like having a nice fifty-thousand-dollar nine-horse trailer all to himself? . . . Oh! Beg pardon, ladies!" The anvil chorus from inside the trailer continued uninterrupted. "Well," said the driver, climbing down from the cab, "let's get him out of there while I still got some trailer left to take back to Tim and Mr. Sheridan."

He opened a pair of wide doors, and we all gathered around and peered in. Aspercel, standing in what looked like a narrow padded cell, peered out. His expression was noncommittal. Hellie, who had raced up the drive ahead of the trailer, said to the driver, "Can I take him out?"

"You got a derrick? We had to use a breast hitch in the front and two guys shovin' at the back to get him in."

Aspercel raised his head and sniffed. Whether he was sniffing in, inquiringly, or sniffing out, contemptuously, was impossible to say.

"Let me try, anyway!"

"The pleasure is all yours, little lady," said the driver.

Helen stepped into the trailer, walked over to Aspercel, and made cooing noises, talking to him as if he were a twelve-hundred-pound kitten. He liked it. I could tell because he began chewing her blond hair. If he hadn't liked it, he would have chewed her arm off. She unsnapped the ropes attached to either side of his halter that held him in *status quo*, slipped her hand through the halter, and said, "Come on, Aspie. Come on boy." She pulled. Nothing happened. She pulled harder. Still nothing happened. She pulled so hard she began to get red in the face. Aspercel was so big and so strong he didn't even have to pull against her to get his way but just stood perfectly still.

"I don't think he wants to get out," said Eleanor.

"*I'll* get him out all right!" said Suzie.

She started into the trailer, but I caught her arm. "I'm sure you could, Suzie, but I'm afraid you won't always be around when we want to get him into or out of something he doesn't want to get into or out of."

"Maybe if you folks'll stand away from the door a little. Maybe he don't like crowds," the driver suggested.

Everybody moved back a few yards. As the horse's proprietor I felt I had some leeway, so I moved back only a foot or so. Having nothing else to contribute, I took a swig of beer. When I lowered the bottle, I saw Aspercel looking at me out of those great big eyes. I held the bottle up.

"Want some?"

He made a gargling whinny noise in his throat. I stepped

into the trailer, and he lifted his head, opened his mouth, and wrinkled his lips. I shoved the neck of the bottle between them. He drained it, shook his head, looked square at me, and blew a shower of frothy spray in my face. While I was mopping, I heard Jack Gardner say, "Of *course,* he's Canadian. In England they give racehorses beer all the time."

"In Canada too," said one of the horseman friends.

"Obviously," echoed the other.

"I'll put the bottle down outside, then see if I can't give you a hand, Hellie," I said.

I stepped to the doorway of the trailer. Aspercel unhooked himself from the floor where he'd become permanently rooted and followed. I stepped out, Aspercel stepped out right behind me. Helen wasn't leading him, he was leading Helen; but I wasn't going to point that out.

"Where shall we put him, honey? In his stall?"

"I'd let him run around in the paddock a bit," said Jack. "Get the kinks out after his trip."

I went over to the open paddock gate, Helen and Aspercel following me so closely that from time to time I could feel his hot wet breath on the back of my neck. The small but admiring crowd followed us. As we turned the big black horse into the lush grass of the paddock and closed the gate, I heard the driver say: "That Mr. Bolton's sure got a way with horses! Next time we get a problem horse at the stables, I'll tell Tim to send for him."

Then I heard Suzie say: "Why, yes, I certainly would if I were you. But be sure to tell him to bring his bottle."

There was an acid quality in her voice a man expects to hear only from his wife.

13

I WILL NEVER FORGET the day of my first horse show, which was Hellie's first big-league show. Partly because it was the only time in my life I've ever willingly let anybody roust me out of bed at five in the morning for anything except to go fishing. At that, the noise of Helen whoopsing her cookies with nervousness and Mary yelling soothing things at her and Aspercel kicking hell out of the back of his stall and whinnying and hollering because he wanted in on the family act made getting up less uncomfortable than staying in bed.

I had learned during the two weeks we'd had him that Aspercel, even for a horse, was peculiar. In spite of being a thoroughbred and all his fancy papers, when he was out of uniform, as it were, he was strictly a family-type horse. Which is to say he could stand being alone in his nice new prefabricated stable just so long; then he'd start banging and hollering. One of us—all too often I—would have to go down and feed him carrots or sugar or a pint of beer.

Ironically, he had taken a great fancy to me. If he was out in his paddock and I started wandering around the place or stretched out in a deck chair on the terrace with a drink, he'd leap over the big paddock fence as easily as I'd step over a crack in a sidewalk and stroll up on the terrace and stand over me, head lowered, chin resting on the back of my chair, breathing hot, oaty air at me. He was, as I had told Mary, a nice horse. The trouble was he overdid it, and I dreaded the day when he decided to crawl into my lap.

But let him catch sight of his onstage costume—his saddle and bridle and stuff—and instantly he did a Mr. Hyde, rearing and plunging and pawing and snorting and in his own way trying to look like four thousand five hundred dollars—and succeeding. That was why I tolerated him. He not only represented four thousand five hundred dollars, which I guess he knew; he also represented that fifteen-grand-a-year raise and a vice-presidency—which he did not know and which I wasn't going to let him find out. I didn't want him to have that kind of hold over me or it would have to be champagne instead of beer. No, sir.

Well, I showered and shaved and hauled on pants and a sports shirt and went down to the kitchen to get my breakfast. Helen was there; her face was pale, and her eyes had dark circles under them. She had on a white shirt without a collar, and in one hand she was carrying her new black top boots; with the other hand she was holding onto her new canary-buff breeches that were half on and half off. I smiled, partly because I was glad to see her and partly because it had just occurred to me she looked like her mother with a hangover. Except for the dangling breeches, of course.

"Popsicles. You've got to pull."

She more or less handed me the belt band of the breeches that had been made for her, naturally ($72.50), and were so tight that she had to button the below-the-knee part before pulling them up, because once they were up she couldn't bend over far enough to reach the buttons. I pulled, and up they came and, as we say at sea, were sheeted home. She gave me the usual wet kiss on the nose, and picked up the boots.

"Please?"

"Please what, baby?"

"Please shine them a little? I've got to give Aspercel his breakfast."

She was to pieces. I *had* shined them before I went to bed. I played it smart. "Sure, you won't even recognize them when you come back."

"Dear Popsicles."

She kissed me again and ran off. Her nervousness was contagious. I flicked my handkerchief over the boots a few times, removing three, maybe four, grains of dust, and stood them against the wall. Mary came in wearing a blue wrapper. Her hair was in those curlers and her face was shiny with soap and morning and lack of makeup. She looked as if she'd been made without any lips. Just with a slot, like a mailbox.

"Freddie, you don't think that horse is going to be too much for her, do you?"

"I hope to God not, but how would *I* know? I've been so busy I still haven't seen her ride, except when she was prancing around the paddock here last Sunday. I thought she managed the horse very well then."

"It would just kill me if anything happened to her."

I knew what it would do to me if anything happened. When she'd been little we had been so very close. I'd get home from work, and she'd be watching at the window for me. We'd go off on all-day picnics together in the woods and hunt for caves that I'd carefully located a day or so ahead. We'd go out in the little outboard I had then, and sometimes we'd fish and some days we'd just forget fishing and sail around the world and visit all kinds of fascinating foreign lands—like Bridgeport. But then one day the enchanting wide-eyed laughing child I'd known so well began to vanish and—overnight, it seemed—a schoolgirl who alternated between tears and giggles, introspection and a sort of mild exhibitionism took her place and we began to grow apart. I suppose that happens to fathers all the time. The awful part is, you don't realize it's happening until it has happened and then it's too late to do much about it.

"Why don't you lay off that Garden Club luncheon and come with us?"

"Because I can't, Freddie. Harriet Whitehouse won't be there and, as vice president, I can't let her down. I've *got* to hostess for her."

"Or she'll tie the can to the idea of you getting to be president next year? Sure, that means a lot, but I think helping me take care of Hellie's more important. Do you know exactly how much I know about horse shows?"

What I knew about horse shows, besides the fact that they were for horses, was what a kid had to do in them in order to be allowed to compete for horsemanship prizes in the National Horse Show at Madison Square Garden. There were only two so-called Hunting Seat classes at Madison Square Garden. One was the finals of something called the Maclay Class. The other was the finals of something just like it called the AHSA Medal Class. Almost all AHSA-sanctioned horse shows had both of these classes. In our area, if a boy or girl succeeded in winning three times either in Maclay Classes or in Medal Classes he qualified for the finals in the Garden. And the reason I knew that was because winning three of those classes was what my success or failure as a big-shot vice-president hung on.

"Freddie, you don't have to know anything. Wolfgang will be there; he's made all the entries for her. All you have to do is get her there. And in case you need to find out anything, I put the Rule Book in the car."

"I don't like it. I don't like any part of it." I sighed. "At least the horse will take care of her."

"What makes you think so? He isn't a Saint Bernard; he's a thoroughbred."

"I know. I also know from the little I've seen of him, which is too much, that Aspercel, even as horses go, is an extremely selfish horse. Aspercel is not going to let anything happen to Aspercel; so as long as Helen is glued on, nothing should happen to her." I looked at her. "I think you'd feel better if you took those curlers out of your hair and put on some lipstick. . . . I know I would."

Now, some people might think this was an unwise thing to say. It was and it wasn't. Unwise in that it made her so mad that I thought she was going to take a swing at me; wise because it took her mind completely off Helen. By the time she came downstairs again, looking like a human being, I had whacked together a splendid breakfast of sausages and ham and eggs and tomato juice and milk. Of course, Helen couldn't eat a mouthful.

Mary packed a lunch—I slipped a bottle of vodka into the hamper when she wasn't looking—and after storing the hamper and a lot of horse junk into the station wagon I backed it down to the stable and we hooked it onto the glossy dark-blue horse trailer that had ASPERCEL printed on it in red letters—red and dark blue being, by an odd coincidence, the colors of the boxes Aspercel tablets are sold in. All our stable stuff—buckets, pitchforks, blankets, headbands of bridles—everything was dark blue and red except Aspercel himself. When I showed his picture to Mr. Dugan a few days before, he opened his mouth and said, "I wonder if . . ." Fortunately, he stopped there.

The next step was to lead the horse into the new trailer that had arrived only last night. It was six o'clock of a wonderfully warm morning when we started this operation. It was seven o'clock of a hot day when it became apparent that one of the things Herr Wolfgang Wilhelm Heinrich von Roetz did not teach his pupils was how to persuade thoroughbred horses to hop into trailers if they didn't happen to be in the mood. It was a rerun of his arrival except that this time beer didn't work. I guess the trailer smelled too new to him. Aspercel would let us lead him up to it by the reins, prancing and dancing; then, when we reached it, he'd prance and dance away. After a hundred tries (I kept count) we got so desperate that I carried my favorite aluminum chaise longue down from the terrace and set it up inside the trailer, got my bottle from the hamper, fixed myself a drink, and stretched out in the chair. Providing him with such familiar surroundings might have worked too, if his neck weren't so long. He came up the ramp of his own accord until he had both feet at the top, but from there he could stretch that old neck out far enough to blow at me. Apparently no force on earth short of atomic power was going to get him any farther. The moment Mary pulled on his reins, he remembered what it was he didn't want to do, reared up out of the trailer, banging his head on the way, broke loose, galloped once around the lawn, reins dangling, then, making loud bursting noises from his rear end, he sailed over the paddock fence, slowed to a walk, and began to graze.

Helen was openly in tears. Mary was on the verge, and I had downed the drink I'd meant as a prop, when I heard a noise that sounded sweeter to my ears than the rattle of falling nuts does to autumn squirrels—the high, ululating, unmistakable roar of a sports car driven at maniacal speed. There was just a chance in a million it was the right sports car. A moment later I heard gears shift, the roar rise a couple of octaves, the sound of tortured rubber screeching across macadam, and Suzie pulled up back of the trailer.

"Hi, all. The Bar-J Ranch where I teach and keep my horse decided to ship up and show in the Western Division at Saybrook today. I remembered Mr. Bolton saying you were going there too with the new horse, so I thought maybe it would be a good idea for me to stop by on my way and see if—*Oh!*"

She had just caught a glimpse of me stretched out in the deck chair, holding a glass in my hand.

I waved a hello, but the ice-look I got told me an explanation was in order. "The vodka was for the horse. To get him into the trailer."

"Mr. Bolton, you just mustn't do that! Stimulants are absolutely against the AHSA rules."

"But you don't understand," said Helen, and tried to explain this was all to make Aspercel go into the trailer.

From Suzie's expression I could see *this* was a phase of horsemanship they didn't teach at the good old Bar-J.

Mary, as always, stepped into the social breach. "You see, Miss Clemens . . ."

"Please, Mrs. Bolton, Sue in the country."

"All right, Sue-in-the-Country. For some reason Aspercel is very fond of my husband." And then she tried to explain the absolutely unexplainable—to no avail.

"Suzie," I cried, "I'm desperate, Helen's desperate, we're all desperate. Can *you* get him in?"

She gave each of us a look as if wondering where on earth we'd been brought up that we couldn't get a horse into a trailer. Then she asked Helen for his halter.

Helen scrabbled in the back of the wagon and produced the halter. Suzie took it and started toward the paddock. When we began to follow, she motioned us away. She opened the gate, walked quietly into the paddock, and sneaked up alongside Aspercel. He jerked his head, snorted, and she said: "Hello, Meatball. Stand still now, huh? And don't snort just to impress me. I want to slip that bridle off and put this nice comfy old halter on. There now."

A moment later she was leading him back toward the trailer. I nipped in and got out the chaise longue and bottle. Suzie, still talking to the horse about nothing in particular in a curious, not unmusical monotone, like a tired priest reading a litany in Latin, led him right up to the trailer and inside. Then she backed him out again.

"Hey!" I protested.

"I just wanted to see if he really is a bad loader, Mr. Bolton. He isn't. But you see you never lead a horse into a trailer by the reins. If for some reason they have to wear a bridle, put the halter on over it. Now we'll bandage him."

My heart skipped a beat. No man likes the idea of four thousand five hundred dollars needing a bandage. I looked hard at Aspercel; I couldn't see any wounds. "Why do you want to bandage him when he isn't bleeding?"

"For travel, of course. So he won't hurt himself if he has to scramble to get his balance if you stop too quick, and so he won't rub his tail raw if he leans against the tail gate. Honestly, Mr. Bolton!"

I suddenly remembered the Agency—and that Suzie worked for me.

"It's all right around here"—I lowered my voice so as not to embarrass her—"but at the show, in fact, any place where anybody from the client's office might overhear us, I think you'd better not refer to Aspercel as 'Meatball.' The agency mightn't think too much of that."

I saw her face fall and the lobes of her ears turn that rabbit pink. "Oh!—Oh, of *course*, sir!"

I felt like a heel. "Ah, forget it. Sorry I mentioned it. What difference does it really make whether you call the bloody horse Meatball or Chowderhead or anything else?"

Suzie's lips came up like a taut bow easing after the arrow is fired. "Like even 'Gelusil'?"

I put my arm around her shoulders, and she leaned against me for a second to show my apology for pulling rank was accepted. I'd made the grade. Then she strolled to her car.

Helen called me aside. "Daddy, could you ask Miss Clemens if I could ride up to Saybrook in her sports car with her?"

I didn't have to ask. Suzie started her engine, gave it a roar, dumped her hat behind the back seat, and put on her goggles. Then, leaning over the edge of the car, she shouted, "Helen, how about keeping me company?"

"Could I? Daddy, please?"

I hesitated. It would mean Aspercel and I would be alone for almost two hours. Anything could happen in two hours, but, hell, I was supposed to be the man around here. "Sure."

Mary walked up, and Suzie and Hellie waved, then roared off down the drive.

"This has been a tough morning, honey," she said. "Let's you and I have just a quick one before you chauffeur Meatball up to Saybrook?"

This sounded good to me. I opened the hamper.

We had our drink and I climbed into the wagon. The trailer gave a jerk as I started up, and Aspercel let one fly with his hind foot in protest. This I could see was going to be some day. I waved to Mary, and we rolled out of the driveway and headed south for the Connecticut Turnpike.

14

ONCE THROUGH the tollgate, I drove at a steady sixty. I didn't stay at sixty because the law says so; I stayed there because Aspercel said so. Every time I'd let her inch up beyond, good old Aspie'd let fly at the tail gate with one of those steel-shod hooves. It puzzled me. Any horse who'd guzzle all the beer he could couldn't be all that law-abiding, so I figured it must have something to do with his comfort, which, as I may have indicated, was something he set great store by. Anyway, as my mind kept wandering to how I was going to manage things at the show, the speed kept inching up without my realizing it and Aspie kept letting fly. It was like driving with a nagging wife in the back seat, and by the time we turned off at Saybrook and began to hunt for the show grounds I'd had it.

Finding the show wasn't as hard as I'd expected. I simply followed my nose along a few back roads until at a crossroads I suddenly began to sneeze. I took a right and the sneezing got worse, so I knew I had it made, and turned off my private loran by taking two antihistamines.

About a mile up the road we crested a hill. In the valley below, there were red-and-white-striped tents and plain green tents and I guess maybe seventy or a hundred vans and trailers. There was one big ring surrounded by a white plank fence with a wide top rail at convenient leaning height, like a bar. There was a big field with a lot of jumps made of fence rails and little stone walls. There were children and grown-ups milling around. And there were horses. The whole landscape was littered with them. I began to sneeze so hard my eyes watered and I couldn't see, so I had to pull to the side of the road to wait for the pills to bite. I closed my eyes so I wouldn't have to see the blur of horses through my tears; this helped. I got out my handkerchief and breathed through it; this helped even more. I looked at my watch. It was nine o'clock; I was late. Hellie'd be horribly upset and probably throwing up all over everything. I couldn't wait for the pills.

I drove on to the gate, turned in behind a big horse trailer, and waited. The trailer moved on and the gateman came over to me. I didn't know if I was supposed to have a ticket or not, but he looked me over, then waved me in. I moved ahead, following the big trailer. I hadn't gone more than a dozen yards before Hellie showed up looking desperate.

"Oh, Father, you're late! Suzie had to go on to her show, and I can't find Wolfgang, and my first class is in five minutes."

"Where do we make camp?"

"I don't know—anywhere I guess in that field with all the vans. But we don't have time. I've got to get mounted."

"Okay." I pulled a little off the beaten path that made a road to the van parking areas, shut off the engine, set the brakes, and got out.

A policeman appeared from nowhere. "Can't park here, buddy."

"Just for five minutes. My kid's got to get on her horse—"

"Sorry, buddy; I said you can't park here."

"That's just one person's opinion," I snapped, going to the tailgate and sliding the hasps back. "Besides," I said, rolling the gate down, "I'm not parking; I'm unloading. That's okay; look it up in the AHSA Rule Book. It's right there on the front seat. Helen, get your saddle. Okay, Meatball, come on out and get to work!"

"*Father!* How can he when Suzie tied him with the halter shank?"

"You want to bet?"

Even as I spoke, Aspercel was backing down the ramp made by the tailgate. I'd been sure with a couple of hours of nothing to do except pick on my driving he'd have untied any knot out of sheer boredom, to say nothing of the approved, quick release slipknot Suzie used. I slid off the light blanket Helen called his cooler, which, for the benefit of us nonhorse types, naturally doesn't mean it's to keep him cool but to keep him warm when he's hot. Hellie flung the saddle over him and disappeared underneath, looking for the girth, surfaced, and buckled it.

"You'll have to tighten it, Father. I'm not strong enough."

The announcer's voice boomed out of a loudspeaker right over our heads. "Class 34 get ready to come into the ring. Class Thirty-four. Maiden Equitation Hunter Seat, fourteen to eighteen not to jump. Get ready, please."

"That's *me!*" Hellie wailed.

I didn't blame her for being desperate. I was pretty desperate myself. All excited and hands tembling, I didn't know then that these maiden horsemen wouldn't go into the ring for another ten minutes anyway. And that the announcer wasn't so much announcing as praying, because, as I later learned was typical, after operating for only fifteen minutes the horse show was already half an hour behind schedule.

"Come on, kid; I'll boost you aboard."

"It's customary to ride with a *bridle*. You *must* know that."

I looked at Aspie's head. He still had on his halter. I'd forgotten all about the bloody bridle. "Oh, bridle, sure. Go get it."

Helen dipped into the back of the wagon, saw a rein protruding from under all the other stuff, grabbed it, pulled, and the bridle came out. Only, thanks to this inexperienced casualness on her part, it came out looking as if someone had been playing cat's-cradle with it. She looked at it, visibly on the verge of tears, and did the silliest thing possible. She handed it to me.

Now, there's a funny thing about bridles—particularly what're called double bridles, which simply means they have two bits and two sets of reins and, this being the only logical horse term I have encountered, are double bridles. Two bridles in one, so to speak. The funny thing about them is that on a horse they look simple, neat, and useful —like a bridle. But as Helen handed this one to me, it didn't look like two bridles in one; it looked like five or six bridles. There were straps running north, south, east, and west. There were reins all over the place. There were miscellaneous loops and buckles and dangling straps that seemed to have no rhyme or reason. I studied it, holding it first one way, then another, while it writhed in my hands. I was just on the point of throwing it to the ground and jumping on it when that loudspeaker right over our heads said, "All entries for Class Thirty-four report to the in-gate please."

"*Father!*" Hellie was on the edge of panic.

"Yes?"

"The reins go over his head first!"

I flung the reins over Aspie's head.

"Now just put the bridle on his head."

I raised it, hoping in some way I could force it around his face and over his ears so it would hang on him any old way, but would hang there. I knew Hellie didn't need it because Aspie was going to do whatever he wanted no matter if it was a double, triple, or quadruple bridle. I couldn't make it stick. All that happened was he peered through the tangle of straps at me with a look of reproach, and backed away.

"The bit. The bit goes in his mouth before you do anything else."

"Oh, the bit." I looked at the bridle. It had, of course, those two bits; one little one with rings on the sides and a big one with, well, connecting rods running down each side. "Tell you what, Hellie," I said, knowing I couldn't possibly get them both in, "I'll put the little one in and we'll let the other hang down as a spare. Right?"

I was shoving the little one into his mouth when I felt a rough tap on my shoulder, and turned. I saw two things: Helen bawling, and the policeman who'd told me I couldn't park there who had shoved his way through a laughing crowd I hadn't even been aware of. He addressed the crowd. "You wise guys who think it's so funny to see a little girl cry couldn't have given this man a hand, could you?" He turned to me. "Even if you are one of those smart alecks with a rule book, I can't stand to watch this no longer. Gimme that thing. You're trying to shove it on backward."

With relief I handed him the bridle. He took the reins off Aspie, gave the whole mess a shake and a couple of twists and, presto, it became a bridle. With an air of assurance his uniform and badge could only have been partly responsible for, he slid the reins over the horse's neck, dropped the halter, slipped the bits into his mouth, and in a single motion popped the bridle into place.

"Okay, miss," he said to Hellie, "give me your ankle and I'll give you a leg."

Here again was the *espéranto de la monde des chevaux,* but Helen, of course, read him loud and clear. Tears still rolling down her pale cheeks, she picked up the reins in her left hand and, standing close to the horse, crooked her left knee. The cop grabbed her ankle, said, "Hup, hup, *hup!*" hoisted on the third hup, and there was Hellie mounted. She gathered the reins, pressed her calves against Aspie's sides in the signal for him to move ahead. He stood stock still. She kicked him. He twitched his tail.

The announcer had been reading off the numbers of winners of the previous class. Now he said, "Class Thirty-four in the ring, please."

"Father, what'll I do? He—he's not going to move!"

I thought I knew how I could make him move. I started to raise my foot, but a man wearing khaki pants, a blue shirt, and a pair of calf-high rubber boots stepped up.

"If you don't mind my saying so, mister, in this part of the country we always take the shipping bandages off *before* we send them into the ring. Different out your way, I guess?"

By now I was beginning to get pretty hot under the collar.

"Yes. Why, yes, it is. We don't like to take chances on horses as valuable as this one."

I squatted down and went to work on the bandage on his left front leg. It ran from his hoof to his knee. For openers I snarled the neat bowknot Suzie had tied. I tried to bite it loose. Wordlessly the policeman produced a pocketknife; I cut the tape and then began to unwind. In less time than it takes to tell, I had Aspercel's leg snarled in about four yards of white woolly stuff.

Again the policeman handed me his pocketknife. "Bandages is cheaper than time," he said. "You can *buy* more bandages."

I boldly sliced Aspercel clear of the bandage, leaving the shorn pieces on the ground. The man in the boots came from walking around behind Aspercel, "Since you were busy I took the liberty of giving you a hand. Hope you don't mind."

He held out four neat rolls of bandage; tail, hind legs, one front leg. Helen pressed her calves in the horse's side again. He reared, danced sideways, gave a plunge, but she sat him steady as a rock. In her two weeks with Aspercel she had got used to his starting off this way; like my old man was used to his Model-T farm truck starting off in a series of twitches and jerks. He calmed down to a dancing jog in a cha-cha rhythm, and she headed him toward an open gate that led into the ring. The crowd dispersed, and I turned to the man in the boots and the cop who was standing beside him.

"You guys have saved my life. Can I buy you a drink out of my station wagon?"

"Later," said the cop.

"I'll drop by after you get parked," said the man in boots. He looked around; we were as alone as we were likely to be at a horse show. "Say," he said, "I don't mean to get out of line, but would you mind explaining to me how come you're here all by yourself to take care of a horse like that?"

I met his eyes. They were gray blue, like Wolfgang's and Tim Riley's. I wondered if the three of them were born that way or if the eyes were a purely occupational characteristic.

"I'm with the Heather Farms outfit," he said. "That big green trailer you can see over there."

Plainly he was giving me his credentials. I looked where he pointed and saw the biggest horse trailer on the grounds. His credentials were okay by me.

"To answer your question," I said: "I'm here alone with my daughter and her horse because my wife couldn't come and my kid's Hessian instructor who was supposed to meet us here didn't."

"That figures," he said. "I just wondered. If you don't mind my saying so, when you first picked up that bridle and saw it couldn't fit on his head I thought for a second there you were maybe going to try to—well, the other end, you know?"

I grinned. "I was tempted. I have never been any nearer to a horse show than the front of a TV set. And I hate horses."

He gave me a quizzical look. "You hate *all* horses? I don't think so."

"Well, all but one, I guess."

"That's more like it. Listen, Charlie—he's the cop—works around horses himself in his spare time. He's got to chase you out of here now or his boss will give him hell. Drive your outfit down and park it next to our trailer. I'll be glad to give you a hand off and on when you need it. My name's Cleve Brown."

"Freddie, Freddie Bolton."

"Glad to meet you, Freddie. I'll keep an eye on your kid 'til the class is over and you get back. She won't have any trouble, not with that horse. I'll be darned if I expected to see a horse like that today. Take him off your hands if you want to sell him. Give you five thousand for him."

"No," I said. "But, well, thanks for everything."

I drove the wagon and the trailer, naturally forgetting to pick up the tail gate first, clanging over into the field where the big green truck-trailer was parked. And now I began to worry. That little money talk had brought home to me again the brody I'd taken. Some people bet their houses on their horses. In the days of the gallant South, gentlemen used to bet their wives and even their mistresses. I was betting much more than that on Aspercel. If, in spite of his prancing and dancing and showing off, Aspercel turned out to be a bust, well, good-bye to a lot of things.

I'd been too busy to worry about that until now. But now I was worrying hard. If Aspercel didn't work out, I would be no more than a funny story guys in the advertising business told each other at lunch or in the bar car on the way home. But even ridicule I could take. What I couldn't take was the idea of Helen's having to share it with me.

I GOT TO RINGSIDE five minutes from the time Hellie had left. There were thirty kids in the class mounted on every size horse you could imagine. Since they were sometimes two and three abreast, it seemed to me that the judge would have to get down on his hands and knees and peer right underneath the big horses to judge the little ones. He solved this just after I got there by having the ringmaster shoo all the little ponies to the middle of the ring and stand there.

That left twelve going around the ring, and now I could see Helen. I thought she looked lovely, stiff and straight, holding her hands and feet just so. And Aspercel, of course, made the other horses look counterfeit. He did everything he was supposed to do, walk, trot, canter right on cue. There was one funny thing, though. Instead of waiting for Helen to give him whatever signal Wolfie had taught her, he seemed to just do whatever the ringmaster in the scarlet coat called for as soon as he called for it. When the ringmaster sang out, "R-e-v-erse, please," he spun around so fast little Hellie almost fell off, and I would swear that as he came by where I was leaning on the rail the stupid animal winked at me.

After five minutes the judge spoke to the ringmaster, and the ringmaster called out that numbers such and such would line up in the center of the ring and the rest were excused. Hellie was one of the ones excused. My heart sank. The Aspercel deal was a bust.

Then I remembered this was horsemanship stuff, and I had learned that in these classes the judge is supposed to ignore the horse and only consider the performance of the child. I hurried over by the gate, but as she rode out, her lips and hands trembling, Helen wouldn't even look at me.

When we got to our trailer and she had dismounted I went up to her. She looked at me through a mist of tears—where was all this self-assurance and poise a horse was supposed to give her?—then buried her face against the great black horse's neck, and wept.

"It's the horse." I shouted bitterly. "It's that fancy horse. *You* looked just swell. Believe me, Hellie, just swell."

Her voice came to me, muffled and miserable. "Dad, don't *speak* like that about Aspie. He was an angel. I—I just hope he doesn't really know I didn't win a single ribbon. It would be too awful for him."

"Of course he doesn't know."

"I *wish* Judy or Mr. Gardner or Suzie or Wolfgang was here."

I wished Wolfgang were here too, so I could break his neck. I had a happy thought; maybe he *had* broken it driving up here. It was so obvious Helen wasn't ready for this kind of competition. This was called a Class B show, which means while it isn't quite as important as an A show, it's pretty darned important—much more important than the ordinary ones, which are called C Shows. It also meant that the kids here were pretty much in the top category in horsemanship. Hellie hadn't been seriously riding for a year yet. She was good—probably—but she couldn't be all that good yet. Wolfgang had somehow let her get the impression that even at this show she'd be in the ribbons. Then, obviously, he'd taken a powder.

"You want to try one more of these horsemanship classes, baby? You don't have to if you don't want to. Maybe you're not quite ready yet. You can quit now if you want."

She lifted her tear-stained face, straightened up, and looked at me out of Mary's eyes. "Quit? Of course I won't quit. It wouldn't be fair to Aspie."

She wouldn't have been up to this a year ago—or two months ago. Maybe the horse *was* giving her something.

"Good girl."

And that was all either of us said. The second class was a repeat of the first, the only difference being she got excused in about three minutes flat. I'd had it. Cleve, the man who'd wanted to buy Aspie, was standing beside me when she rode out of the ring this time, and I asked if he'd go over to the trailer with Helen because there was something I wanted to attend to.

When they'd gone I hunted up the policeman. "Say," I said, "as you just may have guessed, I'm new at this racket. My kid's not getting to first base. Is there any way I can find out what she's doing wrong? Anybody I can ask?"

"Sure, you could ask the judge. He could tell you right off, but he's got his hands full right now. Or you can ask the steward to find out for you."

"Steward?"

I guess I looked as blank as I felt, because the cop laughed and said, "He's a kind of referee and general peacemaker between the judges, the exhibitors, and the folks who run the horse show."

"Where is he?"

My new friend looked around, pointed toward a tent where they sold hot dogs and coffee and stuff. "There he is, the little guy with the blue jacket and gray pants and the badge, drinking coffee. Stewards are great coffee drinkers. That's how they keep busy in between rounds after they've run out of scraps to referee."

"Thanks, pal."

"Anytime."

I walked over to the steward. He had "horse" written all over him, from the ruddy, leathery complexion to the slight bow in his legs—and the blue eyes. Man around fifty, fifty-five, I'd guess. "My name's Bolton," I said, going up to him, "Fred Bolton. I have a kid here and this is her first show. She isn't getting to first base. I wonder if you could find out for me what she's doing wrong?"

He nodded understandingly. He had a pleasant smile, a little like Jack Gardner's. "I think I can. How old is she?"

"Fifteen."

"Been riding long?"

"Not quite a year."

"Instructor?"

"Wolfgang von—"

He held up his left hand, took a sip of coffee. "Say no more. I know right now what she's probably doing wrong, but if you'll walk over to the secretary's stand with me I'll dig out the judge's card for this last class, and check. I'd show it to you but the exhibitors aren't allowed to see the cards." He'd set down his coffee cup and we were walking around the ring. "What's her number?"

"Forty-five. She's riding a great big black horse—"

"Oh, I know. The little girl who's riding Killarney."

"Aspercel! It's Aspercel!"

"Yeah, Killarney. I judged him at the Toronto show last winter. Beautiful animal." He blinked. "What's the matter? Tummy upset because the kid's having a rough time?"

"No."

"I thought I heard you say something about Aspercel."

"That's the horse's name now. We changed it from Killarney to Aspercel."

"Mind my asking why? Seems a funny idea to name a horse after a stomach medicine. Oh, I've got it. That old saying. 'Nothing better for the inside of a man than the outside of a horse!' Right?"

"You've hit the nail on the head."

"By the way, Mr. Bolton. I suppose you've registered the name change with the American Horse Shows Association?" My stomach froze. This could be a major goof. I didn't have the faintest idea whether we had or not.

"My—my wife generally does things like that."

The steward put a hand on my shoulder. "You look as if you're having enough trouble for one day, so I'm not going to ask to see his registration. In fact, the subject never even came up between us, did it? But if you haven't done it, do it. The minute you get home."

"Yes, *sir*," I said, meaning it. I wondered if all stewards were like this. I doubted it. We'd reached the little white-painted stand where they gave out numbers and took your money for last-minute entries. It was crowded with men and women and children and utter confusion, yet in less than two minutes the steward was back.

"I checked the card."

"Learn what she's doing wrong?"

He laughed. "Nothing."

"Nothing?"

"Not one thing. Trouble is, she isn't doing anything right, either."

"I don't get it. Right like what?"

"Oh, like flexing her back and moving her butt and hands with the horse. Stuff like that. The judge wrote opposite her number, 'poses, passenger, stiff.' "

"Damn it! I've paid von Roetz—"

"Take it easy. Got a minute to walk over by the trees there and smoke a cigarette with me?"

"Of course."

"Look," he said, "about your kid, it's this way. Wolf Roetz is certainly one of the two or three top instructors in the East, maybe in the country. He's great at turning out finished riders. Gives them lots of flair, lots of polish. For anyone who rides pretty well he's *the* top. But when kids

104

are new at the game he puts on the polish without teaching them to ride—the basics—first. Little bit like trying to polish a pair of shoes that the shoemaker hasn't finished making yet. That's what's wrong with your daughter."

"Is she any good at all?"

"How long has she been riding—seriously, that is?"

"Seven months."

"She's terrific. If she'd been riding for two years I'd say lousy." He ground out his cigarette.

"I wish there were somebody—the AHSA or some place I could write to and say how helpful you've been, sir."

"That's awfully nice of you, and if you want me to lose my steward's license and my judge's license you just do that."

"Special delivery," I said, and met his grin.

I walked away, head down, thinking, kicking at the dusty grass the way a kid drags his feet on his way to school. I was pretty sunk for Helen's sake, mostly—though I didn't like the idea of facing Harry Tomes at the agency Monday morning and having him ask how my daughter and good old Aspercel made out. He wouldn't ask if we'd won any ribbons. He'd ask how many. Well, it had all seemed like a good idea at the time.

A photographer came up, Leica swinging back and forth on his chest. I recognized Frank, one of the boys we use at the agency for news publicity shots.

"Hi, Freddie. When am I supposed to take that shot that's supposed to be captioned: 'Aspercel wins again. Miss Helen Bolton, daughter of' and all that crap? You know. The one they want where the horse has a ribbon in his teeth or something and she's carrying a big silver tray? Like in the art department layout?"

"I don't know when."

"You look sort of beat, Freddie, like you could use a drink. Want one?"

"I want one. But right now would be a very bad time for me to get stoned."

I started walking on toward the trailer. He came close. "Say," Frank said out of the side of his mouth away from his cigar, "can't these judges be bought? I mean just for one class, so we can get that picture?"

I've always liked the direct approach of news photographers. Basic, like what Helen needed. "I don't think so."

"Too bad." We walked a few steps farther. "Say, it ain't possible this whole Aspercel deal is just one big sour apple, is it?"

"You're making me feel just great. Go away and let me be miserable alone, will you?"

"You mean there's no use my sticking around no longer? We're going to quit on the picture? Christ, Freddie, that horse looks like he cost a lot of sugar. They must have something around here even he could win."

My skin prickled with excitement. *This* was an angle I hadn't thought of.

At this point I saw Cleve walking toward the hot-dog booth. He saw me and came over.

"Be out of line if I give you a tip?"

"Would I be grateful! I was just wanting to talk to you. What is it?"

"For your kid for today the hell with these horse-manship classes. I've been watching. This is tough competition here; she's not ready for it. I couldn't suggest this if we had a horse going in that division today, but what you do, scratch her from the rest of the equitation classes and enter the big horse in the three Junior Exhibitor Hunter classes over the outside course."

"Tell me," said Frank, "as an interested bystander. Why is she going to be any different outside from inside? Or do we still got one big bad apple on our hands?"

Cleve scowled at him. "In hunter classes, only the horse is judged, *not* the rider. On that horse all she's got to do is sit there and steer. If that."

Frank beamed. He even went so far as to take the cigar out of his mouth. Cleve wouldn't know it, but from Frank this was a great compliment. "Stranger," he said, "you know it not, but you are a financial genius. Freddie, put this man on our payroll as an expert consultant."

"Look, Cleve. After the exhibition I made of myself trying to get that bridle on Aspie, I embarrassed Helen so she can hardly bear to look at me. I know perfectly well if I tell her I'm going to take her out of the horsemanship classes and switch her to the Junior Hunters, she'll say, 'Father, you can't do that because Wolfgang said' . . . and, well, you know."

"Sure," said Cleve. "I know. I've got a kid of my own about that age. He was in that last class as a matter of fact. Came in second. But will Ronnie listen to anything I tell him? And I'm the *manager* of that big Heather Farms outfit. His instructor—the guy he *will* listen to—works for *me!*"

For a second we looked at each other in sympathetic understanding. Then I said, "Helen would listen to you if for no other reason than you're not her father. *You* tell her you've persuaded me to switch the classes around."

"Glad to."

"And if she pulls any of this 'But Wolfgang says . . .'"

"I'll tell her I'll fix it with Wolfgang because he's a pal of mine. Naturally, I really hate his guts. Him and his phony accent."

"Put it there!"

I held out my hand. We shook.

Helen—I guess I should say Aspercel—came home with three blue ribbons and one huge blue, red, and yellow job that said "Junior Hunter Champion Saybrook Horse Show" in gold letters that didn't look as if they'd rub off as easily as the 4-H ones. She had also brought home a silver tea tray about two feet square, a silver ashtray, a silver cigarette box, and a hundred and fifty dollars in cash. I hadn't known there were cash prizes in children's classes, since children under eighteen are considered amateurs, but it turned out the cash prize was won by the horse, not the child, so this was okay. Naturally, since Aspie'd won it, Hellie insisted the money be spent buying him something cute, that he'd enjoy having. I suggested twenty cases of Canadian ale, but as I remember it this was followed by quite a silence.

Fortunately, when she and Aspercel—or maybe it ought to be the other way around—were awarded the tray, not only was Frank in the ring taking pictures, but there were also guys from the New Haven *Register,* the Hartford *Times,* the New London paper and a U.P. man. Plainly, I had something.

Winning all this junk had been easy—for me. During the lunch break Cleve and his son Ronnie gave Hellie a quick but complete briefing in what she was and was not to do in the hunter classes. Ronnie walked her around the course, and when they came back Cleve summed up the instructions in two sentences:

"Your horse knows more about how a horse ought to jump than you'll ever know, so don't try to make him do anything he doesn't want to. The only thing he doesn't know is what order to take the jumps in or when to stop. Having seen them together, I really believe that if your father explained *that* to him you wouldn't have to do anything but sit there. But we can't take the chance, so I'm afraid you will have to steer and at the right time say 'Whoa!' and pull him up. But that is *all* you are to do, right?"

"Yes, sir," Helen said.

I went to where Aspie was tied up to the back of the trailer and, just to be on the safe side and hoping to God nobody'd hear me, I explained to him what order he was to take the jumps in. Then I slipped him a pint of beer. About twenty minutes later I was nervously standing at the edge of the field where the outside jumping course was, while in some mysterious way the eight jumps grew higher and higher as Helen's turn approached. "Next horse on the outside course, Number Forty-five."

I saw Aspercel come into the field at a fast canter. I clenched my fists as tight as I could to keep them from trembling. Helen was sitting erect and practically motionless, just the way the steward had said she shouldn't but which didn't matter now. I saw her pull one rein to steer Aspie at the first fence. Then he took off. He was some hunter, all right. He seemed to ignore the jumps entirely, never changing the rhythm of his stride, but merely putting a little more oomph into it as he came to his fences so he would sail at least a foot over the top, land as smoothly as if the fence hadn't been there, and sweep on toward the next one. When he went over the last jump everybody applauded, which I understand doesn't very often happen on outside-course things.

The nearest we came to disaster was in the first class. When he got over the last jump, instead of turning to go between two flags mounted on high posts that marked the finish of the course, he became completely unmanageable and headed right for the edge of the course where I was standing. Thank the Lord I have a really fast brain. The silly beast, having heard the applause and lapped it up, had spotted me and was coming over to hit me for a beer. If he missed going through those two flags, he'd be disqualified. I sprinted and got to the other side of the flags in time. He trotted up to me and completed the course. Having engaged in what for him was a little mild exercise, but like any other ham actor taking it big, he was sweating and breathing hard and snorting as if in agony. He sniffed at my pockets, lifted his head, blew some sweat and spit at me. I patted his lathered neck and said, "Not here, pal. Back at the trailer," and, seeming satisfied and thoroughly pleased with himself as usual, he suffered Helen to ride him out of the gate.

The other two wins were easier because I got smart and watched them from behind a tree where the silly beast couldn't see me. The championship he won automatically, since it was awarded for winning everything else in that department, including a class called Hunters Under Saddle where all he had to do was flop around the ring a few times looking handsome.

With Aspie just tired enough to lay off the back-seat driving and Hellie sound asleep against my shoulder, we got home just as dusk was creeping in over the semidemi. As we pulled up in front of the stable, Mary was waiting for us. "Wolfgang had an automobile accident. That's why he wasn't at the show." For a second I felt guilty for having wished this would happen. Scared, I said, "Did—he didn't break his neck?"

Mary laughed. "Of course not, but he did have to go to the hospital for X-rays. He sprained his wrist. Freddie, when I heard about that I felt terrible about having let you go alone. Was it awful? When he called up about the accident, Wolfgang said he'd heard the competition was going to be pretty stiff. Did you win anything at all?"

Ribbon by ribbon, trophy by trophy I handed her the loot, saving the championship ribbon for last. She looked at the trophies with disbelief at first, then, peering in the dusk, read the engraving on them. She looked up, puzzled. "But none of these are for horsemanship, and Wolfgang said—"

"The less I hear right now about what Wolfgang said, the less apt I am to kill him when I see him. He had no business at all putting her into the horsemanship classes at that show. I tell you, Mary, watching her try to hold on to herself when she was getting the hook—the gate, that is—nearly broke my heart."

"Well, you've done wonderfully." She walked around the wagon and shook Hellie's shoulder with the gentle determination of a Pullman-car porter. "Come on, Helen. Come on, baby. Wake up now and come on in the house."

Helen stumbled out of the car. "I've got to put Aspie away first." She straightened, wide awake. "Oh, golly! Here comes Wolfgang. Oh, what am I going to tell him. Mother, *I* didn't win a thing. I'm so ashamed."

I said, "Nuts," got out of the car, and saw Wolfie's white and now somewhat battered convertible pull up near the house. He was wearing a Band-Aid on one side of his forehead and an Ace bandage on his left wrist. He got out and walked toward us through the darkness.

"Ah!" he said, his eyes lighting up at the sight of the loot. "My favorite pupil." Then he saw the huge championship ribbon and the lettering on it, and his face fell. Of course, in the flash of a second he knew exactly what had happened. He glued a smile on his face. "Well, we didn't come home empty-handed, did we?"

"Nope," I said.

"I congratulate you."

"Thanks," I said, as though he'd been speaking to me, though I knew he wasn't. "I deserve it."

Wolfgang blinked. Something sadistic in him made him ask Helen, "And the horsemanship classes?"

There was a sticky silence. Helen broke it.

"I guess I let you down, Wolfgang. I didn't win anything at all. Nothing."

"She just needs more experience in shows," said Mary.

That wasn't what Helen needed. She needed something Wolfie couldn't give her, that *he'd* been given at Fort Riley so long ago he'd forgotten he even had it. Suddenly a picture floated into my mind. Before lunch I'd had just enough time to drive over to the other show grounds where the western horses were doing their stuff. There I saw Suzie, hat blown off and hanging by its elastic band, her horse Queenie swerving in and out of a lot of poles at a full gallop, Suzie's body following each fast move so closely and so gracefully that she gave the impression she and the horse were a single unit activated by the same brain cells. I knew now where I could get Helen what she needed. I smiled at Wolfgang. You can't blame a guy if his best isn't quite good enough.

"Come on into the house and have a drink and a bite of dinner with us, Wolf? How about it?"

"I'd like to. Very much."

"There are a couple of points where your instruction goes off the beam a little. I'd like to run over them with you and maybe change our lesson arrangements a little?" Aspie had backed himself out of the trailer, and Helen and

Mary were putting him away. Wolfie and I strolled on toward the house. "To sum it up into a small package, it's this way. You just can't polish a pair of shoes until the shoemaker's finished making them. Right?"

Wolfie gave me a long slow, thoughtful look.

"That is very well put, Mr. Bolton. You have a point there. Yes, that is *very* well put indeed."

I laughed, a self-deprecating laugh. "Oh, well, Wolfie old man. After all, words are my business."

16

THE MORNING after that first show I arranged with Suzie for Hellie to go over to the Bar-J Ranch three evenings a week after supper and learn to ride a horse. I'd pick her up when I got back from town, thus leaving Mary free to indulge in civic virtue and wind up her quiet campaign for the presidency of the dear old Garden Club.

Mary was getting more and more upset about this as the annual meeting approached. I wasn't worried. From eighteen years' experience I knew that in spite of her petiteness and femininity, in her own way she was as tough as Aspie. When my Mary wanted her way, she got it.

I knew she was a shoo-in the evening she told me she'd tracked down a lawyer named Blitzstein who'd bought a sort of château a couple of miles from us. Seemed he raised a certain rare breed of orchid—the only ones of their kind in North America—and Mary naturally had conned him into agreeing to let her take half a dozen of his plants out to the Garden Club special convention in Pasadena that was coming up in October. This was a major coup.

But I was not looking forward to Mary's being gone for two weeks or whatever. After the convention she'd take off for her annual fall visit to her folks in Redlands. Every time she'd gone out there in the past I'd wandered around like a lost dog until she got back. I think even people who scrap all the time, which we did not, get like that after they've lived together long enough. Assuming they haven't already killed each other off before then.

But all that was four months off; and this was June, and around Weston like most everywhere else June is just a little different from any other month. Strangers are nicer to each other in June than they are any other time of the year except right around Christmas; friends are friendlier. It's softer. Out in the country a guy walks around his place and sees all the natural stuff like roses and little young trees and things that have made it through the long tough

112

winter on their own and thinks maybe he has a chance too to make it where he wants to go.

I really enjoyed those first weeks in June. Especially the evenings when I'd grab a sandwich on the train instead of a cocktail and beat it up to the Bar-J to pick up Hellie. In spite of how I felt about horses, I got so I actually liked standing at the corral. Me, full of antihistamine pills, Suzie beside me, the two of us leaning on the rail, watching Helen ride, and Suzie calling soft-voiced instructions to her. I liked it even better evenings when we'd sit side by side on a bench outside one of the barns in the deepening dusk while Hellie brought the cow ponies in from the pasture for water and a handout of grain. There was a sort of hush over the land at that time of the evening. It was nature's quiet time. The birds had stopped hollering at each other about who was going to sleep where; the cats hadn't yet started hollering about who was going to do what to whom; even the horses moved on quiet feet across the pasture to the gate and whickered softly as Hellie came for them. There was the wonderful trite smell of new-mown hay rising up from the meadows. Leaning on the corral fence, Suzie and I would talk about all sorts of things, but on the evenings when we'd sit on the bench by the barn, feeling the soft summer night close in around us, we never talked at all. We just sat quietly, close together and, more often than not, we'd hold hands. It was a funny arrangement I suppose. Holding her hand wasn't meant as a prelude to anything; it was just the way we did at that hour. I think we both felt that was the way a man and woman ought to sit together in the dusk on a bench outside a barn. But it brought a closeness to our relationship I would not have believed possible with a girl who still called me Mr. Bolton. But then Suzie Clemens was a most remarkable girl.

The idyllic interlude lasted until Hellie, as the result of her course in basics, which consisted of constantly riding different horses—bareback—could do the barrel-bending bit at a gallop, which she did one Friday evening at the end of June.

At dusk, as usual, Suzie and I repaired to our bench while Hellie finished watering the string of western horses. All of a sudden Suzie disengaged her hand from mine, ending the idyllic interlude.

"Mr. Bolton, I've done all I can for your daughter. She's

ready to go back to Wolfgang now for polishing."

Like an oaf, I blurted out the first thing that came to mind: "But, Suzie, that's awful!"

Suzie, had she been anyone else, would have laughed; but, being Suzie, she understood that whereas it was quite proper for me, her boss, to sit on a bench with her in the dark while I waited for my daughter to finish her chores, it would be not at all proper for me to do exactly the same thing simply because I wanted to.

She nodded. "I'm going to miss these evenings too, Fred —Mr. Bolton."

I smiled. "Did you have to teach her these 'basics' quite so fast? It *could* have taken all summer, you know."

She snapped me back to reality. "Not with Mr. Dugan calling Mr. Tomes every Monday morning and asking if Helen's qualified to ride Aspercel in Madison Square Garden yet, it couldn't!"

I felt the June evening turn chill. "You're kidding. Dugan doesn't really do that, does he? And how would you know?"

"Barbara, Mr. Tomes's secretary. I haven't mentioned it to you, Mr. Bolton, because part of my job is to protect you from annoyances like that so your mind will be free for more important things."

"Suzie, right now there are no more important things. What do you tell Barbara to tell Mr. Tomes to tell Mr. Dugan?"

She giggled. "You really want to know?"

"Of course I do!"

"I tell her to tell him to keep his fly zipped."

"Oh—"

"I know. I'm ashamed of myself. But I've explained that Helen could win her medals or certificates any time you wanted just by picking the shows with the right judges, but that you're a perfectionist and you want her not just to ride in the Garden but to *win* there. Then I explained that she's been having a special course of instruction that's just for experts. I said to tell Mr. Tomes not to let on to you that I'd told him."

And they'd swallowed it! Harry Tomes had, I knew, because although he checked with me on Hellie every Monday lately he'd acted as if he and I were sharing some deep secret. He hadn't pressed me about why hadn't Helen qualified or when was she going to. That had surprised me because Harry really could put the pressure on.

"Suzie," I said in awe and admiration, "you are as much of a con man as I am."

"Yes, but now Wolf's got to get her to the point where she *does* qualify. What—what will you do if she doesn't make it, Mr. Bolton?"

"Why, I will just quietly cut my throat. In the bathtub, probably—according to the books of etiquette—so as not to make too much mess. But I know she's going to qualify."

"How can you know?"

"Because, Suzie, I am going to *make* her qualify. She *has* to."

A lot of weeks passed before I was to realize how that must have sounded. When I did, I just hoped by some miracle it had not sounded that way to Suzie. I don't think so. Suzie was too loyal to permit it.

17

IF I HAD BEEN one of those characters who keeps diaries I would have simply omitted the months of July and August and most of September that year. If in June I'd thought June was good, in July, August, and September I found out how good it really had been. Brother, were those months a grind. In the whole semester there were only two highlights. The day of the Lakeville Horse Show, and Labor Day.

The Lakeville show was on Sunday, August first. It was a Junior Show, meaning for kids under eighteen, which means, like everything else in the cockeyed equine world of which I was becoming a habitué, that they can be well on their way to nineteen provided their eighteenth birthday falls on or after January 1st. Under this same interesting arrangement a horse born before midnight on New Year's Eve is technically considered a year old the next morning. You have to be smart, smart, smart to keep up with this horse crowd.

By the time Lakeville rolled around, we'd been to five shows and I'd begun to feel like a carny who drives his trailer from fair to fair and tries to persuade the suckers to spend fortunes trying to toss round rings around square pegs the same size as the rings. Only in this case I was the sucker who did the spending. Whereas the lucky midway patron brings home stuffed pandas, glass candlesticks and balloons, I carted home silver ashtrays, cocktail shakers, cups, and an occasional tray. If this sounds great, let me state unequivocally it's the most expensive way of acquiring silverware there is.

We had also, the week before, won a Maclay Class—leaving two standing between Hellie and the Garden. In that other one, the Medal, she was still batting zero.

Ever since the first show, Mary had stood by me like a true carny's wife. I'll never know whether this was out of a sense of loyalty or because my performance at that first show and my unique method of handling a bridle had be-

116

come such legend on the horse-show circuit she simply didn't *dare* stay home.

But of one thing I'm sure. Under no circumstances would my daughter have gone alone with me to another show. Which I felt was completely unfair. After all, Aspercel thought me the ideal companion to go to a horse show with. So far as Aspie was concerned, no Freddie, no show. He wouldn't roll. Flattering, but inconvenient for me. Because of this, I hadn't had my boat out of the garage all summer, what with the showing and the fact that as a vice-president at Tomes my working days grew longer and longer, sometimes keeping me up till one or two o'clock in the morning with the tycoons who were kings of the indigestion, tooth-cavity, and underarm-odor empires who were our idols.

As I was saying, by the time Lakeville rolled around I was a veteran. I backed the trailer and station wagon into a spot near some trees, opened the tail gate of the trailer, and told Aspie to get himself out so Hellie could put his costume on. Then I set about arranging creature comforts for myself. These consisted of a marquee, blue and red, of course, that extended about ten feet from the station-wagon roof, a straw rug, on which I set my chaise longue, three armchairs, an ice chest, a portable bar, radio and TV set.

Then I stretched out in my chair and closed my eyes. I knew I was totally expendable from then to five, six, or whenever the show was finally over and it was time to drive home. Unless something came up that had to be paid for, like the veterinary or the blacksmith.

At Lakeville, as everywhere, the minute the strenuous work of making camp and slicking up the horse was finished, Wolfgang showed up and took over. And for this insult I paid him twenty-five bucks per show!

I was half asleep when I heard his voice. "Good morning, Mary—and Helen. How's the old man today? Fine?"

I sat up straight in my chaise. "No, I am not fine! I am worn out. Furthermore, you Wyoming Hessian, I'd have you know I am at least eight years younger than you are."

I knew very well I didn't look it right then, but the funny thing about Wolfie was that he was just genuinely Germanic enough actually to enjoy being told off once in a while. It gave him a sense of security, the way it does children.

"Mr. Bolton, sir, I wasn't asking about *you*. I was asking about Aspercel."

"Well *he* isn't so old either!"

"For a horse?" Wolfie shrugged. "Middle-aged, like me. I expect you're somewhat touchy from overwork, Mr. Bolton, and the high cost of everything? Most of my clients are, you know." He laughed. "All right, Helen, let's run over the classes you're going to be in. Then take the horse to the outside course and school him over the jumps."

I had been dismissed. I was always dismissed when we got to a show. But today it graveled me. "Just a minute, Wolf."

"Yes, sir."

I heard Helen whisper to Mary. "Can't you make my father *stop?* Before he ruins *everything?*"

I said: "This business of schooling him, as it's called, round and round over little jumps he could take with his eyes shut. You and the other instructors and the kids seem to have a passion for doing this. Why? The horse already *knows* everything there is to know about jumping."

"Well, it's—customary. Good for the rider to learn the course, good practice for the horse."

"Look, I don't know what I'm talking about probably because everybody knows I don't know anything about horses—"

"Oh, come, Mr. Bolton. You have learned a lot about horses this summer."

"Well, I know this one horse—Aspie—inside out. He's my pal; I know how his mind works. And I have an idea that if this eternal schooling nonsense keeps up, one day he's going to get a little bored. You know what happens when Aspercel gets bored?"

"I don't think I do."

"*I* do. When something bores him he throws his head in the air and says, 'Ah, the hell with it!' Like being loaded into horse vans and trailers. He got bored with that."

"You give me to think," said Wolfgang. "I hate to admit it, but—about this particular horse—you might be right." He turned to Hellie. "All right, school him over the first three jumps just to get the kinks out of his muscles; then ride around the course until you learn it and he gets warmed up. One thing, however, Mr. Bolton. He got bored with loading, so now only you and Suzie Clemens can load him. If he gets bored with jumping?" He shrugged his shoulders and sauntered off laughing.

"God forbid," said Mary.

Helen rode, and we sat in companionable silence, watching the late-coming trailers and vans roll through the gate and park here and there in the big rolling fields surrounding the ring. The Gardners came over for a cup of coffee. The loudspeakers shattered the morning quiet calling the entries for the first class, Junior Working Hunters, and the four of us drifted over to the outside course and watched without too much interest as Aspercel won the blue, and the Gardners' horse, an almost thoroughbred chestnut, was pinned with the red. I was surprised to realize that nowadays I took the jumping for granted and wasn't the least worried about Hellie, concentrating instead on little things, like the awkward position of one leg. I'd tell Mary and Mary would tell Wolf and Wolf would tell Helen. Strictly protocol, through channels.

After the class we went back to my marquee and were having some more coffee when a rich, burbling sound from the vicinity of the gate made us look up. It was an unbelievably shiny black, slinky, long-snouted DKXE two-seater Jaguar with a New York license.

"Pretty," I said.

"A hundred and fifty miles an hour pretty," said Jack Gardner.

"But who'd want it?" asked Eleanor.

I didn't say me, which would have been the truth. Instead I said, "Yeah, waste of money. Where can anybody go a hundred and fifty miles an hour?"

It came through the gate, and we all watched it burble its way slowly around the ring, stopping every now and then as if its driver were looking for somebody. It stopped, started again, and now as it drew nearer I could see the driver was alone; he had a shock of curly iron-gray hair surmounting a roundish red face, and was wearing an open-necked Hawaiian sports shirt. My stomach did a couple of cartwheels. Tom Dugan! Here in the bright sunlight of a hot August morning!

Tom Dugan had to be met, seen, and heard to be believed. He weighed at least two hundred and fifty pounds, a fair amount of it muscle. He had misleadingly gentle brown eyes, the Irish trick of talking along in a beguilingly naïve fashion, apparently about nothing much at all, and then, sudden as a whipcrack, coming out with a verbal one-two punch that went right to the heart of the subject. What was so unnerving was that, particularly on business deals, you never knew when the one-two was coming. It never did come when you were expecting it; old Dugan saw to that.

How many millions of dollars he had earned since he'd come over from Ireland as a boy no one, not even the T-men, knew. He was smart as the whip he cracked.

One thing for sure: he wasn't here because he liked horse shows.

18

TOM DUGAN was leaning against the ring rail, shielding his eyes against the morning sun and looking around—for me, I imagined. In the few seconds it took me to reach ringside, I faced the real reason his showing up upset me so. Hellie as a horsewoman still was something less than superb. But that was not exactly the impression either Harry Tomes or I had—well—let Tom Dugan get. We'd sort of let him believe she'd started riding before learning to walk. Especially with all those faked pictures of her Harry had hung in my office for Dugan's benefit.

This was one day we Boltons, including Aspie Bolton, were going to have to watch our step.

"Well, Tom, this is a happy surprise. What are you doing out here in the sticks?"

I had come up on him before he saw me, and was pumping his hand as he blinked sunshine out of his eyes.

"Oh, it's you, is it? I didn't recognize you out of your store clothes."

"Yes, sure, yes, it's me, all right."

He took a step away, turning his back to the sun. "You don't sound too sure of it at all," he said. "And it's a bit of a disappointment to find that in private life you're a jumpy, unstable sort of lad. Not at all the cocky, upcoming young executive who handles my advertising for me." He laughed. It sounded like gravel rolling around inside a cement mixer. "You won't believe it, Freddie boy, but for a moment there I thought to myself: Dugan, I thought, this man's very upset at seeing you here. Has he been leading you up the garden path all this time and he's afraid now you're going to find it out?"

I suppose you have to be clever to make the millions Dugan has made, but for once I'd seen the punch coming. I was prepared for it.

"The trouble with you, Tom, is you're such a con man yourself you think everybody must be as slippery as you are."

"Good lad, paying me a compliment like that! Now you

sound more like yourself." He patted my shoulder. "Say, just now I got an idea. You know that toothpaste of ours that hasn't been moving too well lately? Well, driving around the ring I happened to see a great elephant of a horse with all those huge teeth, and it hit me like I'd been struck over the head with a shillelagh."

"No, that I won't do! Not even for you, Tom. Not even for money will I brush Aspercel's teeth with your toothpaste."

"You disappoint me, you do at that. And why won't you do what I want? It could hurt no one. And if the fashion were to catch on, my God, man, we could sell it in tubes a foot long and as thick as your wrist and it would last a good big horse no time at all!" He shook his head. "The *size* of those teeth."

"Look, Tom, come over and meet the family and Aspercel, will you?"

"Of course, I'll be glad to meet your great horse." He chuckled. "I've quite a personal interest in him, you know."

It came to me for the first time that nobody but *no*body outside the office except Mary and Helen had the slightest notion that Aspercel was only technically a little girl's show horse and was, in reality, a big business project. The Gardners—lots of people—knew I handled the Aspercel advertising account. I let them think calling him Aspercel was a—well—sentimental gesture because of all the money I had made from the account.

Nobody knew that the horse was at least seventy-five percent subsidized by Allied Drug money. Nobody knew because of course no pictures of him ever appeared in Allied Drug advertisements. Except for the name there was no apparent connection whatever. But now—today—Tom Dugan could get us ostracized but good, blast Mary right out of the Garden Club, and make me a pariah. What it would do to Helen simply didn't bear thinking about.

For the first time I found myself wondering if I had done something that Eleanor would call "disgustingly unsporting." I'd heard her say this about people and knew what it made me think of them. Apprehensively, I introduced Tom Dugan to the Gardners and Mary; Helen was off eating hot dogs with Ronnie. I wished to God I could flash Tom a warning. He was holding Mary's hand, looking at her benevolently out of misleadingly gentle brown eyes.

"Ah, my dear," he rasped, "I'm so glad to meet Freddie's good wife. We're that close, he and I." Here it comes, I thought. "You know, I should have driven out long before this to watch Aspercel go through his paces. I was that touched by your man's naming him after my favorite product."

I breathed a quiet sigh. Then Jack Gardner put his big foot in it.

"I like Gelusil tablets better myself," he said. "But if Aspercels work better for you, well, what's one man's meat is another man's poison."

Tom Dugan was glaring at him.

"Jack," I said, "Mr. Dugan owns Aspercel tablets. He owns all the Aspercel tablets in the whole world. He *makes* them."

"*Himself?*" said Eleanor. "How cute. I thought they were made by one of the big companies."

"Eleanor, Mr. Dugan *is* the big company. He's Chairman of the Board of Allied Drug."

"Oh, dear," said Eleanor. "And here I was having such fun picturing Mr. Dugan in a little bakery place all done up in aprons, grinding up tons and tons of white powder with mortar and pestle, then looking about to make sure he was alone while he added the secret formula, and then pounding his mixture into thousands and thousands of those little white tablets." She flashed Tom a brilliant smile. "Of course I *did* think that beautiful car *was* a little on the expensive side for someone who made his living that way."

The trappings of great wealth never impressed Eleanor. "Mr. Dugan *I like* your tablets even if Jack doesn't. I serve them sometimes for after-dinner mints."

"What a grand idea! Do you really?"

Eleanor laughed. "I actually did once—by mistake. I had an English maid we'd brought over for the summer, and she filled one of our candy dishes with them."

Tom Dugan's Santa Claus belly was shaking with repressed laughter. "And what was the reaction of your guests?"

"Well," said Eleanor thoughtfully, "it was—noisy. But I will say they cleaned out the dish—ate every one of them."

"I don't think I've ever been so embarrassed in my life," said Jack. "We had an Englishman—a Master of Fox

Hounds type with us. Lord Something-or-Other, who was the house guest of some friends of ours. When he was saying good night, he asked me the name of the mints we'd served so he could take some back to England with him. I simply didn't dare tell him."

"What'd he say about them?"

"He said he'd never had a huge dinner set so well in his life."

The Brain was buzzing. "Tom," I said, "Jack may have discovered a new market for us. Aspercel After-Dinner Mints. We could change the shape and maybe have a little imprint of a hunter jumping a fence."

Tom Dugan's eyes flashed; then he gave me a bland smile and shook his head. "It's a good idea, but no horse. I wouldn't want to be suspected of commercializing a little girl's horse that way."

Had I underrated *him!* One crisis had passed, but the next came hard after—at the end of the Maclay. Today Hellie wasn't striking out; she breezed over the eight fences in the ring, did her walk, trot, and canter business perfectly. Four kids were called back into the ring to swap horses and jump the course again, which is how, when the top riders have performed about equally well, the judge separates the sheep from the goats. It's surprising, I had learned, how often someone who looks like a pro on his own horse looks like a beginner on one he's never ridden before.

Since her lessons with Suzie, during which Hellie rode every horse on the Bar-J, changing horses didn't faze her at all—until she reached the fifth jump. The big Roman-nosed bay she was riding took off one stride farther away from the fence than she expected, and she wasn't ready. Not only was she what's called "left behind"—enough to keep her from winning—but she never got back her balance. The bay stumbled as he landed, and she somersaulted flat on her back in the dust. She lay there still as death. There may have been a groan from the crowd at ringside, or maybe it was just the anguished sound I myself made as I vaulted the rail and ran across the ring. When I reached her the ringmaster in his long scarlet coat was kneeling down on one side of her, the judge on the other. The loudspeaker was calling for the doctor.

I dropped to my knees. "Hellie! Hellie, darling!"

Instinctively I reached out to pick her up, but the ringmaster stopped me. "Don't touch her, Mr. Bolton. She may have broken something."

He unfastened her black coat and with big, gentle fingers loosened the stock at her throat. Her face was the color of putty.

The judge picked up her little hard velvet hunting cap, turned it from side to side. "She'll be all right," he said. "There isn't an earth stain on it. I was pretty sure she fell on her back."

"Is—is it broken?"

"No, Mr. Bolton," said the ringmaster quietly. "She just got the wind knocked out of her. Stunned a bit too, I expect. Here, Mrs. Bolton, she's coming round now."

I hadn't realized Mary was kneeling in the dirt beside me, one of her hands gripping mine tight. "Coming to hurts," she said. "I know. Hellie will feel as if she's strangling."

Hellie's eyes were opening and closing, her nostrils working in and out. An ambulance, muted siren blowing, rolled into the ring. The judge stood up and told it to drive off. "It's not needed and it only scares everybody half to death."

Mary took Hellie's hands in hers. Slowly the lungs filled, and Hellie tried to sit up.

The ringmaster gently held her down. "No, Helen"— ringmasters get so they know the name of every kid riding in the circuit—"before we'll let you up, you've got to move every joint so we can see everything's working. If you like, you can start now. With your toes."

He checked out ankles, knees, legs, arms. She seemed in one piece. "All right, dear," he said, "go have a Coke, and you'll be good as new."

Hellie sat up, nodded. Then she seemed to see Mary and me for the first time. "Gosh, Popsicles, I'm sorry. I don't know how it happened."

Wolfgang, who had just arrived, helped her to her feet. The crowd applauded the way they always do when somebody has a fall and then gets up.

"What happened," said Wolfgang, "is you goofed. On the first four jumps you *must* have felt he was a horse that likes to stand way back and jump. You should have rated him more between fences, slowed him down. You could have placed him properly then. But you just let him go on and then weren't ready when he lit off."

"I am sorry, Wolfgang."

All of us, Mary, Hellie, Wolfie, the ringmaster, and I were walking toward the gate. I stepped back to thank the ringmaster for being so on the ball. He smiled. "You know," he said. "I must have seen this happen five or six hundred times. I always think I'll get used to it. Never. Every time it makes me feel sick inside. The only thing that saves me heaving is being all dressed up this way and right in front of everybody."

Hellie called out her thanks, then said: "Mommy says I have to lie down now but I'll be back for the Medal this afternoon. Don't let the class go without me."

"No indeed, not without *you!*" He excused himself as the announcer blared, "Next horse in the ring please. Number One Eighty-nine. One eight nine."

When I got to the trailer there Helen was stretched out in my chaise longue chatting comfortably with Tom Dugan, explaining what had gone wrong. Watching her, I suddenly remembered how skeptical I was months and months ago when Mary said having a horse would teach her poise.

The young lady I was looking at was, at the moment, as poised as her mother—and believe me, that is poised. The shows and the horse had done that for her, at least. I must remember to apologize to Mary, I thought to myself.

After lunch Tom Dugan took me around behind the trailer—to watch Aspie drink a beer, he said. But when we got there he said: "That business about the fall, I don't like it. None of the others fell off. So tell me this: How well can your daughter ride? Or is this business about her qualifying to ride in the big show in Madison Square Garden with the television cameras and everything just something you've run up out of cobwebs picked on a dewy summer morning to string me along?"

"She's a damn good rider!" I said righteously. "You want to bet me a hundred dollars she doesn't win the Medal Class this afternoon?"

"I've bet enough on her as it is. If she goofs a couple of more times, I'll not like it at all. I've had some big plans start brewin' inside my head today. But she'd better win that Medal—and the next one and the next one and get herself into that Garden horse show. If she doesn't I'll *know* you've just been stringing me along, and I'll like that so little I'd not be surprised if Allied Drug would move its entire account to another agency."

This should have frightened me. Instead, for Hellie's sake, it made me mad. "Dugan, you've never had it so good nor got so much space for so little money as you have since I dreamed up this Aspercel idea and you know it."

"Yes, I know that. And you know what it is? Peanuts. Unless you wind up in the Garden."

"You're an ungrateful Irish—"

His upraised palm stopped me. "Don't speak ill of my homeland," he said. "Incidentally, before we finish our private quarrel and shake hands I want to say you've got a spunky lady with a lot of guts for a daughter, and nothing I've said was meant against her. Just against you, Freddie. *Her* I like."

He held out his hand. I took it.

"You're a mick," I said.

"So are you. But from me that's a compliment. I don't get stood up to very often. Your spunky young lady daughter has got a spunky father."

"Let's hoist one together."

"Done."

We walked back around the open rear end of the trailer and started toward the marquee when Helen called to me from inside.

I stepped into the trailer and found her changing into clean breeches. I held them by the waistband while she did the leg buttons.

"Thanks, Popsicles."

But as I stepped down the ramp realization hit me. Helen had been in there changing all the time Dugan and I had been talking. I hoped to God she hadn't overheard that bit about how if she didn't qualify for the Garden he'd take his account away!

When the Medal Class was called, Helen came into the ring with her mouth set and her jaw thrust out. She had the manner—the whole aura—of a professional setting about doing a professional job. She won the Medal with ease. Naturally. All the rest of the contestants were kids having fun riding in a horse show. They didn't have heavy money riding on them like—like Willie Shoemaker.

19

ACCORDING TO the calendar by which I now operated, Labor Day that year fell on the Monday four horse shows after Lakeville. The four shows had netted us four pretty red
ribbons in the Medal Class and three pretty red ribbons
and one white one representing Helen's performance in the
Maclay. So we were still two Medals away from the Garden, and there were only a few shows left before competition closed for the year. I was getting jittery; and Hellie—
she'd been trying all out; every day she rode the two-mile
shortcut through the fields from the semidemi to Wolfgang's place. At Harry Tomes's urging I'd cut down my
business activity enough to leave town early a couple of
days a week and check up on Hellie and her drillmaster. I
knew my dropping in on the workouts must irritate Wolfie;
I also knew it would convince him I wanted results—
and no nonsense. I was putting the heat on; I had to. And
Wolfie, like all the other instructors, began shopping
around for shows with easier competition, with the result
that every Saturday or Sunday, or both, we went to shows
anywhere that looked like an easy win.

So on Labor Day, as on every Saturday or Sunday nowadays, I got up at dawn. We were going to the Meadowfield Horse Show, way up in the northeast corner of the
state. Saddle-horse country where the Hunt Seat competition shouldn't be too tough. This morning, as on every other show morning, Mary rode up in front with me, and Hellie stretched out on the back seat. Usually both of them
went back to sleep, which allowed me to doze comfortably
at the wheel once we got onto one of the express highways
where I didn't need to worry about crossroads. This morning they both stayed awake. For some reason this made
me nervous. And they didn't talk, which made me even
more nervous. Since we were all awake I felt we ought to
talk, so I opened up at random.

"Boy, isn't this a lovely morning. Look at the sun coming up over South Norwalk."

Naturally, nobody looked at the sun coming up over

South Norwalk. A second after I'd uttered this inanity I was thankful they hadn't, since South Norwalk was to the west and behind us, as we were heading east. To fill the vacuum I kept on throwing out more inanities that also fell on fallow ground until suddenly Helen snapped, "Oh, Father, can't you for heaven's sake stop chattering and chattering? It's driving me wild!"

I told her what I thought of children who are disrespectful to their parents, and she told me what she thought of parents who kept on chattering and chattering when their children want to sleep, and reaching over my shoulder I took a swipe at her, which, luckily, she ducked. Then I heard the sound of muffled sobbing.

The cool draft of close-by icebergs filled the car. "I think that's quite enough," said Mary. "From both of you. You're acting like infants. And"—her voice began to grow shrill—"and I can't stand it! It gets worse every time we go to a show. What's the matter with you two?"

"Going to shows isn't fun any more," said Helen.

"It better be!" I snapped. "Or at least you'd better act like it is."

"Well, it isn't and I hate it." Suddenly the sobs and the anger went out of her voice. "Oh, Daddy, I'm sorry. I do know how much my winning means to you. Ever since I heard Mr. Dugan talking to you that day when I was changing in the trailer I've tried and tried. But I've just got sick of trying. I don't have any friends my own age any more except Judy. I can't go to the movies or to the discothèques or the dances the other kids go to Saturday nights. I don't even get home until nine or ten, and then I have to tuck Aspie in bed. So how can I ever have any fun?"

The terrible thing about all this was that she was absolutely right.

I glanced in the rear-view mirror. Her face was pale, her eyes were fogged with tears, and she was swallowing as if trying hard not to whoops breakfast.

"Hellie," I said, "if you can just get those two silver Medals . . . I'll make it up to you, darling, I promise you. . . ."

There was a mile-long silence. Then Mary, all the usual bubbling gone from her voice, said, "Freddie, you know this really is all rather awful?"

I nodded. I wondered if she knew how awful it was—

and how much awfuller things would be for all of us if I let Helen quit now. I wished to heaven there were some way around it so I could let her quit. And keep my job, which I sure would not if Dugan moved his account elsewhere.

There wasn't any way, and I knew it because I'd already tentatively—just conversationally—tried it out on Harry. With the writing beginning to appear on the wall, I'd suggested switching Aspercel to the Junior Hunter Division in the Garden. I told him that having cleaned up at that Royal Winter Fair Show in Toronto, which was just as big stuff as the Garden, Aspie would be a cinch to win the championship—or at least come close to it. No dice. "Nuts!" he said. "You ever see Junior Hunters on national TV?" Then, without knowing it, he threw some of my own sales talk right back at me. "Now, equitation is different. World series of kid competition and pretty girls. That's glamour. The only thing that's got more glamour are the big-time Open Jumpers."

He was right, of course. Even I knew the names of some of the Open Jumpers—everybody does: McClain Street, Snowman, Uncle Max, Nautical, Gray Aero, Jacks or Better. Since I didn't own any of those, there was no way out for Hellie. And when, four hours later, she rode out of the ring with her second AHSA silver Medal, which left just one more between her and the Garden, I was so relieved I could have prostrated myself in the dust and manure in a gigantic salaam and let her ride right over me.

I was at the gate; so was Wolfie. Did he congratulate her? He did not. He told her all the little things she'd done wrong that the judge hadn't happened to spot. Then he congratulated her—mildly. She slid off Aspie, and I wanted to hug her but didn't dare. Instead I grabbed her hand, shook it, and said, "You were great, Helen. You were terrific!"

"Thank you, Father."

"She was half terrific and half lousy," said Wolfie. "She got a break. Helen, did you not hear me yelling at you for more leg when you went into the third fence?"

"No, I didn't, Wolfgang. I'm sorry."

"The hands are fine now. Not the leg. Next week, starting Wednesday, we work on that every day after your school."

"Yes, Wolfgang. Do I have to ride in the Maclay today?"

130

"Of course. It will give you another chance to practice the legs. I will be at the rail again, and this time, you will listen to me!"

I didn't like that at all, but it was how Wolfgang handled all his pupils; and for most of them the drillmaster treatment produced results. I couldn't interfere.

After lunch, just for a change in atmosphere I walked over to the other side of the show grounds into that field where the adult hunter outside course was laid out. It was a pretty place, and I walked along the edge of the course, aimlessly looking at the crowd. Suddenly who should I see sitting on a small hill off by themselves but Wolfgang—and Suzie Clemens. I had no idea she was at Meadowfield.

She saw me and beckoned to me to come up. I stepped carefully over the reclining bodies of the hunter fans and made my way to the rise.

"I just got here," Suzie said when I reached them. "Wolf wanted me to look at one of his hunters, Mr. Bolton. I've *got* to talk to you." Her eyes fell on a path that led into some woods. "That ought to be a good place. Come on."

Wolf, looking unnaturally bothered I thought, excused himself, and, wondering what was going on, I followed Suzie.

It was a typical woodsy path near a horse-show grounds: decorated with discarded paper plates, paper cups, and paper napkins that a little farther in gave way to empty beer cans and, still further, to empty whisky bottles and more intimate artifacts. Archaeologists digging through different strata know the experience. The deeper they go, the more primitive the remains of human occupancy. By the time we'd gone fifty yards into the woods, the remains were too damned primitive; but Sue walked along with her head up, and after a while the detritus of civilization dwindled, the path became grass covered and cool, and soon we came to a little stream a couple of yards wide that started me thinking about trout. A flattish rock jutted out into the water, and Suzie wiggled along it until there was room enough for me. I sat down beside her and stared glumly into the stream, apprehensive. I had good reason.

"Mr. Bolton," Suzie said, "Wolf's made me a kind of funny proposition."

The tension burst, and I grabbed her wrist.

"That rat! Two wives and four kids and he has the nerve to . . ."

I stopped. Suzie was trying hard not to laugh.

"Mr. Bolton, you're an absolute angel to get so furious for me. If you weren't still my boss I'd just hug you for it, but you're hurting my wrist."

I let go. Something she'd said had just registered with me. "What do you mean—if I wasn't *still* your boss? You think I'm going to fire you just because some . . ."

She held one of my hands and looked at me. The sunlight filtering through the trees gave her the elfin touch again. But she looked like a worried elf, which is a contradiction since elves, having only feelings, not thoughts, can't possibly be worried, which is one of the nice things about elves. "You, you know I'm just unbearably—fond—of you too, don't you? Right now it's awfully important for you to know that."

I was flying blind. Here I'd practically told this kid I loved her in a crazy nice way, and she'd come right back and told me she loved me in some cockeyed sort of way. It's baffling sometimes how many different ways there are to love somebody. I put my hand over her hand that held my hand and stroked it.

"I guess I've gotten sort of mixed up," I said, "I'd appreciate a little clarification at this point. It sounds almost as if you were trying to say good-bye."

Suzie put her other hand on top of my hand that was on top of her hand that was . . .

"I'm not," she said. "Not in the way you think. I'm—I'm trying . . ." Her two hands were hanging onto mine for dear life. "I'm trying to get up nerve enough to tell you I want to quit being your secretary at the Tomes Agency."

"You already have." I guess my voice had a cutting edge in it, because she looked as if she were going to cry. I untangled one hand and put my arm around her shoulders.

In between gulps she said, "I thought maybe you'd like what it is I want to do because, well, for one thing, if I wasn't your secretary it would be all right for me to call you Freddie."

I guess Suzie and I were pretty darn close at that, because I was able to decode this and know she meant that if I wasn't her boss we could be friends like anybody else. Anybody who thinks he can be friends with his secretary is nuts.

"Clarification is still in order. About two hundred years

ago you said Wolf von Roetz had made you a proposition. Like what?"

She was almost herself, but without the bounce. I was surprised that the two of us had been able to kick up such a storm of emotion about the idea of saying good-bye when there wasn't really anything between us at all.

"Of course you know Hellie won her second Medal," she said. "Well, for once Wolf was honest. He gave me full credit. He told me he was great at putting the polish on riders but he felt unless they had the basics it was like trying to polish a pair of shoes the shoemaker hadn't finished yet. I thought that was a pretty clever way of putting it."

"Yeah, so did I when I told it to him after Hellie's first fiasco."

Her eyes tilted up. "That was your line, and he pretended it was his own?"

"Why not?" I grinned. "I pretended it was mine. It wasn't. I heard a steward say it at Saybrook."

She giggled. "Well, the Medal decided Wolf on something he said he'd been thinking about ever since I began giving Hellie lessons. He wants me to be the shoemaker, teach the kids the basics at his place. That way he'll have time to take on a lot more of the expert kids. He'll start me off at a better salary than I'm making now, and I can still teach Sundays at the Bar-J if I like."

I didn't have to think twice. There wasn't any future for her at the agency. Wolf would pay her more, there was a future in it she'd enjoy, and I liked her to call me Freddie.

"I'm all for it. But what about you and the hunters, quarter-horse girl?"

"I'll tell you something if you promise not to tell Queenie."

"I promise."

"Schooling hunters and jumpers is a cinch compared to barrel bending and cloverleaf. I've been practicing evenings at Wolfgang's."

"Well, I'll be damned!"

"I'm going to ride one of them—that big gray that was going around the course when you came up—at the Glastonbury Show next Sunday. Incidentally, will you feel better about my working for Wolf if I tell you it was Hilga's idea in the first place?"

Hilga was Mrs. Wolfie. This cinched it. Around Wolfie now, Suzie would be safe as in church.

"When do you want to start?"

"Just as soon as I can—I'm awfully excited about it." She added quickly, "But I wouldn't leave until you've found someone to replace me."

I thought of explaining that no girl could possibly replace her, but said, "Look, the office manager will assign me somebody. Why don't you plan on starting with Wolf a week from Monday?"

"Can I? Really?"

"Sure, why waste time you can't ever get back?"

"Oh, *Freddie!* You darling guy!"

With that her arms went around my neck and the elfin face came closer and . . . It was a grown-up kiss but a kid kiss, too, because the only place it came from was her heart, and that made it all right. Still, she must have been in some sort of spin, because when she pulled back she forgot the rock was hanging over the stream, and slid off, landing on her seat in six inches of cold water.

"Oh!" she cried. She got up, wet in the most embarrassing places. *"Oh!"* She clutched her hips in anguish. "What am I going to do? I've *got* to see Helen in the Maclay, and I *can't* go back like this. I can't! I'd just die of embarrassment. Oh, Freddie, help me. Please."

"One moment." I closed my eyes. Actually, I was just thinking, the way everybody else thinks, but this looks so much more impressive. It goes big with men like Dugan. In no time at all I came up with a solution.

I eased off my loafers. "We've got to fix it so you look like a girl who fell into a stream instead of a child who—"

"Never *mind!*"

"Like this!" Before she knew what was happening, I was in the stream beside her, had lifted her off her feet and laid her down in the deepest part of the stream. When she realized what was happening to her, she started to swear. When she realized why I'd done it, she began to laugh. She stood up, dripping, jeans clinging to her like skin, shirt and bra wonderfully transparent. But this girl I was really fond of, so I looked the other way and kept looking until she'd fluffed things out a little.

"All clear," she said. "Now do I look like a girl who fell into a stream?" she said shyly. "Please say I look decent."

"Decent but distinctly damp." I laughed, and we started

back along the path through the strata of civilization's detritus, hand in hand. "Now all we've got to do is think up some logical explanation of why a girl like you would fall into a stream."

"We'll simply tell the truth."

I smiled. "With Hellie, yes; with Mary and Eleanor, no. Grown-up, sophisticated women have one hell of a time believing the truth, Suzie. You have to give them something easier."

2 0

TWO SATURDAYS LATER, just back from another business trip, I lay prostrate with weariness in my chaise longue on the terrace. I was alone—that is, almost alone, for Aspie was there, chin resting on the back of my chair, breathing at me—and I was miserable. The next day Mary was taking off for California with the rare orchids she'd wangled from—Mr. Blitzstein, was it?—Helen was staying at Judy's during the three weeks she'd be away, and Aspie was going to live at Wolfie's. Mary had left a note for me saying she'd driven in to New York for some last-minute shopping—spending was more like it—and had taken Hellie with her. I'd left my heap at Joe's Good Gulf Gas Station to get serviced. I was sore at the world, especially Mary. For deserting me to go to California. For not being home when I arrived from Chicago, even though I'd made a plane that got me back five hours before dinnertime, when I'd said I'd arrive.

It was one of those breathlessly hot Indian-summer weekends you sometimes get at the end of September. I finished my drink, went into the house to get another. In the kitchen the radio was playing; a cigarette commercial —Marlboro—came over the air. It gave me a craving for Winstons, my brand. I reached into the pocket of my shorts, fished out an empty pack. I opened the cabinet drawer where we kept cigarettes. There wasn't a cigarette in sight.

"Damn!"

I opened all the other cabinet drawers; purely an automatic reaction, for of course there were no cigarettes anywhere. I went into the living room and looked in every possible spot where a pack of cigarettes could be stashed, desperation growing in me.

"This is silly," I said. "In an hour or so Mary'll be back and I can use her car. . . ."

I took a long swallow of my drink—on impulse I had topped it with two extra ounces of vodka—drifted back out onto the terrace. Aspercel had moved a few yards into the shadow of our one real shade tree and was standing, head hanging down, drowsing, switching his tail in his sleep at occasional flies. I stretched out on the grass beside him, leaning against the tree, and sipped my drink. It was a strong drink, even without the topper that made it into a sort of sandwich: vodka, ginger ale in the middle, vodka again on top. The better it made me feel about life in general, the more I needed a smoke. At the end of a half hour I'd reached the point where I'd have smoked a Sweet Caporal if I could find one. Plainly, steps had to be taken. But the nearest store was in a little shopping center a mile and a half away and the temperature was over ninety and, as I said, I had no car. I finished my drink and suddenly had a real down-to-earth thought. One so eminently practical it surprised me.

"I wonder!"

I sat up and looked at the twenty thousand dollars' worth of horse standing beside me. I had actually been offered that much for him by Wolfgang and a couple of other men, one of them Tim Riley, which, considering he'd sold him to me for forty-five hundred, was really something.

"Why not?" I said. "After all, you *are* a horse, and horses *are* supposed to carry people places. Or wouldn't you know about that?"

Aspie didn't react one way or another. I'd thought maybe he'd resent the implication that anything so deluxe could be thought of as a beast of burden.

"I need some cigarettes," I said. "The cigarettes are a mile and a half away. I have only two legs; you have four. That means it's only three-quarters of a mile for you. How about it?"

Again no reaction.

"Good," I said. I got up and patted his neck. "Good boy, we go. Now it's just a question of settling the details of the voyage."

This took a little thought. If I took him down to the stable and put a bridle and saddle on him, he'd go into his attention-getting act, rearing and plunging and generally leaping around, and I'd wind up in the hospital. On the other hand, if I just climbed up on him naked, so to speak, the way he was, he'd probably be okay. The only thing was, I'd need some sort of a steering gear, like a couple of pieces of clothesline tied to the nose end of his halter on each side. This wouldn't stop him if he wanted to run away, but then the way I rode neither would a set of four-wheel disk brakes.

"I'll be right back."

I went into the house and rummaged around in the laundry and found some clothesline and cut off a hunk. Then I found a white silk sport shirt, put that on as a sop to civic decency on the highway, and went back to Aspie.

I played it cool. "We're all out of beer," I said, tying the ends of the clothesline to the halter, "and there's a nice little saloon down the road a way. Come on, and I'll buy you a beer. After all, you and I never go anywhere together just for fun, do we? It's always just work, work, work."

I had him rigged now. He was holding his head higher but otherwise was still motionless. I stepped back, unhappy. I was faced with another problem. Aspie was a high horse. A very high horse.

"I don't suppose you'd consider kneeling down, would you? Like a camel?"

He blew a little spit and partially chewed grass at me.

"I didn't think so. Okay, I'll think of something else."

I looked around. One of the branches of the maple looked about the right height. I led Aspie under it, reached up and, with a heroic effort, chinned myself. It didn't raise me high enough; I dropped to the ground. I didn't know if he'd stand for it, but there was only one thing to do. I backed off about twenty feet and ran at him and dived upward. I landed on my stomach on his back. He didn't move. Either he was the kindest horse God ever made or he was too surprised to move. I grabbed his mane and, being very careful not to kick him, sort of rolled amidships and sat up. Fortunately, I ended up facing front. The ground seemed a long way down.

Suddenly I was scared purple. I'd seen this huge beast in action. Telling myself that a little child rode him all the time, I managed to keep from letting him know how scared I was. I picked up the clothesline. His head came up, and I felt a quiver run through that magnificent bunch of muscle and bone. He snorted and took half a dozen little dancing steps sideways. He was getting ready to go into his act. Panicked I thought, What would Suzie do?

I knew. "Knock it off, Meatball!" I said. Then I gave him a cuff on the side of the neck, slacked off on the clothesline, pressed my legs against him, and said, "Down to the shopping center, Meatball. Get going!"

The dancing stopped, but I must have overcontrolled, because he started off down the driveway at a brisk trot. I locked one hand in his mane. Now I knew why people always let thoroughbreds wear their hair long. I teetered from side to side. I knew in a couple of seconds more I'd come off. I tried pulling on the clothesline with one hand, but it only made him start in a circle. I was just about overboard when I remembered something else. Making my voice rise about two octaves above normal, I sang out, "W-A-A-A-Alk, please!"

It must have been a good imitation of a ringmaster, because it worked. As always at the shows when he heard that sung out, he dropped into a brisk, steady walk, head up, looking like twenty thousand dollars. I dreaded what might happen if he caught on, but he didn't. He liked being a show horse and showing off. At the foot of the drive I just touched the right clothesline. Good as gold, he turned into the right-hand lane and we were on our way.

21

IT WAS REALLY NICE, riding along the grass at the side of the road. Either my vodka sandwich was working or I was beginning to get into the swing of the thing, because I let Aspie trot a little and even cantered him once for almost a hundred yards. After all, I had always ridden bareback when I was a kid. Apparently Aspie had accepted the fact that I was the boss, because I didn't once have to summon that good old imaginary ringmaster to get me out of trouble. I'd pull assertively on my clothesline reins, and he'd slow down.

I found that riding along the road on a horse gave you an entirely different perspective than did a car. On a horse your head's about ten feet above the ground. You look down on the bushes and straight into the tree branches. For the first time I realized what a lot of birds there were in the trees at the side of the road. I'd never seen any before. Now they were all darting around this way and that and chirping away at each other. Some people passed me in a convertible with the top lowered. I looked down on them, pityingly. I was a giant ten feet tall. The late summery noises—children laughing, women calling to one another across their patches of front lawn—drifted up to me, no hum of tires or muttering of a big engine to muffle the sound. The rhythmic, swaying motion, too, was soothing, once I'd got used to it. From time to time I found I was taking one hand off my clothesline and patting Aspercel's neck and talking to him, making cogent observations on the passing scene.

For the first time I knew why people used horses to get around on one hundred years ago.

As we turned into the shopping center, everybody stared at us in astonishment—why, I couldn't fathom. Aspercel and I ignored them, rode up to the bar and grill, and I said, "Whoa, Meatball!"

He stopped, blew through his nostrils, and hung his head as if overcome with exhaustion from his grueling labors, his flanks moving in and out with simulated hard breathing. All of which I knew was just more of his hamola makeup, because I'd seen him do it at shows after stepping over eight little jumps.

A plump woman in a huge floppy hat walking along the covered sidewalk in front of the bar and grill saw the heaving flanks and shrilled at me: "You should be ashamed of yourself. That poor horse. And on a hot day like this! I've a good mind to report you to the SPCA."

I smiled amiably and a little patronizingly at her. A man on a horse looks down on the rest of the world.

"Go right ahead," I said. "Aspercel will like the publicity."

A man and wife and their three kids had stopped to stare admiringly. The man looked up. "Did you say this horse's name is Aspercel?"

"It certainly is."

"*The* Aspercel? The show horse?"

At my nod the oldest child, a girl around ten, called out, "Can I pet him?"

"He'd love it."

"Can I pet him too?"

"Aspercel!" This from the mother. "*The* Aspercel! Imagine running into him here." She turned to me. "You know, I take them all the time now. I like chewing them."

By now a crowd had gathered. "Say, mister," one man said, "isn't it a little unusual to hop on a real hotshot horse like this and ride down to the store?"

"No bit or reins or anything," a teen-ager in T-shirt and chinos said admiringly. "You must be one sharp rider to be able to control a thoroughbred like Aspercel that way."

"That horse is exhausted," the ASPCA type repeated shrilly. "Aren't you at least going to get him a drink of water?"

"Madam," I pointed to his heaving flanks when he happened to remember to heave them, "when he does that it does not mean he wants water."

"Oh, and what does he want?"

"It means he wants a Knick. The beer with the kick." I heard the woman suck in her breath the way Aspie does sometimes when he'd be getting ready to blow oats and grass at me. I turned to the father of the three girls. "He likes beer with a kick because he's a horse."

"Yeah, I get it. Horses kick."

"You read me. Look, if I get down off of here I may never get back up." I produced a five-dollar bill. "Would you be a real Samaritan and go in and get me two packs of Winstons and two pints of beer in a growler?"

"Sure, be tickled to."

I leaned forward. "He *really* likes Canadian ale best. You see, he's a Canadian."

The ASPCA woman stalked off, and the father went into the bar. The kids kept patting Aspercel, but the other shoppers went about their errands. How fleeting is fame! A horse in a shopping center had suddenly become old hat.

The father came out carrying a bucket of beer, cigarettes, and change. Aspie whinnied gratefully, dunked his nose in the growler, and gulped. When he was done, he heaved a vast sigh and blew froth over everyone. I picked up the clotheslines, leaned to starboard, pressed my legs against him, and we shoved off.

I looked at my watch. It was four o'clock. Better move along a little; Mary'd be home any minute. Up till now, this had been a matter strictly between Aspie and me; I hadn't considered how Mary and Helen might feel about my using our prize show horse for something practical. On reflection, I decided they would probably take a very dim view of it indeed. "Aspie, I think a slow canter is indicated."

I steered over to a border of grass at the side of the road. I leaned forward, trimmed in the mainsheet, so to speak, locked one hand in his mane, pressed my legs against him, and we cantered along for almost half a mile until we ran out of grass. Taking care of himself as always on the hard surface, Aspercel dropped into a slow walk. I rode along comfortably and pretty soon found myself smiling. I'd started thinking about Suzie Clemens and how amazed she'd look if she suddenly roared by and saw me on a horse. She'd faint.

Across my mind a pleasant fantasy began drifting the way the white September clouds were floating across the sky; Suzie coming down the road, fainting, and then me parachuting down to earth from Aspie's back, loosening her clothes and resuscitating her. That's the kind of thinking vodka sandwiches can lead a man into. For about a quarter of a mile I kept dreaming up other minor disasters

142

from which I could rescue Suzie. Pity she didn't like boats. My little boat would . . .

Right then I stopped thinking about Suzie or anything except whether I could live to be maybe fifteen minutes older. Aspie's ancillary equipment not including a rearview mirror, I hadn't seen the State Police car coming up the road behind me. Lost as I was in dreamland, I didn't even notice it slow down beside me nor if the trooper told me to pull over. All I know is that two things happened simultaneously, both of which I could have done without. One, the fool hit the police-car siren. Two, Aspie spun around at right angles to the road and took off. That there happened to be a stone wall with a strand or two of barbed wire on top in his way didn't bother him at all.

By the grace of God and Aspie's long hair and neck I stayed on board. I had no choice. Nobody voluntarily jumps off a vehicle traveling thirty or forty miles an hour. Fortunately, I have pretty long legs. With these and my hands, I just hung on as tight as I could. The siren howled again. High above us I heard a couple of shots whiz by, and from the car, two accompanying bangs. So did Aspie. He didn't like it. He put his ears back, stuck his neck out, and flattened into a dead run. Funny, but this flattening out made it easier to stick on. The motion was more forward and back and less up and down. Another wall showed up at the end of this field. He never even bothered to change stride. I closed my eyes, and we were over without my even feeling it. I opened my eyes. The wind, that all of a sudden had made my mouth as dry as a mummy's scalp, made my eyes water. I half closed them. Unfortunately, I could still see the stone walls approaching, whole rows of them, it seemed to me, some low, some not so low; some with wire over them, some without. It was all the same to Aspercel.

After a couple of minutes I realized he was running with his ears up again, and not quite so fast. Having caught on long ago to the way what passed for his brain worked, I knew he wasn't scared any more but was running crosscountry now for the sheer joy of it. I could understand. This was the first time since I'd bought him he'd had a chance to cut loose, get away from the kid stuff, and do what the Lord and a long line of steeple-chasing ancestors had built him to do in the first place. And though it sounds impossible, I was actually beginning to enjoy myself. We went over another wall, and I found that by sort of heaving myself forward just as he took off it made things even smoother. I was glad to find that out, because the next thing in our way turned out to be a white plank paddock fence that must have been somewhere between fourteen and fifteen feet high.

Did Aspie slow down? He did not. He just kind of bunched his muscles a little as we got to it, and up he went. That time I stayed up a little longer than he did. When I came down I let out a yelp, and for a few seconds I thought he and I had suddenly become the same sex. A few seconds later we were across the paddock, over the companion fence, and pounding across somebody's front lawn. In another five seconds we were going right through somebody's formal garden. On the other side of this I saw a row of glass hotbeds. I guess they looked like a water jump on a race course to Aspie, because of course we soared right over them too. But now we came to something he didn't expect to find on a race course, so he didn't notice it until it was too late. It happened to be a greenhouse.

This he couldn't jump; he didn't try to. Apparently I did. I have a hazy memory of going into orbit and seeing a horse's head far below me on earth; another memory of a horrible crashing sound of breaking glass. Then I was in the greenhouse, and Aspie was outside eating grass. Only, I didn't know it because I'd come down headfirst in the middle of a table loaded with potted plants.

WHEN I CAME TO, I thought quite likely I was dead. Probably as a result of drowning. The subdued greenhouse lighting gave my immediate surroundings a definite underwater cast made horribly realistic by the roots and tendrils of broken plants that trailed over and around my face and hands. Then I saw I was covered with scattered flower petals, and I thought, No, I hadn't been drowned; I was just plain dead and had been given a bang-up funeral. Strewn with flower petals yet. I was deeply touched that people thought enough of me to strew me with flower petals. *That* didn't happen to everyone in the advertising business. But I'd always felt I was a little special.

Then I stopped bothering with thinking. I was very, very comfortable—sort of floaty and cozy. Drowned or just plain dead, it was awfully nice to be right there, lying down. Only slowly did I become aware that I wasn't entirely alone. In my greenish, submarine-like world I could see figures; shapes, weaving to and fro. Three of them, from my angle, looked like reasonably attractive mermaids, but wearing funny clothes for mermaids. A fourth plump one looked like a mermother. A couple of brown-clad gnomes wove their way across my retinas, followed by a tall man, obviously Neptune—Neptune in white flannels and a goatee instead of a flowing beard, but regal just the same. I saw what at first looked to me like a soldier. Then, in spite of my best efforts to forestall it, consciousness overcame me. Soldier, my eye! State trooper!

I sat up abruptly, dripping shards and tendrils.

"You," I said, stabbing my finger at him, "must be the stupid fathead who blew his siren right under my horse's behind and started all this. So help me, I'm going to sue you for every dime I've got."

The tall man in white flannels said to the trooper: "He means he's going to sue you for every dime *you've* got. Poor chap obviously doesn't know what he's saying. Did you really do that, son? Blow your siren right under that throughbred's . . . Well, well, well, you certainly got results, didn't you?"

"I got what it was my job to get, Mr. Blitzstein. I was ordered to pick up a horse thief and I've got him. And just for the record, there are still some laws on the books that make horse stealing a pretty serious crime in this state."

I was about to launch into a more detailed expression of my views regarding siren-happy cops with hallucinations when the name Blitzstein suddenly registered. Wasn't Blitzstein the man who raised the rare, exotic orchids Mary was taking to California tomorrow? Wild-eyed, I looked at the floral ruin around me. Orchids. All around me the tattered remains of orchids. I lay down again and closed my eyes.

From somewhere deep and empty inside me my voice quavered forth: "Mr. Blitzen, are—were—these very special—rare orchids?"

His answering voice sounded to me like the voice of doom speaking from an echo chamber in the lower level of the catacombs. "Why, yes, they were. As a matter of fact, by a shocking coincidence Mrs. Bolton, the lady who reported her horse stolen, was to take them to California tomorrow morning." He gave a ghoulish-sounding chuckle. "I expect she's going to have it in for you, all right. First stealing her prize show horse, then ruining the star exhibit of the national garden club's convention for her."

I kept my eyes closed. The world was not a world I cared to look upon right now. I was faced with a simple choice. Boiled down, of whom was I more scared? The idiotic young trooper whose name I had noted from his plastic identification sign was Roberts and who wanted to pinch me for horse stealing? Or my wife, who would want to kill me dead?

I opened my eyes. The mermaids, obviously Blitzstein daughters, and the mermother, obviously Mrs. Blitzstein; the two gnomes who I now saw were gardeners; Mr. Blitzstein, and the young trooper were all standing silent and staring. I sat upright again.

"It just happens," I said, with all the dignity I felt could be expected of a man in my undignified situation, "that I did not steal that horse. I couldn't steal him if I wanted to. Because it just happens that I am Frederick Bolton, his legal owner."

146

"My goodness!" said Mr. Blitzstein. "You *are* in for it."

"Them orchids," said one of the gardeners. "Is he ever going to catch it from the little woman."

The other gardener nodded portentously.

The trooper grabbed me by the wrist. "All right, out of here now. You've had your fun, buddy."

To my amazement, Mr. Blitzstein put out a hand. "Has it occurred to you, son, that this gentleman, to his own great misfortune, just might turn out to *be* Mr. Frederick Bolton? Have you checked to make sure he isn't?"

Clothed in the comforting authority of his uniform, young Roberts dared give Mr. Blitzstein a pitying look. "Oh, come on, sir! That's the oldest gag on the books—the accused claiming to be the owner of stolen property. Of course we checked. We checked with Mrs. Bolton, and on her own say-so we've got him on two counts. One, this character rides like a professional steeplechase jockey, and she said Mr. Frederick Bolton couldn't ride a Shetland pony across a putting green. . . ."

"What about a formal garden?"

"Not a chance. Two, Mrs. Frederick Bolton testifies to the fact that Mr. Frederick Bolton is in Chicago and will not return to these environs until 7:00 P.M. tonight. Come along now, you!"

He jerked me clean out of the broken flowerpots and onto my feet.

"Just one moment more, please," said Mr. Blitzstein. "As you know, I am an attorney. If the accused would like me to represent him in the matter of these charges, I will be glad to. If for no other reason than that it will give me the opportunity for a private word with him. He is entitled to counsel, and does he need it. Wise counsel."

I jerked the trooper to a halt. "How much would it cost, sir?"

"No cost to you at all. Beyond paying for the orchids, the greenhouse roof, and replacing the formal garden."

I gulped. "It's a deal."

"If you'll excuse us for a few minutes?" His family and the gardeners all marched from the greenhouse. "You, too, Trooper Roberts. As this man's attorney I am privileged; surely you know that. There is only one door to this building. You may guard it. From the outside."

"Well, I guess if you say so, sir."

"Thank you." He waited until the trooper had gone and we were alone. Then he smiled at me. "Of course you really *are* Mr. Bolton, aren't you?"

"Why, yes, of course. But how . . ."

"I have been something of a devotee of cross-country racing. In fact, along with your horse I have two or three timber horses in the stable right now, getting ready for the fall season. I just happened to see you come over those last two fences." He seemed to be having some trouble keeping his lips in line. "In forty years of experience, I don't think I have ever seen a more extraordinary performance."

"Well, they're pretty big fences, I'll admit that."

"Yes. When you took the first one you jumped so much higher than your horse that coming down again in the same field with him would have been a remarkable achievement. Let alone actually making your touch down on his back. Professional steeplechase jockey!" His laughter exploded. "Except for the fact that you actually did jump those huge fences, your wife's evaluation of your horsemanship was positive identification so far as I was concerned."

I was a little miffed. "Well, you see, I haven't ridden in a good many years. Horses started to make me sneeze. In fact, I had to give it up just when I was getting real good."

"I didn't mean to hurt your feelings, Mr. Bolton. I know it took a lot of guts to stay on that horse."

He had seen right through me. I grinned at him. "Now what do we do about me?"

Mr. Blitzstein turned serious. "Well, obviously I could establish your identity in five minutes and that would be the end of the police nonsense. But may I speak to you as a man who has been married for thirty years? To the same woman?"

"Please."

"Well, Mr. Bolton, there have been times during these on the whole rather wonderful thirty years when I would have given anything—anything at all—for the wonderful, quiet, male sanctuary of a nice, cozy jail cell. And I don't *think* my wife has ever been quite as hopping mad at me as your wife is going to be at you when she finds out about those orchids."

"I think you've got something."

"Of course, it could have been worse—for *me*, that is. They might have been my *really* rare orchids. Well, Mr. Bolton, as your attorney, my advice is this: Mrs. Bolton is leaving for the coast tomorrow. Get the troopers to put you up for the weekend. Shall we let them escort you away now? Yes?"

"Mr. Blitzstein, I feel like a heel about the idea of hiding from Mary when she's going away tomorrow for a whole month."

He stood looking thoughtful for a few seconds. Then he nodded. "I quite understand. Here's how we'll handle it. I'll get in touch with her sometime this evening. If necessary I'll see her personally. If I'm convinced she won't shoot you on sight, I'll come down and arrange your release against my better judgment."

"You're a prince."

"Actually, I am. Or was, in Bavaria. But I'll tell you a secret. Being a successful American lawyer is so much more interesting. One gets the"—the laughter began again —"the damnedest cases."

Roberts strode into the greenhouse, clinking his handcuffs. I bowed my head in submission. Mr. Blitzstein winked at me.

23

ANY GUY who lands in the pokey is entitled to one phone call. Generally he calls his lawyer. Or his wife. But I'd already seen my lawyer, and you know how he—and I—felt about my getting even as close as the other end of a telephone wire to my wife. But I am, let's face it, primarily an advertising man, and on the short ride into the State Police Barracks my brain had been turning at the rate of conservatively 10,000 r.p.m.—racing car speed Even leaving Mary out of it, I had some serious problems facing me. One of them was the little matter of holding onto my job. Turning up on a police blotter is not highly recommended for a vice-president of an old and highly regarded advertising firm. The other little problem was related: holding onto the Allied Drug account, to say nothing of the half dozen other big ones I handled now.

Unfortunately, it is a known fact that there is no group in the world quite so sensitive and jittery about public reaction as big radio and TV advertisers. One breath of scandal . . . Obviously the local U.P. or A.P. stringer would take a look at the police blotter of a Saturday evening. Thank heaven, just before we reached the barracks the Brain clicked. Seize the bull by the horns. So Dugan wanted nationwide coverage on Aspercel, did he? Well, I just might be able to arrange that little thing. So when I demanded and got my one telephone call, I dialed the home number of Eddie Harris of Harris Birdwood and Associates, our public-relations firm. Eddie's wife brought him to the phone. All I said was, "Eddie, boy, I've been arrested for stealing a horse."

Laughter, the mocking laughter of disbelief, greeted this one, and he said, "Whose horse? Paul Revere's?"

"No," I whispered. "Mine."

"Are you kidding?" He sounded excited.

"I am not. I'm at the Westport State Police Barracks and I am just about to be locked up and charged with stealing a twenty-thousand-dollar horse. You may have heard of him. Goes by the name of Aspercel. Right, you got it.

What? No, of course not. I was wearing shorts and a shirt, so why would I have my driver's license with me? You don't need one to ride a horse. At least I don't think you do. Take all the necessary steps, will you, Eddie? Bless you, boy!"

We rang off. I turned to Trooper Roberts. "Okay, Officer, I am ready whenever you are."

The desk sergeant called out to Roberts: "Watch that guy sharp, Robbie. He smells like a phony to me."

I walked over to the partition separating the sergeant from us hoi polloi. "Just what do you mean by that, buster? I smell like a phony what?"

"All phonies smell alike," said the sergeant. "It don't matter what kind they are." The telephone rang. He scooped it up. "Sergeant Smith, State Police. . . . What?— Yeah. Yep, Sam. You'll get a scoop on this for working so fast. . . . Yep, that's right. Horse stealing. A real top thoroughbred, too. Aspercel. . . . Sure I'll spell it. It's just like those stomach pills. . . . No, we don't know his name. Guy claims to be Frederick Bolton, owner of the horse, but Mrs. Bolton says Mr. Bolton is in Chicago and isn't due back till tonight. Sure, go ahead, release it, Sam. I'll call you if there're any developments. . . . What? Oh, Trooper Roberts made the arrest. Yeah, Melvin Roberts. Bright boy, Mel. Chased him cross-country for three miles before he rounded him up. Regular rodeo. . . . Do I have any comment? Let me see, Sam. Yeah, you can say I say some people around here think they can get away with anything these days, and I propose to put a stop to it." He cradled the phone, glared at Roberts. "What are you waiting for? Take his fingerprints; then lock him up till somebody shows up to bail him out—if ever."

"Yes, sir."

God bless Eddie, I thought. God bless the U.P. and the A.P., who were sure to pick it up.

Roberts led me away and fingerprinted me. He was a pleasant enough young man once you got him far enough away from that siren button in his car.

"You got a record, mister? These'll show it up within a matter of hours if they're on file."

"They're on file down there," I said.

"Down where?"

"Washington, D.C."

Roberts gave with a low whistle. I could see visions of

fame and fortune dancing in his eyes. Maybe I'd turn out to be a Russian spy.

"What'd you do down there that got you on file?" he asked.

"Worked for the State Department for a couple of years. All Foreign Service officers are required to have their prints on file."

I could see him slump with disappointment. I actually felt guilty about not being guilty. Then I remembered those shots he'd fired in the air. "You'll find it out anyway, so I don't mind telling you. I worked there under the name of Frederick Bolton."

He began to look a little sick. I patted his shoulder. "That's all right. I'm not going to sue you—unless the horse has gone lame or something like that. Oh, Jesus, here comes my wife! Lock me up quick. In solitary!"

Through the glass upper half of the front door I'd seen her. The door opened and Mary walked in. She looked astonishingly composed for a lady strolling into the local hoosegow to spring a husband charged with horse stealing. Incredibly, she didn't even look annoyed. She glanced around, saw Roberts leading me back past the desk sergeant, and cried: "Freddie, thank goodness you're all right! If you'd only let me know you were coming home so early."

I grinned at Roberts.

"Are you Mrs. Bolton?" asked the desk sergeant.

"Of course."

"Identification?"

Mary produced her driver's license.

"Is this man your husband, Frederick Bolton?"

"Of course."

"And you and he and your daughter own this horse, Aspercel?"

"Certainly." She turned to me. "He's back in our paddock, Freddie. Somebody brought him home half an hour ago."

"Okay, Mr. Bolton. Charges dismissed. Please accept our apologies."

"Oh, sure," I said. "And I think you have a very nice police station. Sorry I couldn't pay you a longer visit."

"Don't overdo it," said Mary. "Or maybe they'll arrest you for something else."

Damned if I hadn't been hoping for just that, dreading

152

the moment when she would find out about the orchids. She was bound to find out, and now I'd be right handy for her to shoot dead. When I'd talked to Eddie, I'd muffed the ball.

Like all criminals, I had made one mistake. I had told Eddie to "take all the necessary steps." I'd meant to see to it that when the story broke, it would be slanted the way I wanted it slanted. He, a good family man himself, had naturally thought notifying the prisoner's family—after the story'd been confirmed, of course, and gone out on the wires—was a necessary step. That was why Mary had come for me so soon. I stole a glance at her face. She looked happy. She was not going to look happy long.

24

OUTSIDE IN THE CAR, Mary grinned at me from behind the wheel. I grinned back. "We make a pretty good pair, don't we?" I said. "I flush them out and you shoot them down."

She laughed. "You didn't really ride that horse, did you? And jump a lot of jumps? What happened? Did he just decide to go for a run and you went after him to catch him and the trooper picked you up? And you started giving him a hard time?"

"Mary," I said, "you have less faith in me than that sergeant who said I smelled like a phony. Yes, I did ride the horse. I was out of cigarettes and didn't have a car and I'm just old-fashioned enough to think horses are actually supposed to do a little work once in a while. I was raised on a farm, remember? Look, how is he? Okay?"

"Of course. I don't know who brought him home. Maybe he brought himself."

"He could. He jumps nicely, by the way. Very smooth."

"Freddie . . ." her eyes were accusing, "have you been pretending all this time you don't know anything about horses? Hoping you wouldn't get involved in the horse-show thing?"

I shook my head.

Her voice softened. "If you *did* ride the horse, I'm glad you didn't kill yourself."

"Me too."

"And I'm thankful to heaven some man—he wouldn't leave his name—called and told me what had happened so I was able to get you out of—of"—she giggled—"out of the clink before any of the newspapers could get hold of this."

Here it comes! As often happens when people suggest things, she unconsciously reached out and snapped on the radio. I glanced at my wristwatch; it was coming up five. That meant news. "Oh, let's not have that thing on right now," I said. "Let's talk." And I switched off the radio.

She gave me a funny look. "What about?"

I shrugged but didn't say anything.

"Freddie, there's something fishy going on. You've done something, I can *feel* it." She stopped the car, turned to me. She was suddenly quite pale, and her eyes were intense.

"Frederick, I have an awful sinking feeling that you've done something I am simply going to hate you for. Have you? Was this getting yourself arrested all part of some cheap publicity stunt?"

I shook my head.

"Then why did you shut off the radio? In all the years I've known you, you have never once shut off a radio. Shutting off a radio to you is like desecrating the flag."

She turned the key and pressed the button to the radio. Right away the car was filled with news—Monitor weekend news, going out over almost two hundred radio stations all over the country, into millions of homes and even more millions of cars. It had been a quiet day around the world, not much going on; the newscast was almost over and I was thinking I'd been handed a reprieve when we heard it.

"And now for Monitor's weekly roundup of the lighter side of the news. In Connecticut today a prominent Madison Avenue executive was jailed for stealing a horse. His own horse. We'll have the details after this message."

For the first time in my life I paid no attention to the commercial. And when the announcer came back on, I knew Eddie Harris had really done a job for me. Everything I'd told him was in the story and quite a lot he had dreamed up himself, like stating positively that my daughter was going to ride Aspercel in Madison Square Garden.

The cookie started crumbling.

"Well," said Mary, "that certainly puts Helen in a charming position, doesn't it!"

If it had only stopped there I still might have made it home free. But the newsman from the local radio station had to get in on the act. Right after the Monitor newscaster described my dive through Mr. Blitzstein's greenhouse roof, he said, "and now for an on-the-spot interview with an eyewitness, we take you to Westport, Connecticut." I shuddered. There is something so personal about local news. A lot of Mary's friends would hear what was coming next. The local man came on. "Mr. Goddard, you're chief gardener at the Blitzstein estate?"

"That's right."

"And you were the first person on the scene after Mr. Bolton made his—er—crash landing through the roof?"

"That's right."

"Tell us what you saw."

"Well, there the man was lying in the midst of our flowerpots all broken and glass all over, but him not cut at all."

"How did he look?"

"All right, except he was strewn from stem to stern with orchids. I never saw such a sight."

"I understand Mr. Blitzstein raises some very rare orchids. Were any of these the exotic jungle ones?"

"I should say they were, sir. There were none others like them this side of the equator, and very few of them there. Up the Amazon they come from originally. Beautiful things they are—were, I should say. It's a great pity the world will never see them now."

"I beg your pardon, Mr. Goddard?"

"They was to have been exhibited, these very ones, for the first time anywhere, you know. Through Mr. Blitzstein's kindness they were going to be shown at that big garden-club convention in Pasadena, California. Quite the horticultural event of the year. Now they will not be exhibited anywhere, and that's for sure."

"Anything else you'd like to say, Mr. Goddard?"

"Yes. What is the world coming to? That's what I'd like to know."

"Thank you, Mr. Goddard."

I glanced furtively at Mary. She was sitting absolutely motionless, staring through the windshield. After a moment, without moving her head, she said, "Please drive me home, Freddie."

I opened the door, got out, walked around the car to her side. She still stared through the windshield. "I asked you to drive me home, Freddie."

"I can't," I said. "You're sitting behind the wheel."

"What?" She looked around, and her eyes came into focus. "Why, so I am."

She slid over to the other seat. I got in and started the car. I drove slowly, waiting for the storm to break and the lightning to flash around my head. When it finally came, it was worse than I had expected, for she spoke quietly, in full control.

"I suppose you realize I'll have to resign as president of the Garden Club now that you've made a laughingstock of the whole family. To say nothing of wrecking our prize exhibit." From the hollow sound of her voice she might have been talking from inside a grave—mine?

"What I can't take," she went on, "is seeing that you'd sacrifice anything—me, your daughter, our reputation, anything at all—for money and for your career."

"Mary, *I* wasn't the one who wanted to buy Helen a horse."

"But you have certainly commercialized on it! And—and my beautiful orchids! You've just spoiled *everything!*"

She began to cry; deep silent sobbing that shook her body and tore at my heart. I drove along very slowly, giving her a chance to cry it out. There wasn't any use my telling her that I hadn't meant any of this to happen. But when it had I had simply tried to stave off disaster. A vice-president who gets himself arrested as a horse thief stands a good chance of getting fired. A vice-president who gets his firm's biggest account a million bucks' worth of nationwide publicity is less likely to be. I wondered what Mary would have had me do under the circumstances but thought it would be tactless to ask.

I was just turning into the driveway when I heard her give a good hearty blow into her handkerchief. I hoped that meant the storm of tears was over.

"Hellie home?" I asked.

"No, I dropped her off at the beach. A boy's bringing her home."

"A *what?*"

"A boy. He's quite a cute boy. She's gone out with him a couple of times this past week. I think she likes him."

I was sick of being wrong. I grabbed at the chance to get a little of my own back. "With her father rotting in the pokey, you take my daughter to the beach!"

Her voice grew ominous. "I took her to the beach before I knew you'd been stupid enough to get yourself jailed."

But I pretended not to hear. "And she's been going steady with this boy for a week, and you never breathed a word? You know, fathers like to be told when their daughters start going steady. They—"

She blew. She really blew. She used words she must have got from her father, who must have got them from *his* father, who was a forty-niner on the Yukon. I'm not even going to try to repeat the things she called me. When finally she ran out of breath, she jumped out of the car, ran across the parking lot into the house, and slammed the door shut behind her.

An advertising man has to know a lot about psychology —especially about the psychology of women. That's why they're able to sell homely women beauty creams and stuff. Once in a blue moon they remember to apply some of this psychology to their own lives. I did just that now and came up with a comforting analysis that Mary really wasn't mad at me as *me* at all. She was mad at the world because of the purely accidental wrecking of those orchids. I just happened to be the only person around to vent her wrath on. I also happened to be the fool who triggered the explosion. I went into the house and fixed myself a sandwich, a good stiff vodka sandwich. Then I opened a bottle of beer and went out to the paddock to talk to my pal.

I LEANED ON the paddock fence talking to Aspie for a long time while the sun slid down into the west and the late crickets began to chirp in the grass. Long ago I'd learned Aspie was a good guy to talk to when the going was rough. He was a lot of company when you were lonely, twelve hundred pounds of it. You could ask him anything and be certain he wasn't going to give you the wrong answers. The nearest he ever came to disapproval was when he looked at you reproachfully, and heaved one of his huge sighs, for running out of beer.

Which he did now.

"All right, all right," I said. "You want more Knick with a kick?"

I would swear he grinned at me. I went inside to fix us each another round and bumped smack into Mary coming the other way.

We both backed off in a hurry like strangers who accidentally bang into each other in the subway. We stood there, looking at each other, absurdly embarrassed. Echoes of the scene just before hung between us like smog. It was one of those tricky times when if either person says the wrong thing real trouble can result. Thank God Mary managed a timid, tentative smile—quite a feat for a forceful gal.

"Frederick, what did I say? I must have been pretty mad because I've drawn a complete blank. Tell me what it was, so I can apologize."

After seventeen years of marriage I couldn't utter any part of it, not to Mary. So I said:

"Nothing to apologize for. Took me back to the good old Malamute Saloon."

She blushed scarlet. "Oh, Frederick, you mean . . . Father . . . Grandfather . . ."

"And don't forget Klondike Kate."

"Freddie, I don't even *think* words like that! Oh, dear, how awful!" And she ran out of the room.

Feeling a good deal better about things in general, I

fixed Aspie's and my booze and returned to the paddock. I leaned my nose on the top rail, Aspie leaned his chin on it, and I rubbed his nose and thought about Hellie. So she liked a boy! That I'd believe when I saw it. It was probably some horse nut like Ronnie; it couldn't be just a nice clean crew-cut all-American-boy type. On the other hand, maybe it *could* be—if there were any of them left.

I was roused from my thoughts by the buzz of a motor scooter coming up the lane. I didn't think I knew anybody who went in for that particular form of self-torture. I heard the scooter make a few retching noises as it slowed down and turned into the driveway, then buzz again, coming up the rise toward the house.

I peered, my heart quick with sudden interest. Helen being brought home by a *boy!* I didn't want to miss a second of this historic event. The Vespa came in sight, Helen perched on the rear. Its rider had wavy blond hair cut, if you could call it cut, in an Italian windblown bob.

"Boy, hell!"

I spoke my disappointment aloud, but waved to Hellie, who was clinging to the rider's waist. She waved back and her new friend waved too.

"Hi, Mr. Bolton, sir."

I blinked. The voice, in total contrast to appearances, was a rich basso profundo. An exposed chest under the unbuttoned shirt looked flat and hairy. Still, you can't *always* tell. They pulled up and I saw it undeniably was a boy; a rather beautiful, athletic-looking boy who seemed to be wearing some sort of theatrical costume: the open shirt was lemon-colored silk; there was a long blue scarf knotted around his throat and dangling down his back; and his legs were draped in indescribably filthy once form-fitting blue jeans hanging in tattered strips around his ankles. When I saw two large, dirty bare feet in patched sandals, I knew it was no costume but a symbol of what must be a desperate effort at nonconformism.

"Father, I'd like you to meet Sunny. Sunny Day. He brought me home."

He couldn't be real. "How do you do," I said.

"Sunny thinks you're cool."

And this caricature was driving *my* daughter around!

"Sunny thinks you're just about the coolest parent around."

"Coolest cat in the cockeyed county—sir. No question about it."

160

"Sunny, stop talking goofy." Helen slapped him on the shoulder. "What will Daddy *think* of you?"

"It's a free country, Hellie-baby. I have to just be myself. I haven't any right to try and control Daddy's—Mr. Bolton's thoughts or anybody else's. This is *America.* Thought control is but out."

There was a little silence. I had the feeling that what's-his-name was waiting for applause, as though he had actually said something.

"Sunny's a *thinker*," said Hellie. "A *Prophet*."

Another silence. After all, what was there to say in response to a remark like that? Helen was my daughter.

She turned to the boy. "Of course my father's a genius, Sunny. You'll have to accept that and make any necessary allowances."

Sunny glowed. "Man, he sure enough is a genius. You ask me, Hellie-baby, it *takes* a genius to get pinched for a horse thief in this here jet age." He smiled at me in a friendly fashion. "Sir, how did you fix it?"

"Fix what? I don't fix anything."

"You don't have to be modest with *me*, sir. I'm never modest. I mean what did you do to make it look as if you'd ridden the horse? Hired somebody, and when he got off back of the greenhouse you just slipped inside and heaved a rock through the glass roof?"

"I did nothing of the kind."

Sunny ignored me. "Golly, what a brain. Nobody but an ace advertising man could dream up a stunt like that and grab off all that free publicity. Arranging to get pinched for stealing your own horse! You have to be smooth to do that. Man, I *know!*"

"Sunny's a Prophet," said Helen again. "He knows everything."

One thing The Prophet evidently didn't know was that I was getting ready to bust him one in the nose. I'd gone through enough because of that ride and I suspected I was going to have to go through a lot more. I walked up to this wavy-haired leftover from a Shakespearian comedy, flames coming out of my eyes. He inched the Vespa back a couple of feet, looking scared and, suddenly, very, very young. I checked myself.

Still inching the Vespa backward he spoke. "Gee, I'm sorry, sir. I thought I was paying you a compliment, but I guess I goofed."

"This is *America!*" I said, quoting the silly jerk. "Defamation of character is but out!"

To my amazement he hoisted the scooter onto its stand, fell down on his back in a paroxysm of laughter, slapping his thighs, holding his stomach, waving his dirty feet in the air. Helen stood looking down at him—admiringly! In about a minute, completely composed, he got to his feet, took my hand, and shook it.

"Sir, I thought you were the coolest before. Now I *know!* Hellie-baby, this is a *man!* I *like* it!" He turned back to me. "I get it too, sir. I mean, I guess Jesse James would have got pretty teed off if some punk kid told him he was no train robber. Like that. Especially since Jesse was the best in the business. Right, sir? Well, it's an honor to have met you, Mr. Bolton. I've got to go on home. I'd love to come over some evening and listen to the wind blow when you activate the think-box. Can I?"

He had me punchy. "Oh, sure," I said. "Any time. Of course I'm not home much."

"Well, so long, Hellie-baby!"

He kicked the starter lever, the Vespa buzzed, and he was off down the drive. I saw Helen watching him go; there were stars in her eyes. So what I had been praying for *had* happened! And, of course, it had to happen with *that* comic. All of a sudden the whole day—Mary going away, this happening to Hellie, everything—caught up with me. I put my arm around her.

"Hellie, do you like this boy very much?" It was a silly question. Still looking down the driveway where the scooter had disappeared, she nodded slowly. "You like him—a lot?" She turned to me, "Oh, yes, Daddy. Yes!"

Her face was bright with the aurora borealis radiance of the very first love. I tightened my arm about her shoulders.

"Then I like him too, baby," I whispered.

I felt her arm slip around my waist, and we started toward the house.

We'd only walked a few yards when I heard Aspercel's snort. He galloped a stride or two, his hoofbeats stopped, then resumed a second or so later. He'd jumped the paddock fence and was coming to walk up to the house with us. The trouble with that was he insisted on butting your back with his nose or nipping at your shirt and pulling it until he got exclusive attention. I'd talked to him for half an hour; now I wanted to be alone with Hellie. In my ringmaster voice I sang out, "Reeevarse, please!"

Aspie threw up his head, obediently turned around, and walked his fancy show-walk back toward the paddock.

Hellie laughed. "No wonder when I started showing the judges used to write 'Passenger' opposite my number on their cards. When did you teach him that, Daddy?"

"When I was riding him down to the shopping center to get some cigarettes this afternoon. I was bareback and didn't have a bridle. Hellie, I take it you and Sunny heard that five-o'clock broadcast on the radio?"

"On television. It was wonderful. They had pictures—you know, still pictures—of me jumping Aspercel and of you and me and Mummy at different shows. Mr.—Mr. Dugan ought to just love you to death for that. But"—her voice had suddenly gone flat—"the man said—he definitely said I was definitely going to ride Aspie in the horsemanship championship finals at the Garden. There isn't anything definite about it; *you* know that."

I knew that, all right.

"It's, well, it's sort of embarrassing for me, isn't it? I mean all the kids I've gotten to know at the shows—the ones I ride against. They're going to think that's sort of a funny thing for you to have had the man say. Sort of pre-presumptuous?"

I held her tighter against me now.

"Oh, honey, I didn't have him say it. This whole thing was none of my doing. It *wasn't* a publicity plant; that story about your riding puts me in an even worse spot than it puts you. If you can't win that third Medal and ride in the finals at the Garden, *I'm* the guy who has to try to explain it to Harry Tomes and Tom Dugan."

I felt her tremble under my arm. "Yes, Popsicles, but *I'm* the guy who has to win it. And there's a show tomorrow at Millbrook."

I made a fast decision. "Not for you. Not after what happened today. I wouldn't want to subject you to all the kidding you'd get. What the heck, in two weeks when we show again it will be almost forgotten. You drive down to the airport with me tomorrow when I take Mummy to her plane. I'd like to have your company anyway for the trip home."

"Gee thanks, Dad. And, Popsicles, could I ask Sunny to come along? He likes watching crowds, especially at railroad stations and airports. He says watching strangers makes him feel so superior and that every now and then a man needs to feel superior."

"I had the idea maybe Sunny feels pretty darn superior most of the time."

"Oh, he *does*, of course! But that's because he *is*. He just likes to be reminded about it."

"You can ask him," I said, "provided he'll dress like a human being and put on a clean pair of pants. I suppose he *has* pants and shoes? Or are his folks sort of hard up?"

"*Father!* Sunny's parents have a yacht!"

We had reached the house, and Helen floated upstairs while I made for the kitchen to see if I could wrestle together some supper. All at once a flash of light hit me. I got out the phone book and looked up Blitzstein's number. He answered himself.

"This is Freddie Bolton, Mr. Blitzstein."

"Ah, my favorite client! Where are you? Still comfortably installed in your lovely quiet all-male sanctuary?"

"Not so as you'd notice it, sir. Mary sprung me."

"You *let* her?"

"Let's say the troopers let her. Mr. Blitzstein, my wife's been crying her eyes out about that Garden Club exhibit I wrecked."

"Oh, I am so sorry about that. Anything I can do to help?"

"As a matter of fact, there is."

"Fire away, my boy."

"Well, I just remembered something you said to me before we turned me over to the cops. Something about second-best orchids." I spoke very slowly and distinctly to make sure he'd get it. "Do you think it's very nice for Mary to cry her eyes out about my wrecking your *second-best orchids* after giving her the impression they were your best?"

There was a long, pithy silence. Then he said, "Oh, dear me, I see I have talked too much."

"Or not enough?"

"But Freddie—Mr. Bolton—no one, not even my own gardeners, have been allowed to see these plants. No one in the world but myself."

"Then they really ought to make a smash hit at that Garden Club convention, don't you agree? Mr. Blitzstein, be a sport and give my wife a break. She certainly needs one. Come to think of it, so do I."

I heard him laugh.

"All right. I like your gall, damned if I don't. I'll tell the gardener to let you pick them up."

"Thank you, Mr. Blitzstein." I said it from the bottom of my heart.

"And Mr. Bolton, some more good news. Mrs. Blitzstein tells me that the greenhouse roof is insured; so that leaves only the plants, the formal garden, *and* the lawn for you to pay for." Again the laugh. "So do drop in on me again, any time."

2 6

MARY WAS pretty swell the way she pulled herself together. The next morning I drove her over to pick up the new crate of potted orchids. Mr. Blitzstein was cordiality itself, and explained all over again how rare and how fancy they were, and he gave Mary a typewritten set of instructions about humidity and barometric pressures and of course, temperature and feeding procedures follow.

He went so far as to supply a folding glass air-conditioned exhibition case for them, though he may have done this just for the kick of thinking about the huge excess baggage fee I'd have to shell out on the plane. It weighed two hundred pounds.

We drove home and picked up Hellie and Sunny and then made the long run down the Parkway and over the Whitestone Bridge to the airport. Mary left in a state of mingled anguish and ecstasy. The flowers had set her up enormously, but of course she hated leaving Hellie, and I think even the idea of leaving me alone for a whole month was painful. Only partly flattering, because I knew a good deal of it was fear of what weird mix-ups I might get myself into away from her guiding hand. I could see this; after all, I'd done pretty well yesterday in just one afternoon. When the moment came to actually say good-bye I put my arms around her and found it was all I could do to let go.

In spite of the two kids, I had a lonely drive back to Weston. There was one diversion, if you could call it that; I learned what Prophet means in the lingo of the younger —the much younger—generation. I learned, for instance, that a Prophet can be male or female; that he or she must be cool; must be one whose views on life, religion, folk music, morals, sex (as apart from morals), and smoking pot, are listened to, by admirers who, if of the same sex are Listeners, or if of the opposite, Worshipers. Finally I learned that except under cases of extreme parental duress, a Prophet must at all times conform by being a nonconformist—an eccentric. On this last count, God knows, Sunny Day qualified for the title. On the others I was in no position to tell and fervently hoped I never would be.

We got home around four, and I carried out Mary's instructions to the letter. I dropped Hellie and her suitcase off at Judy's, took Sunny back to our house, where he'd left his Vespa; put Aspie in his trailer and deposited him in the royal suite I'd reserved for him at Wolfgang's. He didn't like my leaving him there. After he'd tried to kick the door of his stall down each time he saw me starting to walk off, I got Hilga to give me a bucket of beer and put it in Aspie's stall. Then I crouched over almost on all fours while he had his face buried in the old suds, and sneaked out. I drove to New York and spent such a heavenly, restful night at the agency's Park Avenue apartment I overslept.

I got to the office late Monday morning. I wasn't quite sure what my reception was going to be. But when I got out of the elevator at the Peat Bog and the tall, svelte, lynx-eyed brunette receptionist who normally barely nodded to anyone less than a senior vice-president batted the lynx eyes at me, I guessed everything was going to be all right. Come to think of it, she was staring at me with the same longing look Hellie lavished on The Prophet. Obviously in my own advertising agency I had become a celebrity! Which, I might say, in a business where models and movie stars are hired by the gross, is quite an accomplishment.

I went on down to my offices. Mrs. Dobson, Suzie's replacement, greeted me with a big grin. Like all the Tomes secretaries, she was smartly turned out and coiffed, but the coiffed hair was gray and she was the motherly type. Needless to say, Suzie had selected her. She was officially rated an Executive Secretary, which improved my status but still was no substitute for Suzie. Mrs. Dobson made me feel like an important, efficient businessman, and seemed to believe I actually was one. Suzie had known better.

"Good morning, Mr. Bolton. Have you come in yet?"

This was the sort of double-talk I'd been getting from The Prophet. "Well, you're looking at me. What do *you* think? *Am* I in?"

Mrs. Dobson laughed. In spite of the chic costume and cosmopolitan corseting she had a pleasant country laugh. The kind that makes you think of small towns and old-fashioned elm-lined streets and wistaria-covered porches on summer Sunday evenings when people are full of supper and brotherly love and are sitting outside for a spell before bedtime. (Creating a mood is very important in the advertising business.)

"I should have asked are you *officially* in. Mr. Tomes, Mr. Dugan, Mr. Harrison, Mr. Johns of Benton and Bowles, Mr. Peters of Triple X cigarettes all want to talk to you."

"Maybe I'd better go home again."

"I think not, Mr. Bolton. Which one would you like me to call first? Mr. Tomes."

She didn't even put it as a question. She pushed a button on her intercom and said, "Barbara, tell Mr. Tomes Mr. Bolton is here now."

I'd hardly picked up the first of a stack of letters before the door swung open and Harry Tomes came in and plumped himself down in his favorite chair, the one facing the picture of his pet racehorse.

"Well!"

This could mean anything, but unaccountably I found myself going on the defensive. "Morning, Harry. We decided to scratch the show yesterday. But there's another one up at West Hartford a week from Sunday. I had Wolfgang get a sampling of the probable entries, and Helen's a dead certainty for that third silver Medal."

"She'd *better* win it, that's all I can say."

I couldn't make out why he had come all over gruff and dictatorial. I thought since he was subject to that sort of suggestive reaction, he must have been reading another novel about the advertising business.

"We'll do our best, Harry."

"That horse has *got* to show in the Garden. In fact, your job here hangs on it. After all, you announced it on the air Saturday. On radio—on TV—everywhere."

"I didn't announce it, Harry! What's the matter, you and Tom not *like* what I pulled off for us on Saturday?"

"You think Tom Dugan and I are *nuts?*"

"Well, sir . . ."

"Of course we liked it, you jackass! In all my years in this business I've never seen anything slicker."

I beamed at him. "Then how about a raise?"

He held up his hand. "I've been waiting for you to

spring this for some time. No, you don't get a raise."

I was mad. And showed it. "Am I supposed to think this little cat-and-mouse act is funny?"

He shrugged. "Your reaction to it is. It's so normal. Sort of reassuring to another highly normal chap like me. Now, if you'll simmer down I'll tell you what I have in mind. Tom Dugan called me this morning to talk about you."

"Oh?"

"Yes, he wants you to come into Allied with him as a vice-president in charge of all their public relations and advertising. It was very sporting of him to speak to me about it first. Because the salary he mentioned is so—well, I'm not going to mention it. You'd be too apt to snap it up."

He didn't say anything for maybe a minute or two, just sat studying the picture of that racehorse on the wall and drumming his fingers on the leather arm of the chair.

"In common decency I've got to come somewhere near matching Tom's figure. But I'm not going to raise your salary. Your work here for the past five or six months and the word that's gotten around the trade has been very productive—and profitable—for the firm as a whole. You haven't once tried to trade on that. As a result, I'm going to take you in as a partner and give you a small percentage on the firm's overall net."

I almost keeled over. I could only guess what this meant in money, but knew it was beyond what I'd ever dreamed of earning. I'm afraid I stumbled quite a bit trying to thank him. Then, as usual, he threw his curve.

"You told the world that your daughter and a horse called Aspercel are definitely and positively going to ride in the Garden. Remember, Dugan saw the kid fall flat on her face at Lakeville. So now maybe you can see why your daughter winning that last silver Medal is just a little important? If she doesn't, Dugan will insist one of three leave this agency. The Allied Drug account—you—or me. And I honestly don't think it would be me. I felt I *had* to point this out."

He got up and grinned at me. "Be of stout heart, Horatius," he declaimed. "Hold fast the bridge and give my regards to your daughter."

I looked at the closed door for a long time after he had gone.

You idiots, I was thinking. You give a guy something with one hand and take it away with the other. "Well, the hell you take it away!" I'm afraid I shouted. "Because I'm not going to let you. That horse is going to the Garden if I have to carry him there on my back!"

THE NEXT TEN DAYS were a nightmare of work. Of course, I was a partner now, and partners are supposed to work harder than mere employees, so they loaded me down with more and more accounts.

By the following Thursday I was limp as a dishrag. Then, right after lunch, I got a telephone call. It was from Wesley Murray, the head of the Weston Country Day School—Director he was called. The call didn't last long, and it went like this.

"Mr. Bolton? Wesley Murray here. I'm very anxious to have a little talk with you at your convenience about Helen. I feel it's important that we get together for perhaps half an hour?"

"Fine," I said. I riffled through the leaves of my desk appointment pad. "Let's see—how about a week from next Tuesday?"

There was silence; then his voice came again, sounding soft—as the voices of headmasters of expensive private schools always sound when speaking to their bread and butter—but firm.

"I think we'll have to make it sooner than that. This is urgent. Say this afternoon? Around five?"

My fingers gripped the receiver. A ghastly memory of the adoring look Hellie gave The Prophet flashed into my mind. No, two weeks ago The Prophet had been non-existent in our lives. Even a really brilliant sexpot couldn't achieve total disaster in that short a time—and find out for sure. And Hellie was still a little girl. At least I hoped she was.

"Is she in trouble of some sort at school?"

"No. Her work's off badly, but at this time of year, right after the long holidays, well . . ."

"Is she sick?"

"Mr. Bolton, I don't know. She fainted today, and I had the doctor examine her. He couldn't find anything wrong with her physically. Do you know of anything that could be troubling her—deeply? I know for instance her mother's away?"

"That hasn't got one thing to do with it! Mrs. Bolton's gone to the garden club convention in Pasadena. You're on the wrong track altogether. Mary and the horse and I couldn't be happier together. And Helen knows it!"

"Did you say . . ." He started out sounding as if he wanted to probe further, but then recognizing he'd stumbled into a domestic situation too complex for an educator with only two or three degrees from Harvard, his voice faded away. He coughed and said briskly, "Shall we make it five this afternoon then?"

"Certainly."

All the way out the Merritt Parkway to the Weston turnoff I planned different approaches and sales pitches to use on Hellie. Naturally, when Wesley Murray asked me if I knew of anything that could be deeply troubling her I could have said, "Yes, Professor, horse shows." I'd seen her relief after my ride when I'd told her she didn't have to show. Of course, it might be because she'd gone ape over this Sunny Day—The Prophet. But no, he could have come to the horse show with us. Maybe, like me, he hated horses and had soured Hellie on horse shows. If *he* had soured her, I knew for a positive fact even if it meant going to pokey again, for aggravated assault this time, he was going to regret it. I would be plenty aggravated.

Okay. When I saw her at the school I would start off sympathizing. Then I'd reassure her—tell her not to worry about fainting and I knew for sure she'd be well enough to ride in the Medal class at West Hartford on Sunday. If she acted as if she were going to blow up, I would simply say: "Helen, my job, my whole future depends on your riding in that class on Sunday and winning it. After all I've done for you, you're not going to let me down, are you?" If she said yes, she was, I would draw on what Harry Tomes would call the old verities: I'd simply turn her over my knee and paddle her. Hard enough to hurt but always bearing in mind that the particular part of her anatomy I would be paddling was not exactly expendable for a horsewoman. She would damn well need it Sunday.

By the time I arrived, the sun was low and a cold, dismal nor'easter was brewing. At a set of ostentatious iron

172

gates I turned and drove up a winding gravel drive to the group of faded-brick Georgian buildings that housed the school. I was all set; wearing an expression of firm yet tender concern I brushed past a couple of private secretaries and strode into the Director's sanctum sanctorum. He was sitting at a big curly maple desk holding a coffee cup in one hand and the microphone of a dictating machine in the other.

"Ah, Mr. Bolton. I'll be with you in just a moment."

Though he was perfectly cordial, all of a sudden I felt like a rude little boy for having dared to march into his office unannounced. Why is it we never can quite shake our infantile awe of headmasters? Even if we know they're jerks, which Wesley Murray strictly was not. He put down the coffee cup, pressed a buzzer three times, and before he'd finished the letter one of the secretaries came in with a cup of coffee for me. I would have preferred a hot toddy, or at least a tranquilizer. Confronted by the Presence, my confidence was oozing away.

I knew Murray was trying to use his dictating machine the way Harry Tomes used silence—to reduce me to a state of malleability. Probably after years of handling het-up parents the procedure was routine. What he actually succeeded in doing was to give me time to realize that the crash program I had in mind for getting Helen over whatever was ailing her might not quite jibe with his philosophy of child rearing and that I'd better keep it under wraps until I could get her alone. Finally, he murmured, "Most cordially, et cetera, et cetera," into the microphone and laid it on his desk. As if he wanted to keep it handy in case he needed it again as a psychological weapon or, maybe, to throw at me.

"Now, sir! About your daughter."

I said, "Yes."

"In our telephone call, I asked you if you knew of anything that could be troubling Helen deeply, and then," he smiled broadly, "and then we seemed to drift off the subject onto another theme entirely. So you see, you never did answer my question. In fact, you seemed quite heated about it."

"I'm sorry if I was rude, s——" I just kept from calling him "sir," "but I resented your implications about our home life. It simply does not concern you."

"Whatever has brought your daughter to a point where Dr. Burnside, the school physician—as well as yours, I believe—recommends immediate psychiatric treatment, concerns me very much."

Trying desperately to control my panic at his words, I said, "Just what did the doctor say? Did *he* have any idea what's eating her?"

Dr. Murray folded his hands on his desk. His hazel eyes as he stared fixedly at me had become uncomfortably penetrating.

"Only in a general way. He said he got the impression she was under some tremendous pressure. Tremendous to *her,* of course, not necessarily tremendous or even very vital to an adult. Since, try as he might, and he went pretty far, he was unable to persuade her to tell him what the pressure—or feeling of pressure—is or what she *thinks* it is, he came to the conclusion that it is entirely imaginary. Which means she is mentally a very sick young lady."

I hadn't realized it, but I had slumped in my chair and was sitting with my elbows on my knees, my head bowed in my hands and my eyes closed. I had them closed not because I didn't want to look at him but because I suddenly could not bear to look at myself. I felt the gentle but firm pressure of Murray's hand on my shoulder.

"Mr. Bolton. These things or similar ones come to try all of us. These—mental disturbances—in our own children are one of the greatest trials we have to face. Believe me, sir, over the years I have been over this same ground with many of our parents here at Country Day. Modern psychiatry can work wonders in a relatively short time. Even with adolescents. You simply must *not* fall into the standard trap of blaming yourself for this situation, Mr. Bolton."

I heard most of what he said, I knew he was trying to help me, yet every word was tearing me apart. I felt guilty! After perhaps another minute I got to my feet. Samson had courage enough to pull a temple down on himself. I was no Samson-but I loved Hellie. That was enough to give me the courage to pull down the temple I had built. It wouldn't take long; it was a pretty phony temple.

"Helen doesn't need a psychiatrist," I said. "She needs a father. Where is she?"

For the first time he sounded flustered. "I don't know that I can permit . . ."

But the strength of my resolve reversed our positions. Suddenly he was the small boy. "I don't mean to be rude, Dr. Murray, and I know you have tried to be kindness itself. But the truth of the matter is you have talked so much you haven't given me a chance to answer the question you started to ask me about three hours ago on the telephone."

He stepped back, looking surprised. Headmasters aren't used to being spoken to like that. But he was sportsman enough to say, "By Jove, you know you're quite right."

"I'm answering it now," I said. "Yes, I do know what's bothering her. I just had no idea how much. It's something nobody *but* me can do anything about and something *I* can fix in less than two minutes. So put your psychiatrist back on his leash and tell me where I can find Hellie."

She was in the empty school library, alone, reading or at least pretending to read, a book. With a twinge I looked to see if by any miracle it was a book about horses. It wasn't. It was a book about folk music.

"Hellie?"

She shut the book with a bang, shot to her feet. She was as pale as a ghost and her lips were twitching. I stood still just inside the room. I didn't dare try to move closer to her.

"Hellie, it *is* this horse-show stuff and being driven and driven as if—as if *you* were the horse—that's got you down, isn't it?"

"Oh, Father—I don't know what happened—ever since the last show every time I've had to ride—I've been *terrified!* And I didn't dare let on to Suzie or Wolf or anybody because I couldn't bear your finding out. I—I—do you want me to ride Aspie at West Hartford Sunday? In the Medal? If you tell me to I will, but . . ."

I took one long deep breath, and thought, Well, Brother Samson, here goes my temple!

"Hellie," I said slowly and clearly, "I don't want you ever to ride a horse again—in a show, around the paddock, anywhere—unless you want to."

"Oh, Popsicles! Do you honestly mean that?" I nodded. "But what about the Garden and Mr. Tomes and Mr. Dugan?"

"The Garden *and* Mr. Tomes *and* Mr. Dugan *and* Madison Avenue and Lexington, too, can all go fly a kite."

She was in my arms, weeping and clinging, frantic with relief. And, like a fool, I felt wonderful. I'd tied the can to my job, to a partnership, to my lovely office, to all the things that were not nearly so important as self-respect and knowing my daughter loved me again.

WE DROVE, Helen and I, all the way to the Gardners' without speaking more than half a dozen words. She sat way over on my side of the car, snuggled tight against me. When we turned into the driveway between the paddock fences, and she said, "Stop a minute, Daddy," I obediently stopped. "All of a sudden," she said, "I feel awful about this. I mean all the money you've spent so I could get to ride in the Garden and now I'm not going to."

I felt awful about it too. "That's okay, honey. Look at all the lovely silver we have to show for it."

"It's—it seems sort of unfair to Aspie, too."

I shrugged. *"He* couldn't care less. What the hell, honey, he's just a horse."

But Aspie wasn't just a horse. He was somehow a great deal more than just a horse. There are animals like that: Balto the serum-to-Nome dog; Man o' War; Battleship; Snowman, Nautical, Jay Trump.

"I suppose," she said, "you can sell him for an awful lot. You'll get back most of the money you spent."

The idea of selling Aspie hadn't entered my head, any more than would the idea of selling Mary or Hellie. Aspie was one of the family. Now I realized I would have no choice in the matter. I would have to sell Aspercel so we could eat while I hunted up another job. The thought made me feel like a cannibal. It was the end of my wonderful noble feeling.

"Yes, of course I can sell him for a lot of money. I've turned down over twenty thousand for him a couple of times."

I drove on up to the house. "Hellie, please don't say anything about your quitting the show racket to anybody just yet. Not even to Mr. and Mrs. Gardner. Just tell them the doctor said you were suffering from tension or something and you're to lay off the riding for a week or ten days. I mean it. Don't even tell Judy."

Even a guy sitting in the electric chair can go on hoping

the governor will gallop up on a white charger waving a reprieve before somebody throws the switch.

"I promise, Daddy." I leaned over to kiss her good-bye. "Aren't you going to stay for dinner?"

I shook my head. That I couldn't face right now. I was too fond of Jack and Eleanor to cry on their shoulders. Besides, I had never let on to them just how commercial the Aspercel business was.

"Sunny's coming for dinner too," Hellie said. "He'll hate missing you."

"Likewise, I'm sure. Although what the sight of his sandals and scarf and beret would do to my appetite I couldn't imagine."

Helen laughed. It was a good sound to hear. "Oh, Popsicles, you're so *passé!* Don't you *know* sandals and scarves and berets are out now?"

The young live at a fast pace. I was *passé* because I didn't know that what was "in" a couple of weeks ago was now "out."

"What is 'in' now?"

"Why, why . . ." She started giggling.

"Come on, honey, what's funny?"

"Oh, Daddy, promise not to tell Sunny if I tell you?"

"Cross my heart and—" I'd been half hoping to die anyway, so let that lie.

"I just this second dug why Sunny says what was out is in now. Sunny dresses as close as he possibly can to the way *you* dress! And do you know what else? He used to write poetry all the time. Do you know what he writes now? *Commercials!* Really dreadful sick-making commercials. He's praying for a chance to show them to you."

"I'm a cool cat," I said.

"You're—" She was looking at me in awe. "Why, *you're a Prophet!*"

You know, it's an awful strain on a leopard to change its spots. I found myself thinking: If I bought one of that nutty kid's commercials and tipped him off, *he* could get Helen back on Aspercel again in time to grab off that Medal. She's so nuts over the guy she'd ride off the side of a cliff if he told her to. But this was unworthy of the new Freddie Bolton father image created less than an hour ago, so instead of staying for dinner after all so I could con Sunny into doing what I wanted, I told her I'd love to see his commercials sometime soon. "You can't tell, Hellie; maybe I could use one of them."

"Oh, Daddy! Can I really tell him that?" She gave me a good-night hug that was almost worth everything I'd thrown away.

Out on the road I drove for a couple of miles without noticing where I was going. For some reason the events of the past few hours upset me. Hellie respected me now; I'd finally earned it. The trouble was, I was going to have to go right on earning it. I turned into a driveway and then realized that from long habit I had driven home. The house was dark, of course, and looked bleak in the darkness. The door of Aspercel's stall had accidentally been left unhooked, and it was swinging back and forth in the wind, creaking and banging against the wall. I walked over to close it, and a rat scurried out of Aspie's straw and peat-moss bedding and slithered out of sight. The whole place had an air of abandonment.

I got back in the car. Guess I'll drive over to Wolf's place and visit Aspie for a while, I thought.

Then I thought: No, I can't face him. How do you go about telling a friend that you're going to sell him?

I remembered the umpteen times I'd read *Black Beauty* aloud to Hellie. What would happen to Aspie once I'd sold him? Would his new owner be kind to him and talk to him and keep him warm and well fed? Would he give him beer? At least, unlike Black Beauty he wouldn't become a cab horse. There weren't any more horse cabs. Or were there? Yes, he *might* become a cab horse and have to stand outside the entrance to Central Park opposite the Plaza all day and half the night in the rain and sleet and snow. Maybe someday when I'd be job hunting I'd stumble by there and see him. If I still had as much as a buck in the world, I could at least go into a saloon and buy a growler of beer and bring it to him. Maybe he'd blow froth all over me again. On the other hand, maybe he'd just think, Oh it's you, you venal idiot! And bite me.

Just ahead, my headlights glinted on the aluminum and glass of a roadside telephone booth. I'd use my office credit card and telephone Mary out in Pasadena. After all, I called her every few days—I *had* to; I missed having her around that much. I went into the booth and had the dime halfway into the slot before I realized this was one of my stupider ideas. How could I call her and tell her that not only was I an idiot but, what was unforgivable, an unsuccessful idiot! How do you go about telling your wife that she'd be lucky if she had a house to come home to? Not if you have a brain left in your head you don't. I couldn't call my wife any more than I could go visit my horse!

I heard a clinking sound. My dime had slipped out of my fingers and gone down the slot. I heard a dial tone on the receiver and listened for a few seconds, feeling I had to do something about it. I'd reached the state of mind where a dime wasn't something you threw away. In a sudden fit of desperation and loneliness I dialed the one number I knew that would bring me the sound of a warm and welcoming voice. The miracle was, I hadn't thought of doing this hours ago.

I HEARD THE PHONE ring in Suzie's house. I could imagine it ringing in the little redwood-stained, paneled living room, in the bedroom where the walls were lined with barrel-bending ribbons (she'd moved the silver trophies out to the living-room mantel), in the midget kitchen that was more like the galley of a yacht than the kitchen of a house. The phone rang five times—six—seven—

"Hello?"

With enormous relief I cried out, "Suzie, this is me!"

My voice must have sounded unnaturally strained because her voice echoed it. "What's the matter?"

"Just about everything."

"Freddie, dear, are you tight?"

Why is it the minute women get fond of a man they seem to think he's tight half the time? "No, I'm not tight, Suzie. I'm just desperate. I—I've got to sell Aspercel."

There was a silence while this sank in. Then her voice came on again. "Freddie?"

"Yes."

"Are you anywhere near here? Because if you are, you come over here right away, hear?"

"That's why I called you, Suzie. I think right now—right this minute—I need you very much."

"Have you had dinner?"

"No."

"Freddie, promise me you'll come directly here when you hang up and not stop *anywhere*. Will you promise me?"

"Promise."

"I'm going to hang up now and start dinner, and you start heading this way."

She did hang up. I stepped out of the booth. It had started raining, with the wind flinging thin needlelike drops sideways. It was fall, all right. I shivered and scrambled into the warm car. I'm going to buy *myself* a decent car when Mary gets back, I thought; those commuter trains are for the birds. And then I realized I was not going to buy myself anything. In fact, I probably would have to sell this car.

After what seemed hours, I saw just up the road lights glowing from the windows of Suzie's Cape Cod cottage. I got out to find the front door open and Suzie holding it. She had on a woolly blue bathrobe with blue pajama legs sticking out the bottom and blue furry scuffies. The wind was whipping the bathrobe tight around her and swirling her hair. And though I knew she was not beautiful, she looked beautiful to me.

I stepped into the doorway and into her arms. She didn't say anything, just held me close; wordlessly comforting, her head squashed against my chest, mine bent so it rested against the warmth at the nape of her neck. There we stood, the wind and rain beating on us, until I began to drip on her as well as on the floor and we went inside. She made me take off my jacket and hung it on the back of a chair in front of the neat cherrywood blaze crackling in the fireplace. She squatted down and adjusted the logs, though they didn't need it.

"So Hellie finally quit? I thought she was getting ready to."

"No, I ordered her to quit. I had to, Suzie. Until I talked to Murray at the school and he told me the doctor recommended a psychiatrist, in a hurry, I hadn't realized the pressure I was putting her under with this horse-show racket."

"Little League kids have a heck of a lot of pressure. Sometimes a whole town's putting pressure on them. *They* seem to be able to stand up under it. Hand me your shirt to dry. You look soaked."

I hesitated, then thought what difference did it make. I skinned out of it and handed it over. She spread it out over a footstool on the hearth.

"Little Leaguers seem to be able to stand pressure, and they're not over twelve years old," she said.

"They're boys."

"And girls can take a heck of a lot more than boys. Believe me, I know. I'm a girl."

"So I've noticed—from time to time."

She swiveled on her little behind and looked up. "Don't resent what I'm saying. You know perfectly well I want to help because I adore you and—and because you're my *friend*. It's just that I can't understand Hellie, well—cracking up like this, doing this to you right at the crucial moment."

I dropped into a maple rocker at one side of the hearth. Suzie wriggled over and leaned against my knee the way dogs do. I began to stroke her hair. I wanted to explain; I guess I wanted to defend Hellie. So, as I'm likely to do once in a while, I fell back on that old dodge, the truth.

"Suzie, remember how exciting it was when I was made a vice-president? And we got the new office?" I felt the head against my knee nod enthusiastically. "I've done pretty well since last April. I've taken in a lot of money, and spent more. Last week Harry Tomes made me a partner, he called it. In other words he gave me an interest in the firm."

"Oh, Freddie *darling,* how *wonderful!*"

In her enthusiasm she clutched my knee with both hands and squeezed.

"Suzie"—I looked into the fire; it was easier to talk that way—"a gigolo is a guy who is supported by rich women. Since last April, to all intents and purposes, I have been supported by a fifteen-year-old girl—and a horse. Little Leaguers *don't* have the pressure of supporting a family, of contributing handsomely to the support of a big ad agency, to say nothing of Allied Drug. If Hellie had never known the whole story, that would be one thing—but she did know."

I knew Suzie so well by now that I could tell just from her slightly bowed head that she was thinking, weighing what I'd said. Then she looked up at me.

"I begin to see what you mean." She gave a little laugh. "I've always thought of *you* as being the one under pressure."

"Well, I was. But all I ever had to do was talk. That's really my profession: talking and thinking. Hellie had to go into the ring and bring home the bacon."

"I take back my crack, Freddie. I guess I might have flipped under *that* pressure myself."

The smell of cherry wood mingled with the rich flavor of steak. They were good smells. A bonger went off; Suzie slithered to her feet.

"Dinner'll be in about fifteen or twenty minutes. Can I get you a drink?"

Only then did I realize that I had forgotten to want one.

"It wouldn't hurt if we both had one," she said. "Several, maybe."

She went off into the kitchen, and I heard the hiss and sizzle as she turned the steak over, then the rattle of ice in a shaker. A moment later she came back with a cocktail shaker and two glasses on a tray. She sat on a little sofa and I sat beside her.

"Skoal."

"To you, Suzie."

We drank. The cocktails tasted fine.

"Now," she said, "what's all this nonsense about selling Aspercel?"

She listened absorbedly, her forehead wrinkled with concentration, as I told her the whole story, ending with Harry's warning of what would happen to me if Aspercel didn't show in the Garden.

"That's the living end," she said. "Boy, are we in a jam."

"*We?*"

"Of course 'we'! You know I've been in this with you from the beginning. If you're in a jam I'm in a jam. That's how it is."

I had a thought. "Look, I'm not a horseman, I don't know angles. You are and you do. I've already told Hellie to keep mum. If there's a chance maybe you could come up with something to bail us out of this, I'll keep quiet in the agency for a while."

The pert puss nodded. "It's a deal. You just do that. Don't let it out to a soul. Can you keep it quiet for maybe two weeks?"

"I'd like nothing better!"

"Okay, I'll come up with something. There's just one thing I've got to find out." She grinned. "If the result of my tests are positive, and you can sell the way I think you can, we're off to the races."

"You're quite a girl, Suzie Clemens."

"Nonsense, I'm happy to help. Besides, I think just being able to share things is good. You seem a little more like yourself than when you crawled in out of the storm. And speaking of the storm, I don't like the idea of your driving back to New York by yourself or going to your empty house in Weston. I have a spare room and I want you to stay here tonight, Freddie, where I can take care of you."

Of course I wanted to. But all I could come up with was

one of my less brilliant lines: "I don't have any pajamas."

"Oh, for Pete's sake!" She put her hand over mine and reading my face said, "What's the matter, Freddie?"

"You really want to know?"

"That's why I asked."

"All right. I'll tell you. It is so cozy and relaxing here with you that, frankly, I'm scared if I once start I'll just drift into the habit of staying here. Then I might not ever want to leave."

"I think I could bear up under that, Freddie." She took a sip of her second cocktail. "But you see, you wouldn't ever *really* feel that way. I'm a state cop's daughter and a professional horseman. I don't belong with the people you go around with nowadays. I never could."

Suzie put her hand in mine. "Of course you know how I feel about you, Freddie?" I nodded. She went on. "I think it began the day we went to the Sheridan stables together when you barked like Tim Riley's terrier. How come I haven't heard you bark since?"

"Maybe because I haven't had anything to bark about."

"How about barking for me, right now?"

I barked, then made the whining noise a dog makes when it's begging for tidbits. Suzie's eyes misted.

"I do like it when you bark," she murmured. "It makes you seem so much less important." She gripped my hand tightly. "But that's just what I mean. You couldn't be expected to go on barking forever—like every half hour, say —so I'd feel secure. That's why you don't need to feel afraid about staying here as often as you like."

"Thanks, Suzie."

"Every guy has to have some place to go where he knows he's just plain loved and no questions asked. This is your place. Now kiss me and we'll go back to being just friends."

I kissed her, long, tenderly, sweetly. And it hurt right through to my brisket, because this time her kiss told me things I knew she would never put into words, things that because I really did love her I would never take advantage of unless a cataclysm took place. At least I hoped I never would.

The bonger on the kitchen timer went off again and she broke away.

"Dinner's done."

It was as good a way as any of ending a conversation

that even when carried on without words was potentially on the dangerous side. Potentially because I never thought about Suzie sexually—except when she had on those tight robin's-egg-blue frontier pants and I saw her from behind. *That* was safe enough, since she had to be going in the opposite direction. Tonight, however, I found robin's-egg-blue pajamas had the same effect on me. I tell you, a man lives in a world fraught with many dangers—some of them damned attractive.

THE NEXT DAY I wrote Mary a long letter telling her about Dr. Murray and Helen and the steps I had taken. I wrote instead of calling because Mary and I had been so close and had rocked along together for so many years that even three thousand miles away she'd sense that my world —the semidemi, our whole way of life—was hanging by a thin rope that Tom Dugan could break with one swipe of his shillelagh. The morning after that I got a telegram.

WILL WAIT AT HOTEL FROM NINE YOUR TIME. PLEASE CALL ME. ALL MY LOVE. MARY.

So she knew. But my tottering world was something I had to face alone and somehow cope with as best I could. I had to prove myself to myself. I never should have agreed to buy a horse for Helen when I couldn't afford it. If I'd only had guts enough, or brains enough, to say no we wouldn't be facing all-around eviction. We'd still have security—job security, that is (and I'd be getting all those coy letters every month from liars who wrote that they were sure I must have overlooked their reminders that my account was now five months overdue). And I'd still be getting no place fast in my cubicle with the grillwork door and with Suzie sitting on the other side of the glass partition, pretending to be a secretary. And I would never have found out she was really a girl. And I don't think Mary would be president of her garden club. And I would never have met Aspie. Why, Hellie wouldn't have learned to have poise. And I wouldn't have become a Prophet with one Listener. Boy, would we all have missed a lot of kicks!

At nine on the nose I called Mary. Before I even said, "Hello" or "This is me," she said, "Freddie, are you all right? If you're not I'll catch the first plane home."

"Of course I'm all right," I said. "Why wouldn't I be? How are the orchids?"

"Terrific. I'm ashamed to say it, but all that ghastly publicity about you wrecking the first batch absolutely *made*

187

the exhibit. Thousands of people came to see them. And everybody asked funny questions about you. In fact, I felt as if I were married to some celebrity—like Harpo Marx."

"The late Harpo," I said, "was also a clown."

"But also greatly beloved," said Mary. Something in her voice told me she knew we were both stalling. "Freddie—is your wonderful job—the partnership—in any danger because of what you did for Helen by telling her she needn't ride in the Garden?"

"Well, nobody's said anything yet."

"Freddie—"

"Okay. Nobody's said anything about my job because nobody knows the horse isn't going in the Garden. I mean Tom Dugan or Harry Tomes. Harry's away. I suppose all hell will break loose when they find out."

"And when they do find out?"

I didn't want to hold out hope based on what I knew in my heart was at best wishful thinking.

"When they find out?" I forced a laugh. "Well, there's always the Foreign Legion. I *suppose* they have a cavalry division, for great horsemen like me."

Mary laughed along with me, and suddenly I felt a lot better.

"By a happy coincidence," I said, "I have to be out of town—all over the Midwest—calling on clients for the next week or so. Tomes and Dugan can't find out about Hellie until I get back. I've fixed that. And a lot can happen in a couple of weeks."

"Like what?"

"What can happen? Oh, well; well, a lot. After all, the world was built in only seven days. By the way, when *are* you coming home, honey?"

"In time for the Garden—oh, I forgot. It doesn't mean anything to us any more."

"No, Mary, it doesn't mean one thing to us, but come home by then, will you? I miss you frightfully."

"Yes, of course I will. And I love you too."

We said good-bye then. We had to say it two or three times because neither of us wanted to hang up first. Finally Mary said, "We're acting like kids. We'll count together, and on three we'll both hang up. Okay?"

"Okay. One—two—three."

I slammed down the receiver. I hoped she had too and hadn't cheated. I picked the phone up quick. She *had* cheated, because I heard the click as she hung up.

I worked my guts out on that trip, selling. I wanted to bring in so much new business that Harry Tomes wouldn't dare fire me even if Dugan threatened to move the Allied account. I returned with enough to make me feel I had just a chance, but I was still scared green.

I got back to the office on a Thursday afternoon. My desk clock, a horrible thing with an oversized silver-plated stirrup iron for a frame that some client had sent me because he thought I liked horses, said four fifteen. There was a message on my desk to call Helen at Wolfgang's, and for just a second I felt a surge of elation. If Hellie was at Wolfie's, she must have got over her equiphobia and be riding again! In that case—I buzzed Mrs. Dobson and told her to make the call.

"Hellie," I said when the light on my phone flickered, "what gives?"

"Hi, Daddy. I brought Sunny over to visit Aspie; he'd never met him. And he brought his commercials with him just in case. Can you come out?"

"If you need me, of course. But what's going on?"

"It's something about Aspie. I want you to look at him."

"Is he hurt?" I said quickly.

"Oh, no, he's feeling wonderful. Too wonderful. Wolfgang says if you're really going to put him up for sale, maybe it isn't a good idea to have him feel quite so wonderful. He is *supposed* to be a child's horse, you know. What time will you be out?"

I sensed that this was all strictly from phony. But even if Helen was pulling some kind of fast one—probably nothing more than cornering me so I'd have to read The Prophet's commercials—I was glad of an excuse to duck out before Harry Tomes knew I'd got back from my trip. I told her I'd be there around six thirty.

At a quarter to seven, I pulled into Wolfgang's place. Even at night it was impressive. The place was ruined architecturally, but made financially, by the huge indoor ring that from the outside looked like Squadron A Armory. Every time I saw it, I thought how I'd been helping Wolfie pay for that. I and fifty other guys who couldn't afford it.

I drove along his winding driveway toward the armory. As I approached, I could see light through the opaque windows so I expected Hellie had lured me into some sort of do. I was surprised to find only Suzie's MGA parked outside. I tooted the horn twice to announce myself, and Helen popped out, threw her arms around my neck, and clung. I could feel she was strung up tight as a fiddle string.

"I've missed you, baby."

"I've missed you, Popsicles."

"Where's The Prophet?"

"Sunny? Oh, he had to go, but he's going to meet us later."

Arm in arm we went into the armory. When I stopped to light a cigarette, Helen tugged at my arm.

"Daddy, please. We're keeping them waiting."

I followed her up to the seats and looked down at the ring, and blinked. Under the floodlights, I saw, arranged in a twisting, curving pattern around the ring, the most appalling set of jumps I had ever set eyes on. They bore no relation to anything I'd seen at the shows we'd been going to all summer. There were sets of white rails that a horse would have to jump a tremendous width to clear. There was a gray "stone wall," made of wooden blocks, of course, that must have been almost six feet high, and a set of three big jumps, close together in a row, and those were only some of the jumps.

Helen put her hands to her mouth and yelled, "All right, Wolfgang. Father's ready!" She turned to me. "This is more or less a duplicate of F.E.I. courses—that's *Fédération Équestre Internationale*" (she pronounced it perfectly) —"about the stiffest jumping course in the Garden."

I felt her hand slip into mine, and suddenly I knew what the surprise was. My mouth went dry and my hands began to sweat with nervousness as a solid gate at one end of the ring swung open and out came Aspercel and Suzie. Only they looked completely different. Gone were Suzie's blue frontier pants and big hat, replaced by black boots with patent-leather tops, fawn-colored breeches, a black, long-skirted coat, a white stock, and a black derby hat. She looked as tiny as Aspercel, his black coat burnished until it reflected the lights, looked huge. He came into the ring with a bounding leap, plunging, rearing, plunging again. His eyes were rolling; froth sprayed from his lips. He looked like a wild animal. Suzie guided him in a circle. Quite obviously it took all her strength to hold him to his plunging canter. She aimed him in the general direction of the first tremendous jump.

"All right now, Aspie."

She spoke in a soft, quiet voice. Aspercel's ears went forward; he flung his head in the air, reared and whinnied like all the stallions who ever shouted their triumphant cries of strength and power. Suzie's voice came again, a little louder. One hand rested on his neck.

"Go!"

With a snort he was off. Ears forward, eyes sharp, strength rippling in every muscle. For all their size, the jumps might as well not have been there at all, and Suzie rode him as if sitting astride all that dynamite, flying the big fences, was what she, like the horse, had been born to do. The only moves she made during two trips around that startling course were to lean back, check him, and steer him into the sharpest turns; and each time they came into the high "wall" she gave a little tug on the reins, slammed her legs against him, leaned over and spoke—to tell him never mind about how good he thought he was, for this jump he'd better hump himself. I don't think in the two rounds he came within six inches of touching any jump. It was the most beautiful sight I had ever seen.

When finally Suzie pulled him up and slacked the reins way off so he could move toward us at a quiet walk with Wolfgang trotting beside him my eyes were so wet I could hardly see. I knew now what I had only sensed that day he and I had taken on all comers, including Mr. Blitzstein's greenhouse: Aspercel was a great horse—perhaps the greatest of his kind there had ever been. He had buffaloed me with his hamming, but the realization of what he was and of what he might become gave me goose pimples all over. He saw me, walked over to the edge of the ring, raised his head, made a little whickering noise, and blew froth at me. I felt as if I'd been knighted.

I could see Wolf and Suzie and Helen were waiting for me to speak first. I guess they thought I was going to be livid for their doing this without asking me. But I didn't speak first after all. Helen did.

"I guess you see now, Father, why my qualifying to ride in the Garden this year doesn't have to mean much to us after all?"

"What?" I was miles away.

She spoke distinctly, as if to a not overbright child: "You see, Father, when Aspie's in training like Suzie's had him since I—I quit, and is getting sixteen quarts of oats a day, he's so full of himself I couldn't possibly ride him. I think I knew in my heart all along, even if I got to the Garden, I wasn't good enough to win anything against all the top kids in America. The very idea scared me sick. But Aspie's good enough to win the Open Jumper Championship at the Garden or anywhere else, which means everybody'll know he's the very best jumper in the whole country. Don't sell him, Father—we *owe* him that chance for all he's done for us. Father, he's just *got* to have his chance. Please say you'll enter him?"

"I got the idea from that ride you gave him, Freddie," Suzie said, "and what you said late that night you—had dinner with me. You said you felt that for the first time Aspie'd come into his own that day."

"So," said Wolfgang, "we went over and measured those two paddock fences at Mr. Blitzstein's. The one near the greenhouse was five feet six. The first one was six feet. So we knew he could jump all right. And, Mr. Bolton, I want you to know I'm not charging you anything for training him. I can't. Honestly, sir, with a horse like this, it's a privilege."

"You will enter him, won't you, Daddy?"

I hardly heard them. I'd gotten aboard my time-and-space machine and was reliving again the few minutes of my crazy ride. I was feeling the surging power under me and the wild, electric exaltation of the horse himself. The very thing that made him lift his head and shout his glory just now when he charged into the ring.

I nodded. "Yes, yes, of course. I think I owe him that much myself."

"We've got to send the entries in tomorrow. Is that all right?"

"Sure."

Then Hellie undid me completely. "And would you mind awfully—because it *was* you really who discovered he was such a terrific open jumper—if we put both our names down—yours and mine—as joint owners? I think Aspie'd like that."

Suzie must have known I was about to dissolve, because she kicked Wolf's shoulder with the toe of her boot and gestured at Helen and the three of them walked away. But

192

Suzie knew the real reason I was falling apart. She had given me back my life—to say nothing of saving Aspie from a fate worse than death—lugging around a cab across the street from the Plaza.

I got to my office around eight thirty the next morning and first thing phoned Dugan at his apartment. This was the moment of crisis. I had a tricky selling job to do, and I wanted to get it over with. The next few minutes would settle whether I belonged in the In or Out basket. I heard him pick up the receiver and answer, if you could call it that, with silence. *He* wouldn't admit he was there on the phone until he knew whether he wanted to be there or not.

"Hello, Tom. Freddie Bolton here. I've had a brainstorm."

Now Dugan's gravelly voice rattled the diaphragm of my receiver. "Is it a brainstorm that's going to cost me money? If so, I'll eat my breakfast first and you can call me back. I hate to spend money on an empty stomach."

"This is not going to cost you a dime."

"Then it must be lousy. If it's lousy, Freddie, why do you call me so early? It would be just as lousy *after* I've had my breakfast, would it not?"

"It's too hot to keep. It's about Aspercel—and Madison Square Garden."

"That's different," said Dugan. "There is nothing wrong, is there?"

He sounded worried. Good! I'd move in on him for the kill slowly, letting his worry build up.

"Oh, no, nothing at all. Why do you ask? What could be wrong, Tom?"

" 'What could be wrong?' the man asks me. Why, the horse could have passed away with the colic during the night. He could have got up to go to the bathroom and fallen down and broken his leg in the dark. He . . . and *you* ask *me* what could be wrong. You should not have to phone me up just as the dawn's breakin' to ask *me!*"

"Well, Tom," I said with what I hoped was maddening slowness, "it's like this. Nothing is wrong *now*. At least I don't think so. But I'll admit something's been worrying the hell out of me for quite a while, and until last night I hadn't had the ghost of an idea how to fix it."

Now he sounded good and mad—and a little frantic.

"Will you for the love of God, man, stop tippy-toein'

around the mulberry bush? Please, Mr. Bolton, if I may make so bold, tell me in words of not over three syllables just what in heaven's name you're trying so almighty hard not to tell me?"

"Okay, we'll start at the beginning."

"Start! Never *mind* about where, just start!"

"Okay, okay. Well, we had a good idea. Right?"

"*Had?*"

The anguish in his voice told me the time for stalling was over.

"Yes, Tom, we certainly had. But there were two things wrong with it."

"*Now* he tells me!"

"Sure, because now I know how to fix it. What was wrong was it lacked drama and there was too much emphasis on the kid and not enough emphasis on the horse."

"And just what, if you please, is the matter with emphasis on a little girl?"

"Well, tell me this. Which is named for the product? The girl or the horse?"

There were a few seconds of silence before the gravelly noise shook the receiver again. "By god, Freddie, you've got a point there at that. Aspercel would be a funny name for a girl." (I didn't say that, when you came right down to it, it was a pretty funny name for a horse, too.) "All right now, get on with this brainstorm that's not going to cost me a dime so you've got to be giving it all this buildup."

"Well, suppose I told you Helen had sprained her ankle and couldn't ride in the Garden? What would you say?"

"I'd say that was as silly a thing as I'd heard in a long time. Can't ride because of a sprained ankle? If she'd sprained her ass, now, Freddie, that would be a different thing altogether."

"Cut it out, Tom. *Let's say she's broken something that keeps her from riding!*"

"Go on, please. Get to the point, now."

"The point is she's heart-broken—not about herself but about her beautiful horse Aspercel not being able to have his chance to perform in front of all those thousands and thousands of people at the Garden. Aspercel just loves being admired, you know. He likes it even more than he likes beer. That's saying a lot, too. . . ."

"Freddie. Tell me straight now. Has that nice daughter of yours broken anything?"

"No, of course not."

"That's what I thought."

"But she's not going to ride, Tom. And it's the biggest piece of luck we've had since I rode Aspercel over those huge paddock fences and sailed through the greenhouse roof."

"I am listening. I am not hopeful. In fact, right at this very second I'm trying to think who to turn the Allied Drug account over to. But I *am* listening, you two-faced con man."

Here goes, I said to myself.

"All right. Here's the pitch. For a long time I've been worrying about this equitation bit. It just has not got the glamour, not for the sort of nationwide coverage I want for you. Let's face it, Tom; we both know that it isn't the kids who get on network TV. What does? The military teams and the open jumpers. Here's where the drama comes in, and, boy, this is no publicity stunt. This is straight. Helen knew even if she did ride in the Garden against the one hundred and fifty or so other top kids—most of them a lot more experienced than she is—who make the finals, she and her horse wouldn't stand a prayer of getting to first base. So what did she do? She bowed out so Aspercel could have his big chance. She's got a cute kid, a girl professional, to ride him in all the big Open Jumper Classes, and of course their picture will be splashed all over everywhere because he's a new star. And he wins the Open Jumper Championship. Superb, isn't it?"

The phone was silent for so long I thought Dugan had hung up in disgust. I was sweating harder than Aspie had ever sweated in his life. I'm no gambler, but I was playing for the highest stakes there are. I'd put down my hand. Now, did I lose my home, my horse . . . or did I win back a fortune?

I heard a crackling sound. I shouted into the phone, "What's going on?"

"Just opening my breakfast eggs, son. I think better on a full stomach."

I was still alive. I waited. From time to time I heard munching sounds, and still I waited. Finally I heard a belch. This was it.

"Freddie, I'm not one who likes to throw cold water all over a bright, upcoming young man." I sagged in my chair. "But, my poor dear boy, you've let yourself be carried away by your own enthusiasm. A dangerous trait that, in a businessman."

"How do you mean I've let myself be carried away, sir?"

"You've let yourself be carried not only away but so far away you cannot even see the glaring flaw that negatives out your whole idea."

"There *isn't* any flaw!"

"Blind you are, man. There's a flaw as big as the Grand Canyon is wide. Your horse. He's a child's horse; I've seen him, remember? Except for a little bouncing around, he's meek as a lamb. Why, the poor beast is no more of an open jumper than I am. Or could I be wrong?"

Then, not sparing the rhetoric, I told him about what I had seen last night at Wolfgang's. I told him also that if he didn't believe me I'd drive him out this evening and let him see for himself. That made him laugh.

"Freddie Bolton, that's not necessary at all. I know at heart you are a con man, which is why I like having you on my side handling my account. But I also know you wouldn't out and out lie to me. At this point."

"Well," I said, my nerves getting to me. "What about it? Satisfied?"

"Will you meet me at the Racquet Club for lunch at one?"

"Of course."

"I want you to tell me that last bit about the horse all over again. Why, it's the grandest thing I've heard since a year ago when Harry Tomes tipped me that Jonah horse of his was going to win the Hampton Cup at Saratoga and I bet heavy on him—and he came in at five to one. Don't be late. I'll be looking for you."

I'd just have time for a quick call to Redlands. I wouldn't be late, that he could be sure of!

I IMAGINE EVERYBODY who has a horse going into top competition worries about whether he'll go lame or get colic or whether he'll just make the grade. But I'll bet I was the only owner who had my particular worry. I was afraid the Garden jumps wouldn't be big enough to keep Aspie interested for a whole week and that he'd simply get bored and say to hell with it!

Wolf and I had entered him in everything he could enter; the cost of entry fees at this point was meaningless. A week before the show, I got Wolf to work out in detail how many classes he'd have to win a first or a second in to score enough points to become champion. Then the two of us got together and figured out, not which ones he was most apt to win but which classes we thought would bore him least. We'd start him only in those and forget about the others.

Of course, I was acting strictly as *Amicus equi,* you might say. I expected Wolfgang as a horseman to be outraged, but I think my brazen arrogance appealed to his half drop of Hessian blood; anyway, as the opening day approached he got so emotional he insisted on paying for all those extra tons of oats Aspie was eating now. It was the first and only time I have ever known Wolfgang Wilhelm Heinrich von Roetz to do anything totally noncommercial. I think he wanted to be able to tell his grandchildren some day that Aspie's first big championship was won, if he won it, only because he, Wolfgang Wilhelm Heinrich von Roetz, had provided the oats.

The day before the show opened—the day she was supposed to arrive home—I got a wire from Mary:

> MOTHER HAD WHAT MAY BE HEART ATTACK AND IN
> HOSPITAL SAN BERNARDINO. THINK SHE IS GOING TO BE
> ALL RIGHT. AM ABSOLUTELY DESOLATE, FREDDIE, BUT
> CAN'T POSSIBLY LEAVE UNTIL SHE IS OUT OF DANGER.
> THURSDAY NIGHT THAT BIG F.E.I. CLASS BEING TELE-
> VISED HERE. YOU AND HELLIE TRY GET SOMEWHERE I
> CAN SEE YOU. MISS YOU DREADFULLY. PLEASE UNDER-
> STAND. ALL MY LOVE.

After business, I drove up to see Wolfie and Aspie. Wolfie was so nervous I was afraid Aspie would catch it, so I gave Aspie a couple of beers, and left. Then I drove over and had dinner with Hellie and the Gardners, and *they* were so nervous they began to get me jumpy. After dinner, Sunny Day came in. Instead of his usual offbeat fast talk, the minute he saw me he said, "How's the horse, Mr. Bolton? Is he all right? God, I get tense just thinking about tomorrow. Is there anything I can do, Mr. Bolton?"

"As a matter of fact, there is." I reached in my pocket, brought out a sheaf of tickets. "Mrs. Bolton's mother's had a mild heart attack, so Mrs. Bolton isn't going to be able to make it to the show. Here's her ticket to my box. You can drive Hellie in after school every day in time for the night jumping classes and back again after the show. Sort of take care of her. Okay?"

I thought he was going to salute he stood so straight. "Take care of *your* daughter, Mr. Bolton? You bet I'll take care of her." I was beginning to feel about this kid the way I felt about that silly horse of ours. "Sir, have you had a chance to read any of my awful commercials yet?"

I had; they *were* awful. On the other hand, so were mine. "I have a new client, one of the frozen-food companies. They have one product I can't even think about without getting nauseated. Clams with sour cream and strawberries. I'm going to have one of your commercials rewritten a little to fit that and we'll use it. We'll pay you, of course."

I expected him to blow oats at me like Aspie. I left and drove up to Easton to the Cape Cod cottage. All the lights were on but I could find no trace of Suzie. I played a hunch and went out to the barn, and there she was at Queenie's stall, her arms around Queenie's neck, and she was sobbing. Though the temperature was down to forty, all she had on were the blue pajamas. She flung her arms around my neck.

"Oh, Freddie, Queenie's been so wonderful to me all these years, and right this minute I ought to be taking her out to the Cow Palace in San Francisco, which for quarter horses is like the Garden, and instead of that I'm riding an Open Jumper in the Garden. I feel so horribly disloyal, what am I going to do?"

"You're going to come up to the house before you freeze to death and I'm minus a rider."

"Freeze to death?"

"Yes, you beloved fool. All you've got on is your pajamas!"

"My . . ."

She looked down at herself, her eyes widening in astonishment, and ran for the house.

I couldn't figure why everybody but me was so nervous. *I* wasn't nervous. And I'd had only four tranquilizers since I'd left the office.

32

THE BIG F.E.I. CLASS that Mary wired was going to be on coast-to-coast television meant the Open Jumper Championship to us if Aspie won. That would give him enough points. He had won every other class he'd been in. In fact, he was one of the few horses, if not the only horse, who had ever gone through a whole Garden show this far without touching a fence. I just hoped he didn't realize it; he had enough of a swelled head as it was. Of course, the papers had played it up big—which was understandable. Neither Aspie nor Suzie was exactly unphotogenic, and she was the only girl riding in the Open Jumper Division. It had reached the point where every night when she and Aspie thundered into the ring, the whole jam-packed Garden cheered.

Our box was crowded on the big night. Suzie and Hellie were with me, along with my new appendage, Sunny Day, and Harry Tomes and his wife and Wolfie and Hilga. Wolfie and I were done up in white tie and tails, and because I was wearing them Sunny was too. Helen had on her first really formal evening gown—complete to elbow-length white gloves. She looked so ravishing I wondered why Sunny wasn't nuts about her the way she was about him. But all the silly ass was nuts over now was the advertising business—and me! My three pals: a goofy horse, a quarter-horse girl, and a Prophet! And you know what? I liked it! Suzie, of course, was done up in her formal black and canary, and patent-leather riding gear.

Throughout the evening, especially as the time for the big class grew nearer, people—all sorts of people—kept stopping by the box to shake hands and wish us and Aspie luck: pro horsemen, kids Hellie had ridden against during the summer, half a dozen or so of the fox-hunting crowd from Fairfield and Goldens Bridge with whom I'd grown friendly since the show started, the president of the show, other officials, industrial wheels who were my pals, and a lot of people I'd never set eyes on before who wanted to be introduced to Suzie. I became aware that the red warning eye of the television cameras was swinging our way a good deal of the time, and I wondered if way out there in California Mary was watching. I couldn't help feeling a little puffed up by all the fuss, and just wished Mary could have been there to share it.

The big class came right after the recess, at ten o'clock, during which the elaborate jumping course was set up. Half an hour before the class, Suzie and Helen and I, with Sunny tagging along, made our way down the ramp to the cellar stabling with its tent stalls and Aspie. We did that before every class he was in so he'd know his three friends were with him all the way. This admiration, plus beer, oats, and hay, were his meat and drink. Wolf was already with him.

There was a crowd around Aspie's stall now. There always was these days, but tonight the Pinkerton men had to clear a path for us to go through and then clear a space where Aspie could get dressed. I went into the stall. Wolfie was rubbing him shiny with a rag. I led him out and held him. He poked his nose at me and popped his flanks in and out a couple of times in case there was any beer around, but of course there wasn't. That had to come later. Hellie leaned up against his neck, snuggling her face against it and cooing at him. Suzie picked up each of his hooves, one by one, to make sure no manure was caught in them. Sunny held things: saddle, bridle, cooler, weight pad (the thing with slots on each side that little slabs of lead fitted into). In the F.E.I. classes, men had to weigh, counting saddles, 165; women, 154; and if they were too light the lead made up the difference.

Aspie stood there, loving every second of it, calm and quiet as an old swaybacked plug in a pasture. Then a trumpet sounded. Moving fast, we went into our standard routine. Sunny slipped the weight pad on his back; Suzie put the saddle on top as Wolf dropped the halter, put the bridle on and Helen fastened the throatlatch on the bridle; quick as a flash, Wolf snugged the girth and surcingle taut. It was done so expertly and so fast that it took Aspie a few seconds to realize he was going onstage—I'm sure that's how he thought of it—and to start his plunging and rearing. The moment he did the crowd scattered, flashbulbs flashed, cameras clicked, and Suzie and I each grabbed a halter shank that was snapped to each side of his bit and hauled on it, each of us alternately and in unison using the rather strong and impolite language he found soothing. To him this meant the first act was over, so he calmed down and let us lead him up the ramp. The loudspeakers called out periodically, "Next horse," then boomed out the number and who owned him and who was riding, and then, "Number So and So, eleven faults," as the horse finished, the outgate opened, and a horse and rider left the ring.

Suzie whispered to me: "I'm scared. People are scoring an awful lot of faults. It must be a really tough course."

"Nonsense!" I grinned at her. "Why, honey, there isn't a jump here that's over five feet seven, and I've ridden him over six feet myself."

"Oh, *you!*" she said. Then she gave me a big grin.

"Think of it this way. We're back at Wolf's place. Hellie and I are the only people in the grandstand. You and Aspie come in to show us—and you never touch a single jump. That course was tougher than this one."

"Next horse, Number Forty-four, Aspercel, owned by Freddie and Helen Bolton—that's father and daughter by the way—and ridden by Miss Suzie Clemens. If they win this one, they win the Open Jumper Championship of the show."

"Remember, Sue," Wolf said, as he tossed her up into the saddle, "time counts on this one. But leave most of that up to Aspie."

She nodded; she was as white as a dead salmon's belly. We unsnapped the lead rope and stepped back. Aspercel gave his great bounding leap into the ring, and the roar that greeted Suzie must have shaken the rafters. Hellie and Sunny and I sprinted for the box and made it just as Sue got Aspie aimed toward the first jump.

We needn't have worried. The nearest Aspercel came to disaster was when one hind leg slipped going around a turn, and there was a groan from the crowd, and when he jumped so big over the last fence that Suzie almost came unstuck. There was another roar as he crossed the finish line, and the high yipping noise horsemen sometimes make, and then still another when the announcer gave his time, which was an incredible six seconds faster than the nearest horse. There were two more horses to come; but they made a shambles of the course, and Aspie was in and Helen was weeping and I was just sitting there sort of stunned. I heard the announcer talking and a lot more applause but wasn't listening. Then I heard him saying, ". . . trophy will be presented by Mrs. Albert E. Hart escorted by Major General Alfred Tuckerman. Will Miss Bolton and Mr. Bolton, owners of Aspercel, please come into the ring."

Still dazed, we stumbled down to the little door in the center of the ring wall. A Pinkerton man, tipping his cap, opened it.

"Hey, dopey," I whispered at Helen. "We can't hold hands. You're supposed to take my arm like a grown-up lady."

"We can too hold hands," said Hellie. "I've got to."

We held hands. When we got to the center of the ring, I gave Suzie a big grin and she gave one back and Aspercel blew froth all over me as usual. The ringmaster tried to mop me up, and about fifteen thousand people laughed, so Aspie rammed me with his nose, then blew froth all over me again, and got a much bigger laugh. A minute or two later, Helen staggering under the weight of a huge solid-silver tea tray, we made our way back to the little door where Sunny was waiting for her. She handed him the heavy tray. I started to follow her, then stopped. I thought the excitement had been too much for me and I was seeing things. I thought I saw Mary standing right in front of me—in a black silk dress with a flowered tulle-veiled hat that made her look like a naughty nun in the springtime. She was looking up at me out of eyes as big as pools, and smiling, tentatively.

"Mary!"

"I had to come back, Freddie. Mummy was, well, almost out of danger, and I—I couldn't stand being away from you for another minute. I couldn't get a plane 'til this afternoon. Then, in Chicago, we got socked in by fog for three hours. I was *dying.*"

I swept her into my arms. I didn't kiss her; Mary never liked public display of private feelings. I just gave her a hug.

"But when did you get here? Just this minute?"

"No, about an hour ago." I started to speak. She put a daintily gloved finger to my lips. "I didn't come to the box because for one thing I wasn't dressed, and for another, this was *your* night. And I—I had a funny feeling that after almost eighteen years I wanted to see you just being yourself without me around to influence you."

She gave a little laugh. "You know, you're not really like yourself at all. You're so—sure of yourself. And all those important people who came up to speak to you, I recognized lots of them from their pictures I'd seen in the papers. I found it pretty hard to believe you were *my* Freddie and—and that I belonged to you. Where did you meet them all?"

"Why, honey, you just said it yourself. You're married to a pretty important person."

"Frederick—" she said ominously.

"Yes, Mary?"

"I think you are perfectly wonderful." She grinned. "Especially for a horse thief."

I threw back my head and roared with laughter.

THE YEAR OF THE HORSE turned full cycle in mid-December. Snow was coming down hard as I kissed Mary, curlers and all, good-bye at the front door and got into the Continental —painted Aspercel blue and red, of course—that our new adjunct, a combined houseman-and-Aspie-valet whose wife did the cooking nowadays, had gotten out and warmed up for me. I started to let in the clutch, when I realized Mary was calling something to me.

"Oh, darling!"

I rolled down the window and stuck my head out.

"What now?"

"I meant to speak to you about it at breakfast. It's about arranging for Helen to take ski lessons. All the girls around here are taking them. They go to Matt Svendon, who's absolutely *the* most, at a place called Hillmount, near Lenox. He's saving a place in the class for Helen. They're starting this weekend, but I thought it only right to ask you first because the lessons really *are* expensive."

I remembered that other morning so long ago when, not having the foggiest idea what I was letting myself in for, I had inadvertently put Wolfie on the payroll. I grinned.

"Why not? Things have been going altogether too smoothly lately. Sign her up."

"Angel!"

I drove out of the driveway, wondering how you went about buying a mountain—and what product to name it after.

more good reading in

THE LAUREL-LEAF LIBRARY

If you cannot obtain copies of these titles at your local bookstore, just
send the price (plus 10c per copy for handling and postage) to Dell Books,
Box 2291, Grand Central Post Office, New York, N.Y. 10017. No postage
or handling charge is required on any order of five or more books.

LAUREL EDITION

The Laurel Charles Dickens
Introductions by Edgar Johnson

DOMBEY AND SON

A moving drama about the downfall of a pompous merchant, with the usual cast of minor characters who provide a humorous background.

95c

PICKWICK PAPERS

The amusing story of that lovable, generous old gentleman, Mr. Pickwick, one of the best-known characters in fiction.

95c

MARTIN CHUZZLEWIT

Nineteenth-century England and America are the setting for this richly humorous novel which features some of Dickens' most outrageous characters.

95c